PRICE OF HONOR

Applause for L.L. Raand's Midnight Hunters Series

The Midnight Hunt
RWA 2012 VCRW Laurel Wreath winner *Blood Hunt*
Night Hunt
The Lone Hunt

"Raand has built a complex world inhabited by werewolves, vampires, and other paranormal beings...Raand has given her readers a complex plot filled with wonderful characters as well as insight into the hierarchy of Sylvan's pack and vampire clans. There are many plot twists and turns, as well as erotic sex scenes in this riveting novel that keep the pages flying until its satisfying conclusion."—*Just About Write*

"Once again, I am amazed at the storytelling ability of L.L. Raand aka Radclyffe. In *Blood Hunt*, she mixes high levels of sheer eroticism that will leave you squirming in your seat with an impeccable multi-character storyline all streaming together to form one great read." —*Queer Magazine Online*

"*The Midnight Hunt* has a gripping story to tell, and while there are also some truly erotic sex scenes, the story always takes precedence. This is a great read which is not easily put down nor easily forgotten."—*Just About Write*

"Are you sick of the same old hetero vampire/werewolf story plastered in every bookstore and at every movie theater? Well, I've got the cure to your werewolf fever. *The Midnight Hunt* is first in, what I hope is, a long-running series of fantasy erotica for L.L. Raand (aka Radclyffe)."—*Queer Magazine Online*

"Any reader familiar with Radclyffe's writing will recognize the author's style within *The Midnight Hunt*, yet at the same time it is most definitely a new direction. The author delivers an excellent story here, one that is engrossing from the very beginning. Raand has pieced together an intricate world, and provided just enough details for the reader to become enmeshed in the new world. The action moves quickly throughout the book and it's hard to put down."—*Three Dollar Bill Reviews*

Acclaim for Radclyffe's Fiction

2013 RWA/New England Bean Pot award winner for contemporary romance *Crossroads* "will draw the reader in and make her heart ache, willing the two main characters to find love and a life together. It's a story that lingers long after coming to 'the end.'"—*Lambda Literary*

In **2012 RWA/FTHRW Lories and RWA HODRW Aspen Gold award winner** *Firestorm* "Radclyffe brings another hot lesbian romance for her readers."—*The Lesbrary*

Foreword Review Book of the Year finalist and IPPY silver medalist *Trauma Alert* "is hard to put down and it will sizzle in the reader's hands. The characters are hot, the sex scenes explicit and explosive, and the book is moved along by an interesting plot with well drawn secondary characters. The real star of this show is the attraction between the two characters, both of whom resist and then fall head over heels."—*Lambda Literary Reviews*

Lambda Literary Award Finalist *Best Lesbian Romance 2010* features "stories [that] are diverse in tone, style, and subject, making for more variety than in many, similar anthologies...well written, each containing a satisfying, surprising twist. Best Lesbian Romance series editor Radclyffe has assembled a respectable crop of 17 authors for this year's offering."—*Curve Magazine*

2010 Prism award winner and ForeWord Review Book of the Year Award finalist *Secrets in the Stone* is "so powerfully [written] that the worlds of these three women shimmer between reality and dreams…A strong, must read novel that will linger in the minds of readers long after the last page is turned."—*Just About Write*

In **Benjamin Franklin Award finalist *Desire by Starlight*** "Radclyffe writes romance with such heart and her down-to-earth characters not only come to life but leap off the page until you feel like you know them. What Jenna and Gard feel for each other is not only a spark but an inferno and, as a reader, you will be washed away in this tumultuous romance until you can do nothing but succumb to it."—*Queer Magazine Online*

Lambda Literary Award winner *Stolen Moments* "is a collection of steamy stories about women who just couldn't wait. It's sex when desire overrides reason, and it's incredibly hot!"—*On Our Backs*

Lambda Literary Award winner *Distant Shores, Silent Thunder* "weaves an intricate tapestry about passion and commitment between lovers. The story explores the fragile nature of trust and the sanctuary provided by loving relationships."—*Sapphic Reader*

Lambda Literary Award Finalist *Justice Served* delivers a "crisply written, fast-paced story with twists and turns and keeps us guessing until the final explosive ending." —*Independent Gay Writer*

Lambda Literary Award finalist *Turn Back Time* "is filled with wonderful love scenes, which are both tender and hot." —*MegaScene*

By Radclyffe

Romances

Innocent Hearts

Promising Hearts

Love's Melody Lost

Love's Tender Warriors

Tomorrow's Promise

Love's Masquerade

shadowland

Passion's Bright Fury

Fated Love

Turn Back Time

When Dreams Tremble

The Lonely Hearts Club

Night Call

Secrets in the Stone

Desire by Starlight

Crossroads

Homestead

Against Doctor's Orders

Honor Series

Above All, Honor

Honor Bound

Love & Honor

Honor Guards

Honor Reclaimed

Honor Under Siege

Word of Honor

Code of Honor

Price of Honor

Justice Series

A Matter of Trust (prequel)

Shield of Justice

In Pursuit of Justice

Justice in the Shadows

Justice Served

Justice for All

The Provincetown Tales

Safe Harbor

Beyond the Breakwater

Distant Shores, Silent Thunder

Storms of Change

Winds of Fortune

Returning Tides

Sheltering Dunes

Visit us at www.boldstrokesbooks.com

PRICE OF HONOR

by

RADCLY*f*FE

2015

PRICE OF HONOR

ISBN 13: 978-1-62639-359-2

This Trade Paperback Original Is Published By
Bold Strokes Books, Inc.
P.O. Box 249
Valley Falls, NY 12185

First Edition: July 2015

Credits
Editors: Ruth Sternglantz and Stacia Seaman
Production Design: Stacia Seaman
Cover Design by Sheri (graphicartist2020@hotmail.com)

Acknowledgments

The Honor series holds a special place in the chronology of my titles. *Above All, Honor* was one of my early works and marks a place in my journey that would prove to be life-changing. I was halfway through writing *Above All, Honor* when I got sidetracked and stopped writing it. I have never written two novels at one time, since I have always written every work from start to finish. Stopping in the middle to write something else (with the exception of short stories, and then just briefly) just didn't happen. But in 1997 I discovered the Internet, and along with it, X-Files fan fiction. Almost immediately, I began to explore writing and posting fan fiction on the X-Files ScullySlash list. Along with that very new adventure came the realization that sharing my work, which I had not done up until that point, added an extra dimension of pleasure and reward to the process of writing. I discovered writing colleagues and a whole new world of challenges.

For a year I wrote nothing except fan fiction on a daily basis, all of which is still available on my website (radfic.com). And during that time, I wasn't writing any original fiction, although I wrote original characters in my fan fiction. Eventually when the TV series died off, I returned to writing original fiction, and one of the first things I did was finish *Above All, Honor*. That book was one of the first I formally published in 2001, and eventually was one of the first to be published by Bold Strokes Books in a revised, expanded edition in 2004. My intention was never to write a series, but I was seduced by requests from readers for more of these characters, and somehow, the series has morphed into ten novels and several story arcs. Each time I start a new "chapter" in the lives of Cam and Blair and all the supporting cast, the characters are at once new and familiar to me and their stories a renewed pleasure. I hope you find the same to be true.

Many thanks go to: senior editor Sandy Lowe for her contributions in keeping me and BSB running on track, editor Ruth Sternglantz for knowing where I'm going before I do, editor Stacia Seaman for always reading with care and attention, Sheri Halal for the expert graphic work, and my first readers Paula, Eva, and Connie for encouragement and inspiration.

And as always, thanks to Lee, who joined the train at the very beginning and is still up for the ride. *Amo te.*

Radclyffe, 2015

To Lee, intrepid traveler and brave explorer

Chapter One

In the foothills of the Bitterroot Mountains, Idaho

Jane had had so many names in her life, she could barely remember the one she was born with. She'd been known as Angela Jones in Eugen Corp, where she'd worked in the Level 4 lab up until the day she'd disappeared with a vial of deadly avian flu virus tucked into a fold of her clothes. In the paramilitary compound deep in the Idaho mountains, she'd been Captain Jane Graves to her fellow militia. She'd liked being known by the name she shared with her father, General Augustus Graves. Now she was neither Jane Graves nor Angela Jones or any of the long-ago names she'd had as a child moving from place to place with members of the freedom movement who'd taught and trained her. The FBI and Homeland Security knew her by those names and were looking for her. And her father was dead and had taken his name, all their names, to the grave with him.

Now she was just Jane.

She smiled as she slid the blades of the drugstore scissors along her neck and closed them on the strands of wet crimson hair scalloped on her skin. She knew her father was dead. She'd seen Cameron Roberts's face in the starburst light of the muzzle flash when Roberts gunned him down. Graves had gone to the grave. No matter. She knew who she was. A name was only a mask she wore, part of her camouflage. She was a soldier, a freedom fighter, a defender of the Constitution. She'd learned that as soon as she had learned to talk, when she'd had the first name, the one she could barely recall. Her father and those who had stood for him had raised her to be a patriot. God, family, country. These were the things that mattered.

Her country, America's America, was being perverted, weakened, humiliated in the eyes of the world by politicians who cared only for their own power and greed, by misguided and self-serving bureaucrats who pretended to care about the common man while undermining the strength and fabric of the American middle class. Her father and those like him understood that a strong America began with its leaders, men who believed in the words of the Constitution and the Bill of Rights, who'd ensure America was for the Americans, and that the world knew it. His vision. *Her* vision. God and country, forever strong.

She was the head of the family now, and she had two missions, each part of the larger goal. She must carry out her father's plan to show the American people, not through empty words but by positive action, the failings of the politicians they had elected to the highest offices in the land. People had grown numb to words but not to the images of their own vulnerability made brutally visible to them on their televisions and computer screens and the front pages of newspapers. Only fear for their own safety would ever change the minds of those who had grown deaf and dumb to the truth. Her father had known this, had taught her this. She and her sister and her brother had been shaped to do their part in the patriotic war. That war had not ended with the destruction of their compound or even her father's murder. The fight had barely begun, and she would not allow the enemy an easy victory. She would continue the war, and she would free her sister.

Jennifer had been the first to fall, not killed, but captured. She was somewhere in DC, in a temporary holding facility, and Jane had only a small window of time to free her before she disappeared into the black hole of the justice system. They had all known this could happen—to any of them. She thought she'd been prepared, but the ache of Jenn's absence was worse somehow than her father's death. He had always been a symbol, a distant force that guided her life. Jenn was her friend, her confidant, the only one who knew her.

Methodically, she collected the fallen strands and dropped them into a plastic supermarket bag to dispose of when she left the motel where she'd spent the last few days waiting for the influx of local and federal law enforcement agents to diminish. She had no idea how many of the others had escaped, or what if anything of the compound remained. All she'd managed to salvage were her rifle, two handguns, and a gym bag filled with a quarter of a million dollars. She'd had to kill the biker who double-crossed them and tried to steal the money her father had obtained from an anonymous political donor to purchase weapons. She couldn't risk contacting any of the other militia, not yet. She couldn't risk returning to the compound, for it might never be a safe place again. She had no home, no refuge. All she had now were her siblings and her father's words resounding in her mind.

She stared into her own flat blue eyes in the pitted mirror above the stained porcelain sink and decided her appearance was altered enough with the ultra-short cut and red dye she'd used. She still had a weapon more powerful than a bullet. She had Robbie, close to the president's inner circle. And she had the phone number of the man who'd provided the money.

She *should* have a new name for this new phase of the mission. She studied her face, smiling softly as the German she studied another lifetime ago surfaced. *Racher. Jane Racher. Jane the Avenger.*

❖

"You should be the one who passes on this trip," Blair said, setting aside the newspaper she'd been pretending to read. She couldn't concentrate on the headlines that seemed only to be a repeat of the ones from the day before, and the day before that. Dire economic forecasts, genocide in Africa and Eastern Europe, protests at home over racial profiling and sexual harassment in the workplace and on college campuses, and cries of moral decline from the increasingly vocal far-right factions. They'd been back in DC not quite three days since Cam and another agent had been taken prisoner and nearly killed, and Cam was still hollow-eyed and pale and limping. The abrasions on her face and hands from showering glass, gravel, and wood splinters were scabbed over but still red. A huge bruise, multi-hued in storm-cloud purples, covered the right side of her chest and abdomen, and the through-and-through wound in her left calf was swollen and angry. "You're in no shape to travel."

"Your father isn't going to delay opening his campaign because of an action no one is supposed to know about," Cam pointed out. "Besides, it's only a week, and we'll be on the train a lot of the time."

"Yes, and the rest of the time we'll be stumping at community meetings and donor dinners and charity balls. We'll be eating bad food, sleeping a couple hours a night, and always running to keep on schedule. You don't know what the campaign trail is like."

"I know I missed all the fun the first time Andrew ran," Cam said, easing down onto the sofa next to Blair. She slowly lifted her injured left leg and propped it on the coffee table, took Blair's hand, and squeezed gently. "I won't be doing any of the heavy lifting. I'll be fine."

"I see." Blair set the paper aside carefully, even though she wanted to fling it across the room. The quick burst of heat welling inside her was familiar, and once, she would've vented, would've pulled away, pushed Cam away. She recognized the anger for what it was now. Somewhere in the course of living with Cameron, loving Cameron, she'd come to understand that the anger that had motivated her to act out when she was a teenager, to put herself at foolish risk when she'd gotten older, to push away those who cared about her, was really fear. She wasn't proud of that, but she was learning to forgive herself for it. She didn't remember when the fear had begun, but sometime between the age of twelve when she realized her mother was not going to get well, and understanding a few years later that her father's job, his mission, put his life at risk, a chunk of ice had settled deep inside her, burning even as it froze. She'd lost her mother. She could lose her father. Love was a risk she wouldn't take, and so she had lived with anger choking her until Cameron made it impossible for her *not* to love. She loved now with everything in her, and the fear of loss was huger than ever. She took a deep breath. "You know, you always say that—that you'll be out of it. That you'll be fine. You realize, it's almost never true."

"Blair," Cam sighed, wondering if Blair had any idea how plainly her emotions played across her beautiful, expressive face. First the anger flared, bright and hot and familiar, darkening too quickly into grief and pain, and finally settling into a kind of calm Cam wasn't sure she preferred. She'd never minded Blair's anger, not once she'd understood its source and realized the fight was part of Blair's strength. She'd only cared when the anger blinded Blair to danger. She threaded her fingers into the tangle of blond waves on Blair's shoulders and sifted the golden strands through her fingers. "You ought to be angry. You're right. Just so you know, I've never consciously tried to fool you. I've obviously been fooling myself, though."

"I don't want an apology. I know by now you're doing what you have to do." Blair slid closer on the sofa and rested her hand on Cam's thigh. "I just don't want you getting into a situation you can't handle because you're not a hundred percent."

"I understand. What if I promise, swear right now, I'll only be there in a supervisory capacity? We've got plenty of excellent people who excel at their jobs to handle anything that needs handling. No boots on the ground this time."

Blair dropped her head onto Cam's shoulder and sighed. "Cameron. I adore you. And I know you mean every word. But this time, if you even think about saddling up, I'm going to tie you down myself."

Cam laughed and kissed Blair's temple. "Is that supposed to be a threat?"

Blair stroked Cam's abdomen and slid her hand under her faded gray T-shirt. "You could think of it as a promise."

Cam took a swift breath, the heat of Blair's fingertips spreading through her, swamping the ache in her bone-weary body with a flood of pleasure. "Believe me, I will."

"Lucinda emailed me the almost-maybe-for real-final itinerary," Blair said. "We leave tomorrow at zero five hundred. First stop, Chicago."

"I got one from Tom Turner too. The next countdown meeting is this afternoon. I want to pay a visit to Jennifer Pattee before that."

"Cam, you could use another day in bed."

"I won't argue," Cam said. "But I'll make it as quick as I can."

"I'll come with you to the White House. I want to talk to my father about what he needs me to do, anyhow."

Cam cupped the back of her neck and kissed her. "We've got the morning to ourselves, then."

Blair shifted on the sofa and slipped her hand higher, caressing the underside of Cam's breast. "I think you should go back to bed."

"I'm not tired," Cam said, her stomach tightening in anticipation.

Blair lightly scraped Cam's lower lip with her teeth, ending with a soft flick of her tongue. "I didn't say you should go to sleep."

❖

Idaho Senator Franklin Russo clicked the remote and turned off the morning news. The local channels were still carrying follow-up stories to the destruction of the local paramilitary compound in the Bitterroot Mountains. They didn't call it a paramilitary compound, but a wilderness camp owned by Augustus Graves, a local businessman who'd perished in the fire. The federal agents had obviously spun many of the details because there'd been no discussion of a firefight, hostages, or casualties. The story in the news was of an accidental explosion of a stockpile of weapons a local survivalist group had acquired in anticipation of future gun restrictions. From what he'd been able to learn from Hooker's contact in the local sheriff's department, the weapons exchange fronted by his money—or rather, the money of several of his wealthy donors—had never taken place. The Renegades, a biker group supplying the weapons, had started a shootout with the militia and all hell had broken loose. He'd helped instigate the gun battle by spreading a rumor that the militia was in bed with the ATF and planned to entrap the Renegades. He'd known he might sacrifice his money, but he'd had no choice once he'd learned the militia had captured a federal agent. As it turned out, not just one agent, but two. He couldn't be involved with something like that. He'd needed distance, and the best kind of distance was the silence of the dead. There'd been no rumor in the news or anywhere else that could lead back to him. The only people who knew of his involvement with the militia were his aide, Derek, who he trusted completely, and his hired gun, Hooker, who he trusted quite a bit less. Still, Hooker had his uses.

Hooker was a mercenary with the kind of contacts Franklin couldn't approach himself. As long as their association with the now-deceased Augustus Graves was unknown, he could continue to use Hooker. After all, he still had an agenda. His presidential campaign was growing in strength, but Andrew Powell was still a popular president among both the left and the center. Only the far right could see Powell for the debauched liberal he was, and in order to strengthen his own position with the less radical contingents, Franklin needed to weaken Powell's. And what better way to shake voter confidence than to show the American people their president was incapable of leading. That he was vulnerable and weak. Franklin's money was still out there, and if Hooker could find it, he just might be able to buy himself another weapon.

CHAPTER TWO

Dusty stroked Atlas's sleek, muscular back and read the question in the dark chocolate eyes that studied hers. *Why are we wasting time in here when we could be working and having some real fun?* "I know, I know. I'm not any crazier about this than you are. But public relations is part of the job, right?"

Atlas flicked an ear dismissively. He didn't care any more for PR or politics than she did. Work was his only interest and his greatest joy, just like it was hers. His long, fluted tail brushed slowly from side to side on the cement floor of the training run, as measured and steady as his temperament. His right shoulder lightly touched the outside of Dusty's left leg. She had him on a short lead, but it wasn't really necessary. He wouldn't leave her side unless she gave him the command to search or release. But since they were meeting a civilian, she wanted to send the message he wasn't a pet and ought to be given the same respect as any other professional. Too many people didn't think twice about approaching a strange dog, even when it was obviously a law enforcement dog engaged in serious work. Atlas would tolerate a stranger's touch if she assured him first it was all right, but it wasn't fair to him to put him in an awkward situation because of a human's ignorance.

"I'll get us out of there as fast as I can, I promise. It's just a couple of questions and a few photo ops. The bosses say good publicity is always important." Dusty wasn't any more eager to be interviewed by a member of the press than Atlas was to be inside when he'd rather be out on the training course. Dog stories were apparently popular with the public and, according to public affairs, created sympathy and support for the federal agencies who employed them, helping to balance the more frequent critical portrayals that seemed the daily fodder of the press. She didn't much care how those outside the unit viewed her. She much preferred the company of her dog to almost anyone.

She and Atlas had been together since he was just weeks old. They'd been living and training together over a year. They understood each other, communicating without words more effortlessly than she'd ever been able to communicate with anyone. They slept together, ate together, trained together, worked together, played together. What else could she possibly need? She stroked between his ears for a second and he nudged her leg.

"Eleven thirty. Time to meet the reporter." She brushed a stray Atlas hair off the front of her dark blue BDU shirt and signaled him to heel. The reporter from the *Washington Gazette* was doing a feature piece on the role of the Secret Service K9 division in the protection of the president. She didn't mind talking about Atlas—she loved letting people know how amazing he was. What she wasn't about to admit was that tomorrow would be the first time she and Atlas took to the field as part of the PPD. She wasn't a rookie, though. She'd worked with protection dogs on the White House grounds before moving to the explosives-detection unit. Atlas was young but seasoned, with one of the best noses in the division. He'd passed all his training certifications with flying colors, and she couldn't wait to get started. Instead of preparing for the upcoming operation, she'd gotten stuck with this.

"Twenty minutes," she muttered and led Atlas down the long hall of the training facility to the conference room at the front of the building. The small room was made smaller by a table too big for the ten-by-fifteen-foot space already crowded with wooden folding chairs and a whiteboard on wheels. The flat fluorescent overheads cast a harsh glow on the off-white walls and scuffed gray tile floor. A metal cart sat in one corner with a coffee urn, a stack of Styrofoam cups, individual plastic containers of cream and packets of sugar, and plastic stir sticks. Otherwise the stark, bare room was empty.

Except for the woman sitting at the end of the table who forced everything else into a monochromatic blur. Even sitting, she looked tall, possibly taller than Dusty's own five-nine. She was ivory complected with dark, dark hair pulled back from her face and clasped at the back of her neck. Shorter strands slanted across her forehead above arched black brows. Lipstick just short of deep red highlighted a wide full mouth. Her high cheekbones, narrow nose, and heart-shaped face were too angular for conventional beauty, but her piercing dark almond eyes were magnetic, mesmerizing.

"Like a Modigliani," Dusty murmured.

"I'm sorry?" The woman stood, her deep green jacket and skirt draping perfectly over a model's body, slender and sleek.

Dusty froze in her tracks and Atlas sat obediently at her side. Feeling a flush creep up her neck, she self-consciously cleared her throat and said a prayer of thanks that her utterance hadn't been clearer. "Ms. Elliott?"

The woman walked around the table and held out her hand. "Yes. Vivian Elliott."

Conscious of her calloused palm meeting smooth cool flesh, Dusty shook her hand. "Dusty Nash. This is Atlas."

Vivian glanced down, smiled. "Gorgeous."

Dusty couldn't shake the disquieting sense that Vivian Elliott wasn't quite real. She'd never seen a woman so beautiful before, not in real life or in any of the dozens of museums and hundreds of paintings she'd viewed over the years.

"He probably prefers handsome," Vivian said, making no move to touch the dog. He was, indeed, handsome. Quick, intelligent eyes, glowing mahogany coat shot through with black over his shoulders and hips, a broad strong head, and tapered snout. "How old is he?"

"A year and a half."

"Young for this work, isn't he?"

"Not for his breed."

"Belgian Malinois?"

"Yes."

Vivian mentally sorted through the research she'd done when prepping for the interview, searching for something that would help her connect to the handler. Agent Nash appeared far less communicative than her dog, whose liquid eyes spoke volumes as he tilted his head and appraised her. Nash's eyes, a startling shade of true green with tiny flecks of brown-gold that matched her windblown collar-length hair, were wary and intense. On most people a green that pure screamed contact lenses, but nothing about Nash suggested artifice or vanity. Her hair was casually cut, her fair, faintly freckled face without any kind of makeup, her uniform standard, well-worn BDUs, unadorned except for the ID hanging around her neck and the unit patches on her sleeves and chest. Agent Dusty Nash was not a people person. "I don't suppose there's any chance we could talk outside, where I could see him work a little?"

A spark flared in Nash's eyes, and Viv congratulated herself. Bingo. It was all about the dog with this one. Not so different from some of the breeders she'd known growing up. "After all, he's the star, right?"

"You do know it's twenty-five degrees out there," Dusty said.

"Does he mind the cold?" Viv teased.

Dusty laughed, and the transformation was breathtaking. Her stoic expression softened and heat melted the coolness in her gaze. "He's bred to work in the mountains. He loves the cold. He'd much rather be outside than inside."

"Does that go for you too?" Viv knew the answer, but she needed to keep Nash talking so the freeze didn't set in again. Not an unfriendly, arrogant disinterest, but something else. A rare air of self-containment, a subtle barrier that provoked Viv's curiosity.

"Yes."

"Then that's what we should do. Let me get my coat."

Viv retrieved her dark green wool topcoat and shrugged into it. She extracted her tape recorder from the left pocket and held it up. "I can't take notes while we're walking, so I'll be taping. Are you all right with that?"

Dusty shrugged. "Sure."

She held up her camera with the other. "Photos, of course."

"Can you just take him?"

Viv considered her approach. Nash wouldn't care about personal publicity. "You're a team, right?"

"Sure."

"He wouldn't work as well with anyone else, or you either, for that matter. Right?"

Dusty's left hand dropped to Atlas's head and he pushed against her palm. "That's how we train. I have to be able to read his actions and the signals he gives when he alerts to something. No one else knows him that well."

"Exactly, and that's what readers really want to see. The teamwork."

"I thought this was about using dogs on protective details."

"It is, some," Viv admitted. "But you know most of that is classified. I'll get some photos on the train to tie in with what we do here."

"You're going?"

"White House press corps," Viv said, pointing to her ID.

"I'll grab my jacket, and we'll go out the back," Dusty said, oddly pleased to hear Vivian Elliott would be traveling with the press on the upcoming trip. "I'll show you some training exercises."

"Wonderful."

Vivian smiled, and Dusty was reminded of her favorite, enigmatically beautiful paintings again.

❖

Blair woke slowly, nestled in the curve of Cam's body, Cam's arm looped around her waist, holding her close. Cam's chest and belly were warm against her back and hips. She laced her fingers through Cam's, drew up her hand, and kissed her fingers. "You awake?"

"Mm," Cam murmured. "Sort of."

"We're going to have to get up."

Cam sighed and kissed the back of Blair's neck. "I know. Five more minutes."

Blair laughed. "You're getting lazy, you know. This cushy desk job of yours might make you soft."

"Nah." Cam burrowed against Blair's shoulder. "Just spoiled. Married life agrees with me."

Blair caught her breath. Married. They were, as of just a few weeks before. She felt the ring on her finger that matched the one on Cam's. Thought about the future, a future so very different from the one she'd imagined a year ago when she'd rarely considered the next day, let alone anything beyond. Her father wouldn't be the president forever, and she wouldn't be an object of public speculation or a potential target any longer. She could have a life like other people. *They* could have a life without danger around every turn.

Cam would probably always have the kind of job she did now. She was driven to serve, driven to protect, but when the administration inevitably changed, she might actually spend more time behind her desk. She'd never completely leave the field, no matter what she said her intentions were. It just wasn't part of her. But there might come a time when someone else really did take the risks. Blair tried to imagine how they would live and thought of the house they'd purchased on Whitley Island. Remote, wild, beautiful. Where they could be alone and she could paint and…

She jolted at an unexpected, nearly frightening image.

"What?" Cam murmured, kissing her again.

"Just thinking."

"Thinking what?"

Blair turned onto her back and found Cam leaning on an elbow regarding her with that serious look she got when she was waiting for Blair to decide to share a secret. Or not. "I was thinking it might be nice to have a child."

Cam's pupils widened. "A baby, you mean."

"Maybe. Or a toddler. Or an older one."

"Adopt?"

"I think so. There's so many kids who need homes." Blair pushed a dark lock from Cam's forehead, searched the storm-gray eyes, and waited. Cam was an only child, they both were, and neither had had an easy childhood—losing parents far too soon. They'd barely begun their life together. Her timing was pretty terrible.

"We have pretty busy schedules," Cam said slowly, carefully.

Blair laughed and kissed her. "I don't mean right away."

The tension in Cam's shoulders eased and her breath came out in a long sigh. "No? When then?"

"I don't know, four or five years. When our life is a little more normal."

"Adoption is fine with me," Cam said. "You don't want to be pregnant?"

"I don't feel any burning need to be. Do you?"

"No. Never pictured it."

"What about children? Did you ever picture that?"

"Blair." Cam eased down on the pillow beside Blair and wrapped an arm around her. "I never thought about being married until you. Beyond that, no. But I'm thinking about it now."

"That's good, then. There's no rush."

"It's a big deal. I know you know that. You might change your mind about wanting to carry a child by the time we're ready to."

"If I do, I'll let you know."

"Okay. Then we have a plan. We'll revise as needed."

Laughing again, Blair slung a leg over Cam's hips and pressed close. Their bodies joined effortlessly, naturally. "I love you."

"I love you."

Blair gave a little shove and Cam fell onto her back. Blair rolled onto her, sliding one leg between Cam's. Smooth and hot skin kissed her wet, swollen flesh and she rocked, enjoying the rush of pleasure that filled her. She braced her arms on either side of Cam's shoulders and worked herself in long teasing strokes to the edge. Cam cupped her breasts and squeezed her nipples lightly, knowing the pleasure would push her even higher. Blair caught her lip between her teeth, felt the tension coil deep in her belly.

"I am so going to come on you in about ten seconds."

"That's right, baby," Cam whispered. "You're so hot."

Blair's vision wavered, heat flooded her belly, and she arched her back. The orgasm started slow and then burst like sunlight, jolting along her spine. She gasped and cried out, her head falling forward, her hair draping Cam's face in a golden veil.

Cam caught her as she fell and pulled her close, reveling in her pleasure. "That was the best five minutes I've had in a long time."

Blair sighed and kissed her throat. "I'm not sure where that came from."

"Who cares, as long as there's more," Cam whispered.

"If we don't get up, we'll be late."

"I suppose we can't keep the White House waiting." Cam stroked her back and squeezed her ass. "But I want the rest later."

Blair pushed herself up, still trembling. "Once we walk out the door, we might not be alone again for days."

Cam kissed her. "We'll find time. Guaranteed."

Blair laughed. "And that's exactly why I love you."

❖

Jane called the last number she'd gotten for her brother. Her heart seemed to stop as it always did until he answered. Now more than ever, he was the one at risk, so close to those looking for her, maybe him too.

"Hey. You all right?" Robbie said by way of greeting.

"Yes. Is it still on?"

"Yes, heading out tomorrow."

"And you're going for sure?"

"Front-row seat." He laughed. "Well, not exactly. Probably four or five cars back, but close enough."

"And the itinerary?"

"Just a preliminary, so far. I expect an update later. I know quite a few people aren't happy about this little excursion."

"Just the usual super-paranoia?"

"Well, given what's happened here and then…out there, security is even tighter than usual."

What happened out there. They didn't talk about their father anymore. He was gone. Now it was up to them. "What about Jenn?"

"I don't know."

The answer was a blade in her heart. "There must be something."

"I know someone who knows a guard, but there's not much news. I think she's still here, but if they move her I'll have no way to get information."

"We're not going to let that happen. She's not going to disappear into some hole."

"You have a plan?"

She did, at least the beginnings of one. She had to set her rage aside and think clearly. Revenge was a dangerous motivator. She'd been taught that. Sweet when accomplished, but dangerous when it clouded judgment. She wasn't a martyr, and she wasn't going to let Jenn or Robbie be martyrs either. "There are options. It might be better if you didn't go."

"You need inside information."

"Yes, but that puts you—"

"In danger," he said sharply. "You mean like you and Jenn? You think I've been happy all these years sitting on my ass scribbling useless articles and ingratiating myself to hangers-on and ass-kissers and perverts?"

"I know it's easier to carry a gun, believe me. But we needed you there, and look what it's accomplished for us."

"Yes. Jenn in a cell."

"That wasn't your fault."

"I shouldn't have trusted the mercenary quite so much."

"We're going to have to trust him again. Is the number for him still good?"

"I think so, yes."

"I'll be getting a new phone later today. I'll text you the number."

"I'll change mine too and let you know."

"Be careful, Robbie."

"You know, you're the only one who ever calls me that. If it weren't for you, I might not remember my name." He sounded sad, lost for a moment.

Jane pushed the sympathy away. "You know who you are. Don't ever forget what we need to do."

"Right," he said briskly. "Well, at least the train will make a nice change from Air Force One."

Jane laughed flatly. "And a nicer target."

CHAPTER THREE

C am braced her arms against the shower wall as the hot water beat down against her back. She ached just about everywhere, but nothing she hadn't felt before and nothing that wouldn't ease in a few days. She removed the bandage on her leg to let the water clean the tract where the wood splinter had sailed through her calf when part of the building where she'd been imprisoned had exploded. She was lucky. Skylar Dunbar was still in the hospital recovering from the bullet wound to her arm and from blood loss. Fortunately the early reports from the surgeon were that no major muscle or nerve damage had occurred and Skylar would not suffer long-term injury. Cam hadn't known the agent very long, but spending twenty-four hours on the brink of death with someone taught you a lot. Dunbar was gutsy and tough, and Cam was glad she was going to be all right.

She was still putting together all the pieces as to just what had happened out in Idaho where she and Dunbar had been abducted. Reports were still coming in from agents on the scene, but the one person Cam wanted to talk to had dropped out of sight. She wasn't surprised. Loren McElroy had been undercover for years and was a valuable asset. She'd disappeared to preserve her cover. Cam had a number for her and had left a message. McElroy would call her, she was certain. In the meantime, she still had a prisoner who was one of the keys to the puzzle.

Jennifer Pattee was connected to that militia compound, and Cam was close to verifying just how close that connection was. Thinking about the upcoming interrogation, she turned off the water and stepped out. Blair was leaning against the counter in a white terrycloth robe belted loosely at the waist, her wet blond hair tangled on her shoulders, her piercing blue eyes studying Cam. A small frown line creased the smooth skin between her golden brows.

Cam grabbed a towel, being careful not to wince when the movement pulled at her sore rib cage. She wrapped it around her torso and grabbed another to towel her hair.

"So how bad is it, and no bullshitting," Blair said.

"Stiff and sore." Cam pushed a hand through her hair and dried off the rest of the way. "The leg feels better."

Blair motioned for Cam to put her injured leg up on a stepstool and picked up a roll of bandage. "It still looks really painful."

"I'll admit I wouldn't want to run very far," Cam said as Blair wrapped the wound, "but I don't expect I'll have to."

"No, I suppose not."

"Thanks. That feels better."

Blair straightened, kissed Cam, and turned to put the medical supplies back into the narrow closet in the corner of the bathroom. "Are you going right to the White House?"

"No, I'm going to stop at the detention center first."

"Maybe I'll see you for dinner, then."

Cam cradled Blair's shoulders and pulled Blair against her. Wrapping her arms around Blair's waist from behind, she kissed the side of her neck. "The countdown will probably run long. I don't think we've gotten the final itinerary yet."

Blair laughed shortly and covered Cam's hands with hers. "Why aren't I surprised? You know Adam is always adding last-minute stops for Dad."

"I know. Eisley's a real pain in the ass."

Blair rested her head back against Cam's shoulder. "He is. But he's really good at his job."

"I suppose. If you end up staying later, I'll see you when you get home."

Blair turned and let her robe fall open, pressing naked against Cam. Her skin was warm, her body strong and supple.

Cam groaned softly. "Come on."

Blair's eyes flashed and she smiled a satisfied smile. "I want you to be thinking about me this afternoon."

"Like I wouldn't be?"

"Just making sure."

Cam clasped the back of Blair's neck and kissed her, a long, serious kiss. "Mission accomplished."

Blair breathed heavily, her lips faintly parted. "Yeah. Me too."

Cam grinned and brushed a thumb over her chin. "See you later, baby."

"See you later, Commander."

❖

The building where Jennifer Pattee was being detained looked nothing like a prison. It was a square glass-and-steel structure like most of the federal buildings surrounding the Capitol. The upper floors were all administrative offices of midlevel attorneys, aides, and other justice employees. But the second basement level, accessible only by a key card that a select few people carried, was a different matter.

The elevators opened on a ten-foot-square, tile-floored lobby directly across from a guard station. There were no chairs, no signs, no water coolers. The two uniformed officers sat in a well-lit glass cubicle scanning banks of monitors that displayed relays from the exterior and interior of the building as well as the four detention cells behind the adjacent steel doors.

Cam presented her credentials and one of the officers keyed in the code to the doors. They swung open and Cam walked through. Only one of the cells, their interiors dim behind plain metal doors with rectangular windows, was occupied. She settled at the bare, brown laminate table in the small visitor's room and waited for the guard to bring Jennifer Pattee in. Cam hadn't seen her for almost a week. Her appearance was much the same as the last time. Her shoulder-length dark hair was clean, her heart-shaped face pale and faintly shadowed. Her eyes were still clear and angry and sharply intelligent. She sat across from Cam in her gray jumpsuit, her shoulders upright, her hands still cuffed in her lap.

"Are you being taken care of adequately?" Cam asked.

The former White House Medical Unit nurse smiled wryly. "I'm being fed and allowed to shower and given clean clothes. I wouldn't mind a computer."

"Who would you contact?"

"I like to surf the shopping sites and read the news."

"What about a phone call?"

"Who would I call?" Jennifer echoed.

"How about Augustus Graves?"

For a fraction of a second, Jennifer tensed, and if Cam hadn't been looking for it and hadn't spent a large part of her career in investigations doing interrogations, she would've missed it.

"Who would that be?" Jennifer asked.

Her question implied she cared about the answer. She was usually too smart to engage in any conversation. "He was the leader of a militia group out in Idaho. I thought since you grew up there, you might've heard of him."

"I don't know anything about Idaho," Jennifer said.

She was lying, of course. Cam was nearly 100 percent certain that Jennifer was related to the woman who'd taken Cam prisoner and undoubtedly would have killed her had she the opportunity. The two of them looked alike. She didn't know how Augustus Graves fit into the picture, but she was certain they all knew each other.

"In that case, you won't be disturbed to learn that he's dead."

This time Jennifer Pattee didn't move. She'd probably already been mentally preparing herself for some kind of news once the name had been mentioned. She was very well trained, but the autonomic nervous system was something few people could control completely, if at all. Her pupils flickered rapidly. The news had triggered an adrenaline surge.

"Let me tell you about him. It might ring a few bells." Cam relaxed back in her seat. "Graves was an Idaho businessman who owned a large tract of land up in the Bitterroot Mountains. He built a compound on that land. A big one, big enough to house a few hundred people. A militia. Before it got blown up a couple nights ago, it appeared to have been pretty self-sufficient, with an infirmary and an armory and barracks. Pretty sophisticated stuff."

"I don't know him," Jennifer said flatly.

"Interesting place," Cam went on. "I ran into one of his senior… officers, I guess you could say. A woman. She reminded me of you. Looked a little like you too. I didn't get her name, but maybe you know it?"

The fingers of Jennifer's right hand closed slowly, a small tell. "I don't know any of these people. I don't know anything about Idaho."

"You know," Cam said slowly, "I said I didn't know her name. That's not exactly true. I know the name she used when she worked at Eugen Corp. Angela Jones. The one who stole the virus that you were carrying when you were apprehended. Help your memory at all?"

"I already told you. That was a mistake. I have no idea what the virus was for or why I was given it."

"Lots of coincidences. Are you interested in knowing what happened to her?"

"No," Jennifer said, no inflection in her voice. "As I said, I don't know her."

Cam leaned forward, forcing Jennifer to look into her face. "You know her. She's a cousin…no, closer than that. A sister. Don't you want to know if she's alive or dead?"

Jennifer's pupils were pinpoint. "No."

"She wanted you to be released. She wanted to trade me for you. She made a mistake when she did that. She brought the hammer down on that compound, because we don't negotiate with terrorists."

"Terrorists," Jennifer exclaimed.

"What would you call them?"

"Patriots," Jennifer snapped.

"Yes, I suppose you would. Tell me, Jennifer, how patriotic is it to attempt to kill the president of the United States?"

Jennifer's lips pressed together. She'd made a mistake, speaking out.

"She's your sister," Cam said with certainty. "And before too long, I'll know exactly who both of you are. If you don't want her killed, then help me find her before she does something else."

"I can't help you."

"All right. Not yet." Cam stood. "But don't wait too long."

Cam signaled to the guard to return her to her cell. Jennifer Pattee and Angela Jones hadn't been alone in devising the thwarted attack on Andrew Powell. It'd taken a lot of money and significant inside help to pull it off. She didn't know how close the other conspirators were to the president, but she couldn't rule anyone out except those she trusted absolutely, and those numbers were few.

Anytime the president was exposed, he was vulnerable. Now he insisted on kicking off his reelection campaign with a grassroots appeal to the heartland via a train ride, despite that being a security nightmare. But the Secret Service and Homeland Security were the best protective organizations in the world. Everyone would be ready when game day arrived.

❖

Viv waited in the doorway of a small equipment room while Dusty pulled a navy nylon bomber jacket from a locker and shrugged into it. Atlas sat beside her, the cadence of his tail swishing back and forth increasing when she donned the jacket.

"He seems to know what's about to happen," Viv commented.

"He does." Dusty zipped the jacket and murmured a command. Atlas followed at her side as Dusty joined Viv in the hall. "There's nothing he'd rather do than work."

"Sounds like a perfect partner."

"Couldn't find a better one."

Clearly Dusty Nash meant every word. She and the dog were more than a team, they were a unit, apparently self-sufficient in every respect. Viv knew dog people. She'd been raised around them. Her mother bred champion Labradors. Some were used in police work but more often they worked in service areas. Their gentle nature and less threatening demeanor made them better choices where a great deal of social interaction was required. The Malinois were far more aggressive and tended to work better one-on-one with their handlers in solo situations, like Dusty's, or in small units, as they'd been employed in the Middle East.

Dusty was like a lot of dog people she knew, more comfortable with animals than people. But she got the feeling it went further than that, as if Dusty had an invisible barrier around her that kept her apart. Viv had always been drawn to the quiet solitary types, like her father. She'd come to recognize at an early age that when praise or a smile or a gentle touch was given from someone like him, it meant even more. She wondered if there was anyone Dusty smiled for. Realizing she'd been daydreaming, Viv put her game face on. "How often does he need to train, now that you're a working unit?"

"We train a little every day," Dusty said, leading the way through a set of double doors into an open lot behind the group of low buildings. "Requirements are a minimum of ten hours of active training every week unless we're deployed."

"I don't imagine he thinks of it as work," Viv said.

"For him it's just fun."

"How about you? Is that what you do for fun too?" Viv realized a second too late her comment might be construed as flirtatious, and maybe it was.

Dusty regarded her solemnly, the merest hint of question in her eyes. "It's not work for me either. It's what I enjoy doing."

"He lives with you, I take it?"

"That's right."

"And how is he…" Viv searched for a way that wouldn't make it too obvious she was probing for personal information. "With family?"

"He behaves himself with strangers. He's good with people, but not overly friendly. That's just normal for his breed."

That was nicely sidestepped. Viv made a noncommittal noise and followed along, hunching her shoulders against the brisk wind. The training area looked to be a hundred acres of field bordered on one side by woods. They veered away from the woods and along a narrow path that led to a group of buildings, more like sheds really, where a number of vehicles were parked haphazardly in tall grass.

"I already placed a hide earlier today," Dusty said. "I was planning to bring him out for a little work before the Office of Public Affairs contacted me to meet with you."

"A hide?"

"An explosive-impregnated package."

"Is it dangerous?"

Dusty shook her head. "There's nothing to arm or trigger the explosives. It's the odor we care about. Atlas detects bombs by scent. He's incredibly good at recognizing just about any kind of explosive."

"Right. He alerts to the scent cone, isn't that it?"

Dusty gave her a long look. "That's right. Not many people actually know that."

"I did a little reading before I came," Viv said. "And my family's in dogs. My mother raises and trains Labs, mostly for service but a couple go to handlers for law enforcement. Usually search and rescue, cadaver, sometimes protection."

"Really? Labs?"

"Uh-huh."

"They're good dogs. A little distractible."

Viv laughed at the understatement. "Oh my God, don't you know it."

"That's why they're not the best dogs for bomb detection."

"How old was Atlas when you got him?"

"The pups are separated from their mothers earlier than normal so they bond with the human from a really early age. After I worked with some of the graduate dogs for a while, I got to choose my own for training. He was three weeks old."

"He's been with you his whole life."

Dusty leaned down and unclipped Atlas's lead. He panted softly, his ears perked and his eyes bright.

"Atlas, find it." Dusty pointed at a bus twenty-five yards away, and he tore off like a missile fired from a fighter plane.

"Yeah, his whole life," Dusty murmured as she trotted after him.

Viv ran to keep up, cursing the heels on her suede boots. She hadn't anticipated anything quite so strenuous. She clutched her recorder in one hand and kept her coat closed at her throat with the other. The wind bit through the wool as if it was sheer cotton. Dusty, hatless with her jacket partially unzipped, appeared impervious, her gaze riveted on the dog. She slowed and Viv pulled up beside her, trying not to gasp. A few more weekly sessions at the gym seemed in order.

Atlas trotted along beside the bus, halting occasionally to hunker down and crawl partway underneath, then backing out and resuming his methodical foot-by-foot search along the carriage.

"What's he doing?" Viv fumbled her camera out and got a picture of Atlas sniffing along the wheel well with Dusty a few feet away, her hands on her hips, her face in profile, staring into the wind in utter concentration. They were both beautiful animals.

Dusty glanced over. "Checking the exterior, the undercarriage, the wheel wells, the body, the places where someone could plant a charge. He'll finish inside if he doesn't find anything outside."

"Will he?"

Dusty grinned and that breathtaking transformation happened again. She went from remote and cool and icily striking to warm and sexy. Viv stared as Dusty tilted her head much as Atlas had done earlier, studying her in return.

Viv's face heated against the cold wind, and she hoped Dusty would write off the flush in her cheeks to the weather and not her embarrassment at being caught staring.

"There," Dusty murmured, her focus back on Atlas again. "That's a good boy."

Atlas sat and woofed once, his head extended and his nose pointing to the grille at the front of the bus.

"Different breeds, different dogs, will alert in different ways," Dusty said as she strode toward Atlas. "Once he alerts, he sits, his focus on the find."

"How often does he miss?"

Dusty grunted. "Never."

"And that's what you'll be doing during the president's trip? Atlas will be checking the train?"

"Atlas will be checking everything."

CHAPTER FOUR

Hooker slid onto the stool next to the county sheriff's deputy and motioned to the bartender to refill the deputy's beer. Early afternoon, the place was almost empty, the lights turned down low and the windows too grimy for much of the low, flat winter light to penetrate. The deputy, wearing two days' worth of beard, mud-caked boots, and a sweat-stained, rumpled uniform, glanced at Hooker and grunted in greeting. The man was Hooker's best source inside the local law-enforcement network, and he'd been combing through the wreckage of the militia compound just like every other LEO in that part of Idaho for the better part of a week. Hooker wanted to know what they'd found and, even more importantly, what they suspected, without giving away his stake in the game.

"Sounds like you've been pretty busy up there," Hooker said.

The ruddy-faced middle-aged man, his salt-and-pepper hair cut close, his heavy straining belly showing his fondness for brew, grunted again. "Fucking waste of time."

"Puts you boys in a tight spot. I don't imagine anybody's too eager to start arresting their neighbors."

"No point to it," the deputy said. "No way to prove who was up there that night, no way to prove they were even doing anything illegal, unless you can tie those illegal guns directly to them. Which we can't."

"I heard the bikers were the gun connection."

"Looks like it, and that's their style."

"What about the Renegades? Are you picking up any of them?" Hooker sipped the beer the bartender put in front of him. It was a little too early in the day, but he made a show of it.

"The ones who could ride away, did. That left us with the dead and a dozen wounded. The ones in the hospital swear they don't know anything about any guns and were innocent bystanders."

"What happened to the guns?"

"They're locked up in evidence. The ATF will try to track them, but they won't get anywhere."

"So the whole thing is pretty much going to die down."

"The feds are pretty interested in finding out who was backing the buy, but since there's no money to trace and no one's talking, things will probably end up dead-ended."

"Huh," Hooker said. Someone had the money, someone who'd been in the compound that night. His boss wasn't happy about losing their donors' money, although they'd known the risks when they'd manipulated the bikers and the militia into believing each was double-crossing the other. All the same, losing a quarter of a million dollars wasn't something to write off easily. "Maybe the militia was fronting the buy and one of them made off with it."

"Most likely." The deputy drained his beer and Hooker signaled for the bartender to fill him up. "Wherever it went, it's gone, and I don't think anyone's gonna be looking too hard."

"How'd the feds get pulled into it so quick?"

"Some big shot from back east poking around is what I heard." The deputy scoffed. "Like they don't have real enemies to be going after, they have to come looking at Americans."

"They sure managed to find the place quick."

"Probably the firefight between the bikers and the militia brought down the heat."

Hooker wasn't so sure. He'd never been to the compound, but he knew how well hidden it was. Graves always arranged a meet somewhere on neutral ground, and he couldn't see Graves letting the bikers anywhere near the place. But the Renegades had shown up in force, and the feds had found the location in record time too. To him, that spelled inside information. But then, maybe someone in the militia got cold feet and tipped off the feds. Every group had its traitors. At least nothing was coming back on the senator, and that meant his job was secure for the time being.

"Yeah, you're probably right—bunch of hotheads on both sides. Waste of time." He left a ten on the bar, slapped the deputy on the back, and waved to the bartender on his way out. He was halfway across the street to his truck when his cell phone rang. He waited until he was inside the cab to grab it.

"Yeah?" he said, turning on the engine to get some heat going.

"I still have the money," a woman said. "Unfortunately, I don't have any guns."

Hooker straightened, trying to place the voice. Youngish, maybe the slightest bit of a Midwest accent. "I understand things didn't go well at the exchange."

"Is that what you call murder?"

"Sorry. I know you took some losses."

"That's done now," she said with a chilling absence of emotion. "I still have business to finish."

"What, you still want to try for guns?"

"There's no point to that, not without the soldiers to use them."

"What exactly are you talking about then?"

"You didn't give us the money because you support our cause. People like you want something. I want to know what General Graves promised in exchange for the money."

"I'm just a middleman."

"Then I suggest you find out from the man on top. If you can't, I'll take the money somewhere else to someone who can help me."

"Wait a minute—"

He swore as the line went dead. The senator was not going to be happy.

❖

Blair nodded to the uniformed officer at the south gate of the White House, crossed to the mansion, and called Lucinda Washburn, her father's chief of staff. Lucinda guarded her father's time with an iron fist, and even Blair had to check with her before getting in to see him. She understood. Besides, Luce never kept her waiting unless he was really, truly busy.

"Hi, Luce. Is he free?"

"For about two hours. Have you had lunch?"

"Uh—no."

"Neither has he. I'll have something sent over. He's in the library."

"Thanks."

"Make sure you eat."

Blair laughed. "Roger that."

Lucinda disconnected and Blair walked to the library, nodding to the agent and military aide outside the closed door. She knocked and entered. Her father sat in a red-cushioned, wing-backed chair in front of the fireplace, reading a thick file. His shoes were parked beside the chair, his sock-clad feet up on a hassock.

"Hi, Dad."

"Hi, honey." He smiled when she settled in the matching chair across from him.

"Playing hooky?" she asked.

"Hiding," he said, removing his reading glasses and setting them and the file on an antique table next to him. "How's Cam?"

"Healing. Stubborn. On her way to the countdown."

Andrew Powell, in his early fifties and looking a decade younger, his hair still golden brown, his blue eyes sharp and clear, laughed. "Back to her old self, then."

"Almost. I tried to get her to stay home."

Andrew nodded. "I suppose you had about as much success as she did in getting you to stay behind."

Blair smiled wryly. "That would be a good bet."

"The trip should be relatively straightforward and not too strenuous."

Blair laughed. "Dad. Have you forgotten what the campaign trail is like? If we even manage to stay on schedule it'll be a miracle, and you know Adam is going to end up adding extra venues all along the way."

"Still, Cam shouldn't have to do too much."

"You're probably right." Blair set her concerns aside. Her father did not need to worry about Cam. That was her job. "Some of the opposition has been making noise ahead of your arrival that you're making the trip due to slipping approval ratings. Do you want to address that out in Chicago?"

"Familiar song." Andrew snorted. "I think we should stick to our original plan to press our platform and not engage. Responding only gives credibility to their arguments. They're going to be fighting like dogs over a bone for the next few months until a clear contender emerges. Until then, addressing their issues and arguments is fruitless."

"I'm surprised Russo hasn't made a statement yet," Blair said. "He's clearly the man the press is pointing toward as the next candidate."

"He's still pretty far right, but he's got momentum, no doubt," Andrew said. "We've got people watching. I hope he does come out on top. He'll have a hard time winning over the center."

"You know we're going to take some heat over the wedding in a few places out there," Blair said.

Andrew shrugged. "Gay rights is always an issue. We've dealt with that before."

"But not like this. Come on, Dad. Don't pretend I haven't put you on the spot."

Andrew leaned forward, his gaze deep and intense, a look of such certainty that even television cameras couldn't mute it. That look had won over a great many voters. "Your personal life does not create a problem for me. The country already knows my views. If anything, what you and Cam have done only makes us stronger. People respect those who live by what they preach."

Blair's chest tightened. She'd spent so many years resenting her father's ambition, his driving need to lead. She refused for so long to acknowledge what she knew in her heart—he sacrificed too. The burden of power, of responsibility, wore on him. "You never let me down."

"I wish that were true." He shook his head. "You're more likely to get heat than me."

Blair grinned. "I can't wait."

He laughed. "You're going to give Adam fits, you know."

"Oh, I'll be good." Serious then, she said, "I'd never do anything— at least not intentionally—that would reflect badly on you."

"I know. And I'm sorry you've had to think about that first for all these years."

She waved her hand. "Dad. How many people in the history of the world have been able to say their father was the president of the United States? It's okay."

"Thank you for that."

"So we're all good. We'll take Middle America by storm." Blair looked at her watch. They had an hour. "Any chance we could sneak away for a burger somewhere?"

He grinned. "We can try."

❖

"This has been great," Viv said, standing in the hall of the training facility, unspeakably grateful to be inside, out of the wind. "Atlas is incredible. I love how he zeroed in on everything out there."

Dusty stood with her jacket slung over her shoulder and Atlas's lead lightly looped in her hand. "He was showing off for you today. He knew you were watching."

Viv extended a hand. "Do you think he'd mind me petting him now?"

"I think he'd like it a lot." Dusty gave a command to let Atlas know he was off-duty, and he gave a vigorous shake, as if relaxing after a strenuous workout. He sat again as Viv knelt slowly and held out her hand.

Atlas nosed it and she petted his head. "You are such a gorgeous guy." She looked up at Dusty. "I can't wait to see him on the job again."

"You probably won't see much of us," Dusty said. "We'll be doing most of our work when the train is stopped, and you'll be off covering the president."

Viv frowned and straightened. "Would you let me know when? I can stay behind, at least a couple of times. You're the story. My story, at any rate."

Dusty felt a flush of pleasure, a rare sensation and a little disorienting. Putting Atlas through his paces for Vivian had been easy. She loved to work him and loved to show him off for an audience. But there'd been more to it today. She'd been aware of showing off herself a little bit. She liked the way Vivian watched them, both of them, as if they were both special, both interesting. Even the biting cold hadn't seemed to put her off. The idea that Viv wanted to see her again— Dusty caught herself. That wasn't really what Vivian had said. She wanted to see *Atlas* again. It was all about Atlas. "Sure. If you want."

"I do. Maybe we can have breakfast or lunch on the train. Compare notes and you can let me know a good time."

"As long as it's cleared," Dusty said. "And the shift leader approves."

"Goes without saying. I'll talk to the public affairs office tonight, to let them know I'll be doing some follow-up."

"So I guess I'll see you tomorrow or sometime," Dusty said, feeling awkward and wishing she had something to say that would keep Vivian there a few minutes longer.

"Absolutely." Viv held out her hand. "Thanks again. It's been great."

Dusty took her hand, squeezed gently. "Right."

"Well. I should go." Viv stepped away.

Dusty nodded.

Viv took a few steps, halted. "You're busy now, right?"

"Uh." Dusty swallowed the sand in her throat. "I've got countdown—the advance briefing. For tomorrow."

"Of course. So, what about tonight?"

Dusty's breath came a little faster. "I'm sorry?"

"Tonight? Are you working?"

"Not after the briefing."

"So how about dinner?"

"Dinner?" Dusty was aware she was parroting everything and sounding like an idiot.

"You. Me." Viv smiled and pointed a finger between them. "Dinner. You can tell me how you ended up in the canine division. Research."

"Sure. For the article, you mean."

"That too," Viv said softly.

"Okay," Dusty said, aware of venturing into unknown territory. "Okay. I'll call you, when I'm free."

"Give me your phone," Viv said.

Wordlessly, Dusty handed it over. Unexpected pleasure swept through her when she saw Viv push numbers into it.

"There," Viv said. "You can call me. And it's Viv, by the way."

Dusty stared down at the phone, Vivian's name and number in her contacts. That was the only number on her phone that wasn't work related. She looked up to see Viv studying her. She swallowed, nodded. "Okay. Viv. I will."

"Don't forget."

"I won't forget," Dusty said quickly.

"Good. I'm looking forward to it." Viv gave a little wave and walked away.

Dusty stared after her and said softly, "Me too."

Atlas nudged her leg, and she looked down into his gleaming eyes. "Yeah, yeah. I know you're still the star. It's just business."

But the buzz in her middle stayed with her, a strange new feeling she liked.

CHAPTER FIVE

V iv parked in the lot reserved for the press and walked the short distance to the entrance to the West Wing, stopping at the guard post to show her press credentials. As always, the pressroom was busy, with some people talking on their cell phones, others working on tablets or laptops, others huddled in small groups drinking coffee and speculating on the newest developments in the political scene. She was relatively new to the White House beat and focused more on op-ed and feature stories rather than straight White House political reporting. Although her editors had been skeptical at first that humanizing the political process was necessary or even possible, she'd pointed to the popularity of TV shows focused on the inside world of Capitol Hill, arguing that the public had a fascination with what happened inside the White House, an institution—much more than just a building— shrouded in secrecy and mystique. They'd assigned her to the beat with a watch-and-see attitude. Now a lot of people were watching.

Her pieces were getting some of the highest hit rates online of any of their Washington coverage, and the power people at the paper were reaching out to contacts to get her deeper and deeper inside. She liked watching the inner workings as much as anyone, and she felt as if she had the best of both worlds. She was there when world-changing events happened, and because of her emphasis on some of the individuals involved—people like Dusty Nash and her dog—her stories brought a special touch to the sometimes cold facts that resonated with readers. Some of the other reporters ignored her completely, relegating her articles to the category of fluff, and she couldn't pretend it didn't bother her. She had an ego and ambition, after all, but she knew what she was doing was valuable and good reporting. Her editors knew it too, so she really couldn't complain about a few arrogant people. Much.

She draped her coat over a chair at one of the communal tables and went for coffee. She'd write up her notes and start outlining the article while waiting to see what else was happening. Something was always happening at the White House. To miss a breaking story was a reporter's worst nightmare.

And while she worked, she could wait for Dusty's call.

Dusty Nash. She smiled to herself. What an interesting woman. Viv poured coffee into a ceramic mug and added a little half-and-half. As she stirred, she thought back over the past few hours. She'd gotten some really good stuff, but that wasn't what occupied her mind and created the almost-forgotten tingle in her middle. She kept seeing snippets of Dusty's face—her intense focus as she watched Atlas search for the explosives, the quick nod and quicker grin when he succeeded, the brilliant smile as unexpected and breathtaking as the sun breaking through on a cloudy afternoon. And even more surprising, the mild confusion and endearing discomfort in her eyes when anything personal came up.

Dusty had seemed completely unconcerned about making a good impression, or any impression at all, for that matter. She exuded a fascinating combination of confidence and unworldliness, along with an unabashed unsophistication that was a rarity amidst the glitz and glamour and power of the Hill. Most interviewees couldn't wait to take center stage. Dusty's disregard for the spotlight was as refreshing as it was charming.

Viv carried her coffee back to the table, extracted her recorder from her coat, and plugged in her earbuds. Like most reporters, she was impervious to distraction and usually able to work anywhere, but she kept needing to rewind while taking notes after losing herself in the soft drawl of Dusty's voice. She couldn't place the accent. Texas? No, not broad enough. Softer, lazy almost. Definitely someplace in the South. She'd have to ask her about that. They'd touched on nothing personal during the afternoon. She always injected some personal background into her articles—that's what gave them the personal flavor readers craved, but this was about more than the article. This was for her. She was curious. More than that. Intrigued.

She'd always been drawn to one-of-a-kind things. She'd been a collector as long as she could remember—bottle caps, stamps, old coins, hand-painted hat pins—matchless things of beauty, elegant in their simplicity and precious in their uniqueness. Dusty wasn't a thing, not someone to be collected, but she was unusual and altogether fascinating. And it seemed they had a date.

How had she ended up with a dinner date with an attractive, mysterious Secret Service agent? And had she really asked first? How totally unlike her. Viv smiled, shook her head, and rewound yet again.

"Working on something good, Viv?" Gary Williams sat down across from her with his own cup of coffee. Gary was a White House regular, putting most of his stories out on the wire services. He was in his early thirties, a little bit older than her, handsome in a smooth kind of way—blue eyes, dark hair carefully cut, a trim body thanks to regular gym workouts. Friendly but not pushy.

"Just getting started," Viv said. "I miss anything around here this afternoon?"

He sipped his coffee and shook his head. "Everything's pretty quiet. Just the usual pre-trip stuff."

"Did we get the itinerary yet?"

He laughed. "We probably won't get that until we're climbing onto the plane tomorrow."

She laughed with him. "I guess you can always hope."

"Some of us are going out to dinner tonight. You interested?"

Viv hesitated. She was friendly with most of the reporters on the White House press beat. She had to be, spending so much time with everyone. Still, she was careful not to spend too much time with any one guy lest they get the wrong idea. When she'd first arrived, she'd had to pointedly decline a number of dates. Gary had never seemed interested in going in that direction, though. "I would, but I've already got plans."

He raised an eyebrow and grinned. "Something exciting, I hope."

She smiled. "Maybe."

"Well, have fun, then." He stood. "I'll see you in the morning."

"Right," she called as he walked away.

She turned the recorder back on to listen to Dusty's soft, sexy drawl again. Something exciting? Yes, without a doubt.

❖

Cam's cell rang as she was leaving the office she rarely used in the Ops Center for the countdown meeting at the Secret Service command center. She'd missed a lot of the advance team reports while in Idaho, and though she was totally confident that everything was set to go, she needed to hear it herself. Blair and Andrew were not just any protectees, and a gnawing fragment of doubt worried the back of her mind. She didn't recognize the number on the caller ID, and since she had a few minutes, she took the call. "Roberts."

"Loren McElroy. Got your message."

Cam stepped out of the corridor into an empty office to take the call from the undercover agent. "Thanks for getting back to me. Are you doing all right?"

"Not *doing* much of anything." McElroy sounded like an all-star sitting on the bench during a playoff game. "We're in a holding pattern until some of the excitement dies down. A lot of the crew I was with went down during that fubar, and the higher-ups don't want me surfacing too soon."

"How about Skylar?"

"She's up and about and complaining."

Cam laughed softly. "That sounds pretty good, then."

"So far the docs say she's going to be a hundred percent."

"Good, I'm glad to hear that."

"I owe you."

"Actually, I owe you," Cam said. "If you hadn't contacted the right people when you did, we would've been in trouble."

"Let's say we both scored points, then. You got Skylar out of there alive."

"Fair enough. Now I need a favor."

"Name it."

"I need to know what you know, off the record, about Graves and the woman who took us. We know her as Angela Jones."

"I only saw her once before that last night," Loren said. "When we first set up the exchange, Graves was calling all the shots. Showed up personally to make the deal. Then we got a call that one of his captains was taking over. Turns out it was her and she was pretty antsy about security. She wanted neutral ground, that kind of thing."

"Do you know who she is?"

"Not her name. But she had to be pretty high up and totally trustworthy for Graves to delegate any responsibility to her."

"What about him? Background?"

"We know he was ex-military," Loren said. "Special forces. The funny thing is, the trail gets really muddy before Desert Storm. It's tough even for us to trace military records if black ops are involved, but I don't think you'll find anything on him prior to 1990. He might've been in the military, but not by that name."

"Every time we try to run backgrounds on Graves or the major players, we run into dead ends," Cam said.

"Maybe at this point it doesn't matter."

Cam frowned. "How so?"

"Graves is dead. I take it the woman isn't. The one thing we know for sure about these people is they're fanatically dedicated to their cause. Whatever Graves was going to do, she's going to want to finish."

"And we don't know what that is." Technically that was true, but Cam's gut said Graves and Jones and Jennifer Pattee were all part of a larger plan. And she knew what—or who—their target had been.

"I can draw a few conclusions," Loren said.

"Go ahead."

"It's guesswork."

"Pretty educated guess. You know more about what's been happening out there than anyone."

"Not anyone," Loren said. "Skylar's been working this for a long time. You might want to talk to her too."

"I will if I have to," Cam said, "but for now I'd rather leave her to concentrate on getting well. If we read her in, she's likely going to want to start working it from your end."

"You're right, so thanks." Loren paused. "I don't think there's anything too complicated about my picture. It's the old story—follow the money. The militia got an infusion of cash to buy guns from the Renegades. Where'd it come from? Why? Why arm a bunch of crazies if you aren't planning to use them as your private army?"

"So you think someone was pointing them somewhere—like a loaded gun?"

"Yeah. And there's nothing around here that needs that kind of firepower. There's no war happening here. But somebody wanted some kind of violent action somewhere else, to make some kind of statement."

"I can buy that. But why not go for bombs, like in Oklahoma?" Cam said. "Maximum effectiveness with minimum manpower. A couple of guys and a truck full of fertilizer."

"Not as personal maybe—sure you get mass casualties, but maybe that's not the goal."

"So what were they going to do with a couple hundred automatic weapons?" Cam said.

"Maybe that was for defense *after* the action. Those are sniper rifles, and it only takes one sharpshooter to do a lot of damage."

Cam wasn't old enough to have lived through the assassination of John F. Kennedy by a lone gunman with a sniper rifle, but that scenario was every Secret Service agent's nightmare. One individual with a line of sight from any of a hundred vantage points getting off a shot. Their job was to find every one of those vantage points and make sure no one else could use them. She had to trust the Secret Service to come out on top if that was the plan.

"Best guess as to where the money came from," Cam asked.

"Had to have passed through a number of hands to reduce the risk of the militia using it for leverage."

"Private money, you think?"

Loren was silent for a long moment. "I can't prove any of this, you understand."

"Best guess," Cam repeated.

"Private money with a political purpose. I'd look at who would benefit locally from a major political disruption nationally."

"You know what you're saying."

"I do," Loren said quietly. "And since you're involved in this, then I'm guessing I'm not that far off."

No one knew about the thwarted attempt on the president's life, and Cam wasn't about to confirm it. But she didn't deny it either. "Be careful if you go deep again. This isn't over yet."

"I'll keep your number handy."

"You do that. Like I said, I still owe you."

"I want them as much as you. It's personal now."

"Yes," Cam said quietly. "It is."

❖

The maid came into the Russos' dining room just as Franklin and his wife were finishing dinner. "Excuse me, sir," she said diffidently.

Franklin wiped his mouth on a linen napkin and set it aside. "Yes, Maria?"

"There is a gentleman on the phone, sir. He apologizes but says it is important and insists on speaking with you."

Franklin frowned. "Did he say who it is?"

"No, sir."

Franklin sighed. He couldn't take the chance something had come up affecting the campaign, although he thought Nora would let him know of any problems. Still, with the race for the primaries heating up, he had to be available. At least he'd have an excuse to leave his wife to whatever it was she did in the evening. He rose with a practiced smile. "I'm sorry, my dear. You'll forgive me."

She gazed at him almost vacantly, her eyes faintly dulled by whatever medication she'd been prescribed this time. Or perhaps it was just the extra pre-dinner cocktail she probably didn't think he'd noticed. Her family money and political influence had proven useful over the years, but her usefulness had worn thin. He left her still seated at the table, walked down the hall to his office, and picked up the extension on his desk. "This is Franklin Russo."

"Hope I didn't drag you away from dinner," Hooker said.

Franklin crossed the room and closed the door. "Why are you calling me on this phone?"

"Because you're not answering the other one."

"What couldn't wait?" Franklin snapped.

"How about two hundred and fifty thousand dollars?"

Franklin poured two fingers of scotch and carried the short, heavy glass to his desk. "What are you talking about?"

"I got a call from one of the militia. She says she has the money."

"Do you believe her?" Franklin sipped the scotch.

"No reason not to," Hooker said. "It sounds like she wants to bargain. Otherwise, why call? Why not just keep the money and buy a nice cabin on a river somewhere."

"What does she want?"

"No idea. What do you want me to do the next time she calls?"

"Find out what she wants, string her along. Arrange a meeting or something and get the money back."

"You think she's just going to hand it over?"

"I don't care," Russo snapped. "This is our chance to come out of this clean with no losses. It's your job to figure out how to do that. And for Christ's sake, don't call me on this line again."

He slammed the phone down and slugged back the rest of the scotch. He hated loose ends. Hooker might be able to take care of this one, and then there'd only be one left. Like his wife, Hooker was close to outliving his usefulness.

Chapter Six

Cam nodded to the agents already seated in the briefing room and took a seat next to Paula Stark, midway down the right side of the table. Tom Turner, the boss of the PPD, stood at the end of the table waiting for everyone to settle in. Evyn Daniels, the lead agent on the advance team, sat on his left side and the assigned shift leaders opposite her. As the room slowly settled, Tom stood and clicked on the remote for the projector. He was a tall, thin African American in his mid-forties, his demeanor serious most of the time, although when he relaxed, which wasn't often given his duties, he was famous for his stories about some of the now-legendary agents when they were still young, green, and occasionally stupid. Cam liked and respected him, even though they'd been at odds a few times in the recent past. They'd aired their differences and agreed that above all, beyond any personal considerations or ego, all that mattered was the safety of those they were sworn to protect.

Beside her, Paula Stark sat straight and attentive, her dark suit crisp and pressed, her cap of dark hair recently cut, and her brown eyes intently focused on Tom. Paula had replaced Cam as the boss of Blair's security detail. She was young, still shy of thirty, but experienced beyond her years and completely dedicated to her work. Cam trusted her with the most precious thing in her life—Blair's safety. She tried very hard to stay out of Paula's road in matters of Blair's security, affording her the respect she deserved, even though they had begun as mentor and trainee. Paula was far beyond that now, a seasoned agent, bloodied in battle more than once. Cam couldn't help but worry when Blair was soon to be put onstage in high-risk situations, but having Paula in charge helped. As if reading her thoughts, Paula leaned close.

"I'm meeting with Egret after this to review her itinerary. We'll have everything squared away before takeoff in the morning."

"I don't doubt it," Cam said, meaning it. Paula would do everything possible to assure Blair's safety.

But they all knew what they prepared for was not the danger. The unknown was the enemy—the unexpected, the surprise, the illogical or irrational. Entire teams were devoted to anticipate what seemed beyond imagining, and the process never ended. Every day new technology or new weaponry or a new wave of fanaticism empowered their adversaries. No matter how well they prepared, they could never prepare enough when lives were at stake. So they would review the details, and review them again. As many times as it took.

"All right," Tom said, pulling everyone's attention to him. "Here's the itinerary to date."

A few dry chuckles sounded through the room. Everyone knew they'd be making adjustments on the fly once the trip was under way. Suboptimal but normal for this president. Tom laid out the stops, venues, and timetables planned for the eight-day, two-thousand-mile trip.

"The route follows Amtrak's Southwest Chief commercial line from Chicago to Flagstaff. The tracks will be cleared for us forty-eight hours in advance of our next stop." He put up a map and clicked on the red flags marking cities along the route and the distances from the train stations. "Twelve planned stops along the way in Illinois, Iowa, Missouri, Kansas, Colorado, and New Mexico."

Tom handed the remote to Evyn Daniels. "Here's where we stand with the advance."

Evyn brought up a schematic of a train on the screen. "This is Thunderbolt. Twenty-five cars."

"Jesus," one of the agents muttered. "That's a long parade."

No one commented on the obvious. It was a very big, slow-moving target.

"We couldn't get it down any smaller."

"Maybe we could cut out the press cars," another agent suggested with a hopeful note.

"Ah," Evyn said lightly, "for this trip the president might consider them more important than us."

"His campaign manager sure will," someone shot back.

"Okay," Evyn said, serious again, "here's the present order of the cars."

She reviewed the lineup of the cars, from the president's working and private cars down through the USSS sleeping cars, press cars, dining, staff, cook cars, and special divisions: canine/EDU; CAT/ERT counterattack teams; fire rescue; communications; transport. She flicked the laser pointer. "Our command car is here and the medical car here."

Wes Masters, the first doctor and head of the White House Medical Unit, frowned. "That's too far from the president's cars. And we need our base car moved too. Can you get us closer?"

Evyn glanced at Tom, who nodded. "Talk to me after—we'll see what we can arrange."

Wes nodded at her partner. "Good enough."

"As noted," Evyn said, "Eagle's itinerary is not firm. Egret has appearances at every stop too. Simultaneous event coverage. Per usual, count on going OTR at any time."

The lead agent handling vehicle movement and driver assignments said, "We'll need to factor in time to refuel the backup limo and SUVs while the Beast is deployed on these off-the-record trips."

"You'll be refueling while the train is stationary. We won't be carrying much in the way of fuel."

"We'll have to pull off-shift agents for that," he grumbled.

"Can't be helped."

Cam listened as Evyn worked through the rest of the advance—where safe houses were located along the train route, which hospitals would be used for emergency evacuation, where the local law enforcement and field office agents would meet the motorcades when the president left the train for his scheduled appearances, the motorcades' primary and secondary routes. Out of habit, Cam searched for holes in the planning, not really expecting to find any. She didn't. Evyn Daniels was a superior agent and destined to be a boss before long.

"Anything else?" Evyn said.

Phil Virtucci from the canine division said, "Every time Eagle leaves Thunderbolt, we'll have multiple primary sites to surveil—Thunderbolt, the motorcade, his destination. Lot of ground for the dogs to cover in a short amount of time."

"One team will stay with the train and the other accompany POTUS in the motorcade," Evyn said. "Locals will be working the public sites."

Virtucci grunted. Canine teams were only as good as their handlers, and while most local teams were excellent, many communities were just phasing in the new divisions.

Stark said, "What about Egret's appearances? We'll need dogs then too."

Evyn nodded. "We'll be using locals for that too."

Paula frowned but nodded. "All right."

"Aerial surveillance?" someone asked.

The aerial security boss outlined timing and extent of the no-fly zones along Thunderbolt's route and over the presidential appearance locations, the satellite image coverage, and ground-to-air defenses.

"We'll also be employing local evac birds in case of a medical emergency," Wes Masters said. "We can handle anything in the medical car until evac arrives. A full team will travel with both Eagle and Egret."

Turner reviewed the shift assignments again, advising the teams they'd be sharing sleeping quarters when off-shift. That brought a few grumbles from the agents, who preferred assigned sleeping quarters.

"Can't be helped, if we want to keep this train at some reasonable length," Turner said, sympathetic but unbending. "Any other questions?"

No one had any. The trip was an unusual one. Some of the agents had never been detailed to a train trip before, but in the end, the various moving parts were all the same. The difficulty with evac routes was a challenge, but they'd have local agencies and their own agents from regional field offices backing them up along the way for the entire trip.

As the agents began to move away from the table, Stark turned to Cam. "His itinerary is a matter of public record. There's no way to vary the route once we get started."

"That's the problem with rail travel," Cam agreed. "You've got one route and not much you can do about it. But should we run into any difficulty, we'll evac by motorcade or air, so we've got alternative routes that won't be public knowledge."

Stark grimaced. "Still leaves us out in the open in the middle of nowhere. Some stretches there's nothing around for a couple hundred miles."

"That's why we tried to talk him out of the train idea. But…" Cam shrugged.

"Yeah." Stark straightened. "Well. That's what we get paid for."

Cam rose and they walked out into the hall together. "How's Renée?"

"She likes the counterterrorism unit," Stark said of her FBI agent partner. "Anything that keeps her in the action keeps her happy."

"I get that," Cam muttered.

"Anything new on the other investigation?" Stark asked quietly.

Stark was one of the few people Cam trusted completely, and because she was responsible for Blair's safety and Blair was a logical secondary target, Stark was read in on everything that posed a security risk to the president. "Making a little progress, but nothing substantial yet."

Stark looked around to be sure no one was nearby. "Do you have the same feeling I do? That something else is coming?"

"Yes," Cam said quietly. Stark had good instincts and she wasn't surprised Stark felt it too. The gnawing unease that portended trouble.

"And I guess there's no way Egret would stay—"

"Not a one," Cam said.

"Okay then," Stark said firmly. "Game on."

Cam nodded. "Game on."

❖

Dusty waited with the other agent handlers for the boss to show up and begin their briefing. Atlas was in the kennel. She'd pick him up and take him home after dinner. Dinner with Vivian Elliott. Part of her didn't really believe any of it was real. She had to stop herself from checking her phone to see if Viv's number was still there. She glanced at her watch instead. Getting late. Maybe she should call Viv and tell her things were running long. Maybe Vivian would change her mind. Maybe she'd decide she'd gotten all the information she needed for her article. Maybe, maybe, maybe.

"Hey, Nash, how did the interview go today?" Willy Chu, a small, energetic agent with a crop of black hair perpetually in his eyes, dropped into a chair beside her.

"Fine," Dusty replied. Willy was easygoing and never seemed ruffled by anything out in the field. Dusty got along with all her fellow agents pretty well, but she wouldn't exactly say she was friends with any of them. They were there to do a job, and most of them were closer to their dogs than each other. If she had to name one who was closest to a friend, she'd have to say Willy. They'd started at about the same time and often shared the same shifts. Spending hundreds of hours together naturally led to conversation, and somewhere along the line Willy had surmised Dusty's second choice for companionship after Atlas wouldn't be one of the guys.

"I was glad they pegged you to do it," he said, "until I saw the reporter. Tough duty."

"Not really. She knew a lot about the dogs."

Willy gave her a sad look and shook his head. "Did you talk about anything besides Atlas?"

"No, not exactly. You know, she was here about the dogs."

"Yeah," he said. "Definitely a wasted opportunity having you do that interview."

"I don't know," Dusty said, shrugging. "I guess I could cover anything I forgot at dinner tonight."

Willy drew up short. "No. Really?"

Dusty grinned, an odd surge of satisfaction shooting through her. "Really."

He whistled and clapped her on the shoulder. "Take it all back. You done good."

Dusty laughed and settled back as Virtucci came in. It felt good, better than good—great—talking about Viv. Thinking about her, even when she wasn't around. Looking forward to seeing her again. She remembered the little smile Vivian had given her right after she'd put her number into her phone. As if something had transpired between them that pleased her. She wanted to put that smile back on Viv's face again. She wondered if she'd be able to, without Atlas to help out.

"All right, everybody, listen up," Virtucci said.

Dusty jerked her attention back to the briefing. She didn't think about Viv again for forty-five minutes as Virtucci outlined the itinerary, the shift assignments, and the provisions for the dogs on the train. She and Atlas were working the middle shift to start, and their assignments were split between traveling with the motorcade and securing Thunderbolt when they were stopped. Both high-threat situations. Whenever Eagle was en route, whenever the train or vehicles were stopped, they were targets, either for long-distance attack or potential explosive placement. She'd be busy. That was good, she liked being busy.

When he was finished and all the questions were answered, the briefing broke up. After seven. Maybe it was too late for Viv. Probably would be. They all needed to be up and out early for the flight to Chicago. She stepped into the hall and made sure no one was around before tapping in the number Viv had given her. One ring…

"Hello?" Viv's voice was bright and a little breathless.

Maybe.

"Hi, this is Dusty."

"Hi. Are you done?"

"Yeah. I'm sorry it's so late. I should have called sooner."

"No problem, I've been working. Are you hungry?"

Dusty realized she was, although the stirring in her stomach wasn't hunger. The tight, twisting sensation was excitement. "Sure."

Viv laughed. "Well, that's good then. Shall we meet somewhere?"

"I need to feed and walk Atlas. Then I'll be ready to leave."

"All right. What's your favorite food?"

"I don't think you want to know that."

"Please don't say McDonald's."

"Like I said…"

Viv groaned. "Seriously?"

"Why don't you pick. I'll eat anything."

"Sushi?"

"Even that."

Viv laughed again and warmth spread through Dusty's chest.

"You mean it?" Viv asked.

"Sure. Yeah. I can do it."

Viv named a restaurant not that far away.

"Thirty minutes?" Dusty asked.

"I'll be waiting."

Viv's voice had gotten low and husky, and the warmth spread. Dusty swallowed hard. "I'll be there."

CHAPTER SEVEN

Viv debated between taking a table at the window and one farther back in the darker corner. A light snow was falling outside, and the scattered flakes drifting through the muted lamplight was a nice view—kind of warm and sensual. On the other hand, they'd have more privacy away from the customers moving through the restaurant and the passers-by on the sidewalk glancing in the windows. And here she was, dithering about atmosphere when she'd just met the woman and didn't even know if this was a date. She almost snorted at her pathetic attempt to fool herself. Of course it was a date. She knew it, even if Dusty didn't. Yet.

"I think the one in the back," she said decidedly.

"Very good." The manager plucked two menus from a stack at the end of the sushi bar and led her through the narrow aisle to the table.

"Can I get you anything while you wait?" he asked.

She knew the menu and the wine list by heart. The restaurant was close to the White House and a favorite place for the press corps to grab takeout or a fast sit-down meal. She ordered her usual glass of white wine.

"One moment," he said and disappeared with practiced efficiency.

A waitress returned far less than a moment later with her wine. Viv sipped, surprisingly content just to relax and wait. She didn't even bother taking her phone out of her pocket to check her mail. She chose instead to enjoy the swirl of expectation building along her spine, something she rarely experienced. She wasn't averse to dating, she just didn't have the time or the inclination to *make* time for the few people who had caught her interest in the last year or so. She'd been dating a gallery owner steadily before she'd gotten the White House press assignment. Back then she'd been hustling to win a slot on a regular column, and she'd taken whatever story assignments had come her way. Since there weren't all that many, her hours were fairly regular. Once she'd caught the White House beat, her work hours doubled overnight and her schedule descended into total chaos. She canceled dinner dates, had to jump out of bed in the middle of the night—occasionally in the midst of intimate moments, and finally missed one too many art openings or evenings at the theater. Her lover delivered an ultimatum that had been as unexpected as it had been unfathomable. Choose between her job and her relationship. She'd been too shocked to do anything more than say she was sorry, but there was no way she could give up her job. She didn't add: not for a relationship that was nothing more than pleasant. Pleasant wasn't something she had time for any longer. Pleasant was undemanding companionship, good conversation, a shared meal, a mutually satisfying evening in bed. Pleasant was nice but not critical, and ultimately expendable.

She sipped her wine, savoring the woodsy flavor and the warmth that stirred in her middle. Warmth that was only partly due to the wine. She was looking forward to the possibility that a meal with an interesting woman presented, anticipating the discovery, the surprise, the excitement. Things she hadn't experienced in a long time. Things she hadn't realized, until just this moment, she missed.

"Is this seat taken?"

Viv blinked and heat rushed to her face. Dusty stood a few feet away, her hand on the back of the empty chair across from Viv, a whimsical glint in her eyes.

"Oh my God," Viv said, hoping she hadn't been ignoring her. "I was daydreaming and didn't see you coming."

Dusty took mercy on her and pulled out the chair and sat down. "A good daydream?"

Viv suspected her face was on fire at this point, but something about Dusty emboldened her, made her take chances. She turned the wineglass in her hand, her gaze meeting Dusty's questioning one. "A very good one. I was thinking about you, actually."

Dusty's lips parted, a half-smile dancing across her face. "Really?"

Viv nodded.

"I think you might be the first one who's ever done that."

Viv caught her breath. Dusty had changed out of her BDUs into a white shirt, dark jeans, and a leather bomber jacket. Droplets of melted snow shone in her windblown hair. Everything about her from her down-home good looks to her trim, solid body was sexy. Was it possible Dusty didn't know how incredibly good-looking she was? How amazing her complete lack of artifice, especially in the world of façades they inhabited? "I can't believe that. I bet you've had girls dreaming about you since high school."

Dusty slowly shook her head. "I don't think so. I wasn't much for conversation."

"Girls love the strong silent type."

"Just girls?"

"Women too," Viv said, walking closer to the edge.

"I've got the silent part down, I think." Dusty laughed.

"I think maybe you've got it all down."

"Are we flirting?"

Viv's heart gave a little rush. "I think so. How does it feel?"

Dusty pressed her palms to the white linen tablecloth and gently brushed the wrinkles from it, smoothing it across the surface of the table. Viv imagined those hands smoothing their way down her body and wasn't sure she could sit through a meal without totally losing what control she had left. She'd already risked more in a day than she had in a year with Kate.

Dusty looked up, her expression completely unguarded. "It feels really nice. I don't think I'm very good at it, though."

"You don't have to try. You don't have to do anything at all." Viv couldn't help herself. She took Dusty's hand. It was warm and dry. Calluses formed a tiny ridge across her palm. Dusty's fingers closed around hers and a thrill ran up her arm. "I'm looking forward to getting to know you. Just be you and that will be perfect."

"I…" Dusty shook her head, staring at Viv's fingers wrapped around hers. She'd never sat in a restaurant holding a woman's hand before. She'd had a date or two when she was in college, but she'd never felt comfortable. She knew there were things she was supposed to be doing or saying, but she was never really certain what they were. She hated the feeling of having disappointed and not knowing why. Then, work became all-consuming, so it hadn't mattered. It mattered now. She traced her thumb over the top of Viv's hand, caressing each knuckle, marveling at the delicate bones beneath the soft skin. "I think you might decide before dinner's over there's not all that much to find out about me."

"I think you're wrong," Viv said quietly, "but let's not worry about that. Let's relax together before all the craziness starts and enjoy dinner. You can tell me how you picked Atlas out of all the other pups you could have had."

Dusty laughed, and the worry slipped away. "You know it's easy for me to talk about him, right?"

"I noticed that, but I really want to know the answer too."

"I'll make a deal with you."

Viv's eyebrows rose. "Oh yes? We're bargaining now, are we?"

Dusty nodded, enjoying the little bit of play. Surprised how easy Viv made everything. "We are."

"All right then. What are the terms?"

"I'll answer your question, but then you have to tell me something about you."

Viv was quiet, and Dusty started to worry she'd made a mistake. Maybe she'd asked too much, too soon.

"All right," Viv said quietly. "That's a deal."

"All right then." Dusty let out a long breath, relieved. "There were only four pups in Atlas's litter. Three males and a female. The female was feisty and adventurous, but on the whole, the males are better for this work. They're a little bigger and heavier and sometimes, but not always, more aggressive. So I only looked at the males."

"And Atlas was the most outgoing and inquisitive?"

Dusty shook her head. "No. Atlas was the one who hung back a little and studied me. All the other pups climbed around, sniffing and playing, but not him. He assessed."

Viv imagined Atlas as a tiny puppy, studying Dusty with that tilt of his head, as he'd done with her earlier. "He's careful."

"Yes," Dusty said instantly. "One of the most important things in a bomb dog is focus. They can't be distracted by other dogs or crowds or stray scents or noises."

"How did you know he'd be good at the work?"

"I visited him every day. I took him out into different environments. One day we went to the mall, another to the train station. Sudden noises didn't bother him, people rushing by didn't bother him, other dogs sniffing around didn't bother him. He looked around, he was interested. But he didn't get excited, you know? He's steady."

Viv smiled. "Steady. I think I like the sound of that."

Dusty pointed a finger. "Are you playing with me?"

"I might want to at some point," Viv teased, "but not right now. I really mean it. The steady part appeals."

"Why?" Dusty asked.

Viv sipped her wine. Why. It was a simple question, one so rarely asked. People so rarely listened or really wanted to know what lay beneath the surface. What mattered. "I think because when I was younger, my life was anything but steady. Our whole household was… hectic. There were five of us kids, all pretty close in age, and life was often unpredictable."

"Unpredictable?"

The waitress came by before Viv could answer and they gave her their orders. She was glad for the chance to collect her thoughts and rein in her runaway emotions. She hadn't expected Dusty to be so perceptive. Her lack of artifice didn't mask naïveté, but a clear-sighted intuitiveness and sensitivity. She was frighteningly insightful, and Viv ought to feel exposed and vulnerable. She didn't. Rather, she felt seen, and she liked it.

Once again, she stepped to the edge.

"My father was a long-distance trucker, and he was away from home for weeks—sometimes months—at a time. He showed up in the middle of the night and he'd wake us all up, despite our mother telling him to wait till morning. All of us kids were ecstatic to see him—like Christmas morning every time. He had a personality bigger than life and everything was a celebration. He'd bring presents that I didn't realize at the time he couldn't really afford. That always created strife with my mother, who struggled to keep the household going while he was gone. Sometimes he'd be on a long-distance haul through Canada to Alaska, and he wouldn't be home for months. My mother worked two jobs, but sometimes we'd move while he was gone. I always worried he wouldn't find us." She sighed. "He always did, until the time he didn't come back."

"What happened?" Dusty asked quietly.

"I don't know," Viv said. "I was fourteen, and he just didn't come home again. My mother searched, and later, my older brother and sister did too. He just disappeared. I think he decided to unburden himself of a life that wasn't fun anymore."

"I'm sorry," Dusty said.

"That was fifteen years ago," Viv said. "My mother moved on, found a steady guy. I finally had to give up being angry. I'm pretty much over being hurt too."

"My parents are farmers," Dusty said. "My father inherited the land from his father, who inherited it from his father. My mother is the daughter of the town librarian and never went beyond high school. Town population three thousand. There were sixteen kids in my graduating class. I could've been a farmer, but I wanted to be a Secret Service agent."

"However did you decide that?" Viv asked.

"I saw a special on television about the K9 division. As soon as I saw the dogs, I knew that's what I wanted to do."

"How old were you?"

"Ten."

"And you never considered anything else?"

"Never."

"No regrets?"

"How could there be? I've got the best dog in the world, and the best job."

Viv laughed. "They knew what they were doing when they picked you for the interview."

"Maybe. But I think I'm the one that got lucky."

Viv drew a quick breath. "Now who's flirting?"

Dusty smiled, pleased. "I guess that would be me."

"I guess it's my turn to tell you something else," Viv said.

"No." Dusty leaned back as the waitress placed the sushi boat on the table. "That was free."

"Rain check, then?"

"Yes." Dusty brushed her fingers down Viv's arm. "We're leaving at midnight so the dogs can clear the landing site. I don't know when—"

"I'll be covering the breakfast speech. After?"

"Yes," Dusty said instantly. "I'll look for you."

"I'll look for you too."

❖

Jane stretched out on the single bed in the Motel 6, her fifth cheap, nondescript room in as many days, and turned on the local news. The story about the camp was winding down, with only a twenty-second spot that added nothing to what she already knew. Of course, none of the news was accurate, but at least she knew the intense law-enforcement presence would be dying down.

Her father had taught her how to hide in plain sight, and no one gave her a second look when she walked to the diner down the road or stopped at a nearby gas station to fill her Jeep and the extra gas cans she kept in the back. Her father had planned well in case they'd need to disappear, and after she'd hiked down the mountain carrying her weapons and the money, she'd collected the vehicle and the IDs from the cache he'd left behind. She had his IDs with her, even though he wouldn't need them. She had ones for Robbie and Jennifer too, and when the time came for them to disappear again, she'd take care of it. It wouldn't be long now.

When the news ended, she called Robbie.

"Everything all right?" he said instantly.

"Yes. With you?"

"No change. We're set to leave here at four tomorrow, arriving in Chicago around six thirty. He's got a breakfast conference downtown and then a big ceremony to launch the train."

"You have the route?"

"Yes. I'll scan it and send it to your phone."

"I'll be heading out in the morning," Jane said. "Just one matter of business to finish up here."

"Don't take any chances. I don't want to lose you too."

"You won't lose anyone, I promise."

"I know, I know."

His anxiety was palpable. He wasn't a warrior, not like her and Jennifer. He'd always been the one who'd rather stay inside with a book than crawl through the obstacle course her father set up in the woods behind the house, carrying a .22 and shooting at human-shaped targets. He could handle a weapon adequately, but he'd been the obvious choice to infiltrate the communications network. His natural talent for journalism had been a bonus. She trusted him, but he'd never been in the midst of an action before.

"I'll text twice a day, twelve-hour intervals. Don't worry," Jane said. "You'll do fine."

"You've always been most like him, you know." Robbie sounded both wistful and apologetic.

Jane blinked at the unexpected moisture blurring her vision for an instant. "Then trust me. We'll all be fine."

"Don't worry about me."

"I'm not. Keep me updated on any changes in the itinerary."

"See you soon," Robbie said.

Jane disconnected and two minutes later the phone buzzed. An instant message appeared with a map showing a blue line connecting Chicago to Flagstaff. Red dots along the way denoted towns where the president would stop. She calculated three days driving eighteen hours a day, and she'd intercept at just the right place. All she needed now was the right weapon.

Chapter Eight

B lair said good-bye to her father at the elevator to the second floor of the residence and walked out the west entrance toward the street to catch a cab.

"Blair!" Cam caught up with her on the sidewalk. "Want some company?"

"Your kind." Blair kissed Cam quickly on the cheek, slipped her arm through Cam's, and snuggled close, looking for warmth in the biting wind but mostly just wanting the pleasure of her hard body up close. "Is this a happy accident?"

"Ah...not exactly."

"Stark called you?"

"Mm-hmm."

"I suppose Dad is in trouble now too?"

Cam laughed. "You do know it stresses the shift when Eagle goes off the record, right? And both of you..."

Blair chuckled. "It was only a burger."

"Right. A burger that required a motorcade, half a dozen agents tear-assing across town to clear the place before he got there, press corps piling into SUVs and creating havoc in the streets, and probably a dozen more gray hairs on Tom Turner's head."

"Tom doesn't have any gray."

"He will if you keep encouraging your father to go AWOL."

"You know he loves it."

"I know," Cam said. "Just promise you won't do a burger run when we're out on the campaign trail."

"You always said that impromptu public appearances are the safest because no one expects him. It's not like anyone was waiting at Five Guys for the president to walk in."

"That's true, but you can never be sure that somebody who just happens to be there won't take it upon themselves to make a move. The only way to be safe is to predict and plan for—"

"Any contingency." Blair sighed. "I know. I know you're right. But I know what it's like to be caged in. And it's got to be a lot worse for him."

"His choice," Cam pointed out, not unkindly. "And it's not about just him. It's about the office and the—"

"You're right. I'm sorry."

"Don't apologize." Cam slid her arm around Blair's waist and pulled her under her arm. "I know it wasn't your doing. Besides, Andrew knows better. But it would be good sometimes if you could talk him out of it. He's too much of a public president as it is."

"It's important to him, to his image. And it's really important now. I hate to say it, but I agree with Adam. Part of Dad's problem has always been his background. He's an intellectual, he comes from money, he's seen as part of the elite. He's not like that at all, but he has to work to appeal to a certain spectrum of the population. A big spectrum."

"Agreed. But nothing is worth risking his safety." Cam kissed Blair's temple. "Or yours."

"All right. I'll be the grown-up this trip."

"Thank you. And I know Tom won't say anything, but he'll secretly thank you too."

"Are you done for the night, then?"

"Yes. Wheels up at five. We'll have to leave for Andrews around four."

"Did you eat?"

"A sandwich in the canteen."

"Cam, that's not food. What about takeout?"

"I'm okay. You?"

"Guilty. Two burgers and fries."

"I think I might hate you."

"I'll make it up to you."

"Really?" Cam stepped off the curb and flagged a cab. As it careened across the lane of traffic toward them she stepped back onto the curb, putting herself between Blair and the road. "How?"

"I'll leave that for you to think about."

Cam opened the cab door as two black SUVs pulled into line behind the cab. She couldn't see through the smoked glass but she knew the position of the occupants. Stark rode on the passenger side. Mac

Phillips drove. The shift was in the follow car. She'd been aware of them following her and Blair as they'd walked from the White House. Giving in to Blair's need for a little bit of freedom had meant putting up with cab rides. The shifts didn't like it, but they liked Blair evading them even less. This way at least they knew where she was, and cabs were another unlikely source of problems. When Stark had called her to tell her Blair insisted on walking partway and catching a cab, Cam had waited for her at the White House so she could walk with her. Stark felt better about that. So did she.

They settled into the backseat and Cam gave the driver their condo address. Blair curled against her, slid a hand inside her topcoat, and rested it on her abdomen. Cam looped an arm around Blair's shoulders. Being close to her was the most comforting experience she'd ever known. "I love you."

Blair stroked Cam's middle. "I love you too. Are you all right?"

"Yes. Just…happy."

Blair rubbed her cheek against Cam's shoulder. "Me too."

The cab pulled over, Cam paid the driver, and before they could step out, the SUVs moved in quickly behind them. Three agents jumped out, bracketed the two of them as they got out of the cab, and walked them toward their building. Cam nodded to the agent nearest her. "We'll be in for the rest of the night."

Brock nodded. He'd stand post in the lobby until the next shift arrived. The others would be with the cars until they were ready to leave for Andrews and the trip to Chicago aboard Air Force One. Until then, she and Blair would be alone.

Once inside the apartment, Cam shed her topcoat and took Blair's. She hung them both in the closet by the door and took off her blazer. Blair kicked off her shoes and leaned against the back of the sofa that separated the kitchen-dining area from the living area. She braced her arms on either side of her hips and gave Cam an appraising look. Cam unbuckled her belt. Blair's gaze dropped to her hips as she slid the leather slowly through the loops and draped it over the back of the sofa. Watching Blair watch her, she unbuttoned her shirt, pulled it from her pants, and left it hanging open.

"Want me to keep going?" Cam said.

"Oh yes."

"Then you have to follow me into the bedroom."

"At the moment, I'd follow you just about anywhere."

Cam laughed and held out her hand. Blair took it and Cam led her down the hall to the master bedroom at the far end. She motioned for Blair to sit on the edge of the bed, and once Blair was settled, watching her again, she slowly undressed, removing each article of clothing and draping it over the clothes stand in the corner.

"Now you." Cam pulled Blair to her feet and swept down the covers. Blair wrapped both arms around her neck, her sweater pleasantly rough against her bare nipples.

"You undress me," Blair murmured.

Cam slid her hand under the waistband of Blair's pants, slowly caressing the firm curve of her ass. Blair moaned softly and kissed her throat. Cam eased the cashmere up Blair's abdomen, over her breasts, and, backing away a step, slipped the sweater over her head. She draped it at the foot of the bed and released the clasp on Blair's bra, drawing the straps down her arms and off. She kissed Blair again, then made her way down her throat, kissing her way to the hollow between her collarbones. She cupped her breasts, massaging both nipples with her thumbs.

Blair arched her back and groaned. "God, I love your hands."

"I love the way you feel." Cam lifted her breasts and kissed each one before kneeling and pressing her face to Blair's abdomen. She wrapped her arms around Blair's hips and tugged her close, kissing the curve of her abdomen and the tight line of her hipbone where it disappeared beneath her pants. She kept kissing her as she worked the zipper down and, with her thumbs hooked over the waistband, pulled her pants and underwear down her thighs.

Blair stepped free, kicking the clothes away and parting her thighs. Cam murmured her approval and stroked the valley at the junction of her abdomen and inner thigh. Blair gasped and her hips tightened. Cam held her steady with both hands on her ass, guiding her closer to her mouth each time she kissed her. When she stroked along her cleft, Blair gasped again.

"I won't last," Blair warned.

"I don't want you to."

Cam teased her, feeling the tension build in her tight thighs, speeding up as the muscles beneath her hands clenched and released, clenched and released.

"I'm almost there."

Cam tugged her in and Blair came hard in her mouth, gripping her head, fingers buried in her hair, rocking and shouting. Cam closed her eyes and pressed her cheek to Blair's lower belly as Blair quivered. Her heart pounded as if she'd just run a hard mile.

"Bed," Blair gasped, light-headed and weak-kneed. And hungry, so, so hungry.

Cam stood and guided her down, climbed in after her, and yanked the sheets up with one hand as she stretched out above her. "More?"

"In a minute." Blair sighed, stroked Cam's back, and ran her fingers along the divide between the tight muscles of her ass. She pushed her thigh between Cam's, felt the wet, and the heat. "I love how hot you get when you make me come."

"Every time." Cam buried her face in Blair's neck and thrust against her thigh. "I love making you come."

"You can get as close you want," Blair whispered in Cam's ear, "but I want to fuck you when you're ready to come."

Cam groaned. "Anytime. Now is good."

Laughing, Blair pushed until Cam rolled onto her back. She followed her over and cupped between her thighs. Cam pushed into her palm and she filled her. Tight. Wet. Hot. Her breath stopped. Her heart stuttered. So beautiful. Slowly she stroked.

"Fuck," Cam gasped.

Blair laughed and pushed deeper. Cam tightened around her, her belly went hard, and her back arched. Keeping steady, Blair stroked her through the orgasm and kept stroking her until she came again.

"Done." Cam groaned again.

Blair curled up beside her, hand still between her thighs, cupping her as she settled. "I think you've got me going again."

"Handy," Cam murmured, turning on her side and drawing Blair's leg over her hip. Blair pressed against her thigh and moaned. Cam cupped her from behind and stroked the undersurface of her clit. The want returned full force, energizing her. Blair was hers and she could never get enough.

"God," Blair gasped, sliding up and down, "I'm going to come again."

"Yes," Cam whispered close to her ear as Blair shook in her arms.

Cam held her close as she drifted toward sleep. Tomorrow she would have to share her. Tomorrow and the days that followed, she'd have to depend on others to protect her, but for tonight, nothing and no one could touch her.

❖

Hooker answered on the first ring. "Yeah?"

"I'll be at Danny's Diner outside Emmett for the next hour. I've got fifty thousand dollars with me."

"What about the rest of it?"

Jane laughed. "I'm not walking around with it."

"Is it safe?"

"Yes, and there's nothing you could do to me to make me tell you where it is."

"Whoa. Whoa. No need to go there."

"Let's not pretend we both don't know who we're dealing with." The minute hand on the chrome clock behind the counter, its face dimmed with years of grease, jumped forward another notch. "Fifty-eight minutes now."

"How do I know you're not a cop?"

"You'll recognize me, if you look carefully."

"What?" He sounded genuinely confused.

"You know," Jane said, sipping the surprisingly good black coffee, "I thought your voice sounded familiar. Now it all makes sense, why my…Graves dealt with you. You've got an important boss."

She was guessing, but she knew in her heart she was right. The kind of men her father had been forced to associate with for the sake of the mission never did their own dirty work. They used men like the one she was talking to—cowards and traitors at the core.

"I don't know—"

"I guess it's a little too cold for ice cream this time around. You can buy me a burger instead."

The line was silent for twenty seconds. "You're a long way from home. Angela, isn't it?"

"That doesn't matter now."

"Are you sure you're not being watched?"

"I'd know. And if I was, they wouldn't be *watching*. They don't have that kind of patience."

"I'll be there in forty-five minutes."

"I'll order the burgers."

Hooker laughed flatly. "Fine. Make mine with cheese and fries."

Jane hung up and signaled to the waitress. "I'll have a refill on the coffee. I'm waiting for a friend." She ordered cheeseburgers for both of them and fries for Hooker. "Give it half an hour."

"Sure, honey," the waitress said without giving her more than a glance and hurried off to slap the ticket down on the counter in front of the short-order cook.

The burgers came, and five minutes after that Hooker walked in. His hair was a little longer than when she'd seen him in Georgia and his body bulkier in a dark brown canvas coat, work pants, and boots. A day's worth of stubble blunted his heavy features. But his was a face she couldn't forget. She'd last seen him when she'd handed him a vial of live virus, but she'd imagined killing him a hundred times since then.

She thought about reaching for the semiautomatic nestled in the waistband of her pants at the base of her spine and shooting him as he walked toward her. He was the reason Jennifer was in prison. He'd handed off the delivery to a go-between who'd botched everything. If he'd made the exchange himself, keeping the number of people involved to a minimum, no one would've known. The president would be dead or severely compromised, and Jennifer would be free. Her father would be alive. And they'd be another step closer to victory.

He deserved to be punished, another lesson she'd learned in childhood. Simple justice, an eye for an eye. But right now, he was her only connection to the people who could get her the kinds of things she needed to finish the mission. He looked around, studying the few patrons in the diner. At close to nine, most everyone was off the roads and inside where it was warm. A few truckers sat at the counter, hunched over coffees and plates of food, and two teenagers occupied one side of a booth at the very end of the long railroad-car-styled room, necking. He studied her with no expression, walked down the scuffed red-and-black-tiled aisle, and slid into the booth across from her. He glanced down at the burger, then back at her. "You cut your hair."

"I need a contact between here and Colorado Springs to provide me a product."

Hooker took a bite of the hamburger. "Not a bad burger." He wiped his mouth and picked up a fry. "Guns?"

Jane shook her head. "Explosives."

Hooker took a bite of a fry, then popped the rest into his mouth, chewed and swallowed. "That's not an easy choice of weapon—you need to get close to somebody—and you're likely to get blown up yourself."

"That's not something you need to worry about."

"I've got two hundred and fifty thousand reasons to worry."

Jane reached down beside her, picked up the wrinkled supermarket bag, and placed it on the table next to her plate. She put her hand on it. "You give me the information I need, and you'll have fifty thousand less reasons to worry."

"It'll take some time."

"Six tomorrow morning. I'll be gone after that, and I'll find another way to get what I need. When I meet the contact and receive the product, I'll wire you the money."

He shook his head. "Cash now. Information in the morning."

"Ten now, the rest upon delivery." Jane slid the bag into her lap and extracted the ten grand she'd secured with a rubber band. She tossed it under the table onto the seat beside him. She'd figured he'd want an incentive. She doubted his boss would ever see that money. "I'll call you at six. Thanks for dinner."

CHAPTER NINE

Dusty glanced at her phone. Almost 2200. "I guess we ought to get going."

"I know," Viv said. "Three thirty's going to come awfully early."

Dusty made no move to get up and neither did Viv. She didn't really want to go, but Atlas was waiting for her. He'd be fine in his kennel at the training center, but he was used to going home earlier and having her around almost all the time. They were rarely separated because she rarely did anything other than go to work and spend the evenings reading or walking Atlas through the streets for hours on end. He loved the walks and she loved watching—the people on the sidewalks, the monuments glinting like bejeweled palaces, the night sky turning from hazy orange and red to deep purple and midnight black. The splashes of colors were like the paintings in the museums she visited over and over again on her days off. Those were about the only times Atlas didn't come with her. There'd been a time, briefly, when she'd been young, that she'd thought she might want to be a painter. Her parents hadn't exactly discouraged her in so many words, but her father had gently pointed out that being an artist was no way to make a living and besides, there was no money for the kinds of materials she would need, to even see if she was any good at it. She'd contented herself with absorbing the natural canvases that sprang up around her every morning and night through the ever-changing seasons in the countryside.

"What were you thinking of just then?" Viv said quietly.

A flush crept up Dusty's cheeks, heating them. "Sorry."

"Why? You don't have to tell me, by the way, but you don't need to apologize either."

"No, I…" Dusty pushed a hand through her hair, knowing she'd probably blown the evening. "I was just thinking about paintings."

Viv's eyebrow lifted. "Paintings? Why?"

"I was thinking that I didn't want to leave, and Atlas would wonder where I am."

"Oh," Viv said quickly. "I'm sorry. I almost forgot about him. I've been selfish keeping you out here so late."

Dusty shook her head. "No, it's not that. He'll be fine. But I was thinking that I don't usually leave him except when I go to the museums."

"Oh. The paintings." Viv smiled softly. "I remember now. That remark about the Modigliani."

"I wasn't sure you heard that. I shouldn't have said that out loud." Dusty grimaced. She was making things worse. Why was it so hard to say what she meant instead of bits and pieces that came out all wrong?

"Why not? I'm flattered."

"You are? Because you're very beautiful, and I said—"

Viv reached across the table and grasped her hand. "Dusty, being compared to a magnificent work of art is not an insult."

"I know, but you know, the Modiglianis are not exactly lifelike."

"Not realistic as in a photograph, no, but they *are* memorable."

"And striking," Dusty said softly. "Mesmerizing."

Viv's eyes, so beautifully shaped and deep, deepened further. A faint blush tinted her cheeks. "There, you see. How could any woman be insulted?"

"I'm glad you're not."

"What else do you do? I mean, besides the walks and museums."

"Not very much." Dusty shrugged. She patted the pocket of her jacket and pulled out an eReader. "I like to read."

"I imagine if a routine day is anything for you like it is for us, you spend a lot of time sitting and waiting."

"Standing and waiting, usually."

"Oh, right. Okay, let me guess." Viv's brow furrowed. "Something tells me you're not reading thrillers or suspense. Not a work-related topic. You probably just can't suspend disbelief long enough. History— maybe. But—I really think it's…romance novels."

Dusty straightened. "How would you know that?"

"Because of the paintings. You're a sensualist."

Dusty laughed. "Me? No."

"Yes, I think you are." Viv tilted her head, her eyes alight. "But all right. You tell me why you read them."

"I like the connections people make in the books," Dusty said quietly. Probably because she didn't make very many in her own life. Her parents had been loving, but not very communicative, and she'd always been a little different. Too different to make close friends.

"You see?" Viv said quietly. "What could be more sensual than that?"

Dusty didn't know how to answer. Her heart was beating too fast for her to think. Why did it seem as if Viv was looking right inside her and seeing everything she'd always felt but never figured out how to say to anyone?

"We'll have to go to the museum sometime," Viv said after a minute of silence. "You can show me your favorites."

"You'd like that?" Dusty asked.

Viv stroked the top of Dusty's hand as naturally as if they'd been touching for a long time. "I would. Very much."

"What about you?" Dusty didn't want to move her hand in case Viv realized what she was doing and stopped. "What would you like to do? We can do a museum one day, and then next time…" She hesitated, but the intent look in Viv's eyes spurred her on. "What would you like to do the next time?"

"Oh, that's easy. A Nationals game."

"Really?" Dusty laughed. "I guess we don't run to type."

"Is that right?" Viv feigned indignance. "Are you trying to say a lady can't enjoy baseball?"

"Sorry. It's just that you're so elegant and refined and—" Dusty broke off. "I think I'm making a mess of this."

"Not yet, you're not," Viv said softly. How could any woman object to the things Dusty said about her? "But you know, I'm not really a lady. At least, not all the time."

Dusty looked down at Viv's fingers outlining each of hers. "A game would be great." She looked up. "Except baseball season is quite a ways off. You'll have to pick something else."

Viv nodded, a big red caution sign flashing before her eyes. Dusty wasn't playing games, she wasn't flirting. She was totally honest. How amazing. How scary. "I'll let you know when I've decided."

"Okay. Whatever you like."

Viv wasn't about to say what she'd like. First of all, she didn't kiss on the first date, and she certainly didn't have sex after one dinner date. But she couldn't help thinking about it, sitting across the table from Dusty. With every minute that passed, with everything new she learned about her, she found her more attractive, more intriguing. Physically she was gorgeous—tight bodied and strong—with piercing green eyes that focused on her with such intensity she felt as if she were the only woman in the room. Hell, the only woman in the universe. Dusty's gaze made her feel at once incredibly desirable and desired.

Then in the next moment, Dusty would hesitate, looking slightly abashed and uncertain, and that vulnerability was so touching, Viv wanted to stroke her and assure her she was doing everything right. Just imagining stroking her sent heat coursing through her until glowing embers settled in the pit of her stomach and slowly spread everywhere. The desire was surprising because it felt so good and had been so long. She wanted more of that hot, heady sensation, but she wasn't going to rush. Whatever happened between them, she wanted to savor every moment.

All she had to do was convince her body that waiting was a good idea. She released Dusty's wrist in a fruitless attempt to temper the wanting. "My car is nearby. I can drive you back."

"It's okay, I don't mind walking."

"It's dark and cold. Please, I'd like to."

"All right then. Thanks." Dusty signaled for the check, they split it and then walked outside. Viv drove Dusty back to the center and pulled up in front of the main building. The only lights were those that lined the walkway leading to the kennels in the rear. She could scarcely believe she'd first laid eyes on the place a little over twelve hours before. That she'd just met Dusty, who she hadn't stopped thinking about all day. "I'll look for you in Chicago."

"Would you mind if I texted you?" Dusty said quietly.

"I'd like that a lot."

Dusty put her hand on the door handle. "I will, then." She hesitated, turned toward Viv. "Thanks for asking me to dinner."

Viv caught her breath. Moonlight shone behind Dusty's head, illuminating the side of her face and the corner of her very sexy mouth. To hell with it. Viv leaned across the space between them and brushed a kiss across Dusty's mouth. She lingered just an instant, memorizing the shape and texture of her lips. Warm and soft and silky smooth. She leaned back, the roaring in her head making it impossible to think. The heat in her belly bloomed higher. "Believe me, tonight was my pleasure."

"Mine too," Dusty said, her voice husky. "Good night, Viv."

And then she was gone, striding rapidly down the walk and disappearing behind the building. Viv put her hands on the wheel and stared out the windshield. Somehow, her world had taken on a very different flavor. She was seriously in lust and dangerously in like. Both feelings were incredibly pleasant and equally terrifying.

❖

The incessant beeping shattered a very lovely dream having something to do with being naked on a sandy beach under a blazing sun with Cam rubbing warm oil all over her butt. Blair groaned, rolled over, and slapped at the offending instrument. "No."

Cam sat up, disgustingly alert as she always was the instant she came awake. Perhaps the only habit of hers that Blair took issue with. "It's time."

"Five more minutes," Blair muttered.

Cam laughed softly and kissed her. "You can have ten. I'll shower first."

Blair pulled the pillow over her head and turned away.

"It's time, baby," Cam murmured again way too soon, kissing Blair's ear. She drew the covers down, stroked Blair's back, and kissed the side of her neck. "The shower's all nice and warm and ready for you."

Blair rolled over and sighed. "It's still dark."

"That's because it's three thirty in the morning."

"I'd forgotten how much I hate this."

"It's not too late to change your mind."

"Yes, it is." Blair put a hand in the center of Cam's chest and pushed. Nothing happened, of course. Cam was a rock, and under most circumstances she found that immensely sexy. "I'm going and it's too early to argue."

"Then you have to suffer along with the rest of us." Cam patted her butt, without benefit of the warm oil and sunshine. Or the beach and naked part. "Up and at 'em."

"Yeah, yeah." Muttering, Blair climbed out of bed and headed for the shower. The hot water helped revive her and fortunately, once awake, she got up to speed quickly. She finished dressing the same time as Cam. They grabbed their luggage and rode downstairs where Stark was waiting in the lobby. She looked bright and chipper as usual.

"Morning," Stark said, walking to the door just ahead of Blair. One of the shift agents opened the door and they all trooped out to the waiting Town Car that idled at the curb. An agent opened the trunk.

Cam and Blair piled their luggage inside and climbed into the backseat. Stark sat in front and the driver pulled out with the two follow cars right behind. Her father would fly from the White House to Andrews Air Force Base in Marine One. Everyone else would convene at Andrews by car—the rest of her and her father's immediate security detail, the military aide, the president's doctor and the medical team, the White House staff, a select number of the press corps, the communications officers, and the stewards who prepared all the president's food. Everyone else would fly commercial to Chicago or in the C-17s along with the cars, equipment, dogs, and everything else that was necessary for a trip with the president.

Blair pulled up the latest schedule from Lucinda to make sure nothing had changed for the morning. Once they reached Chicago, she was to join her father for their first public appearance, a breakfast with select donors and political fund-raisers.

Cam took her hand. "Are you ready?"

"Yes." This trip felt a lot different than the first time she'd taken to the campaign trail with him. She'd been younger, for one thing, and something of an unknown. She wasn't any longer. She'd been secretly a little resentful that first time too, having to take the place of her mother and help her father create an image that the public could relate to. She understood the need, but as much as she believed in him, as much as she loved him, she'd resented being forced into a role that required her to hide who she was.

Maybe that was why she'd had the affair with the French ambassador's wife. Foolish and immature, looking back at it now, although Margot *had* been beautiful and surprisingly inventive in bed. Blair wasn't hiding now. And she probably hadn't even had to hide then. Her father had never asked her to. His campaign manager certainly had, and others had been less than subtle in suggesting that she keep her private life private. Well, that bird had flown. She took Cam's hand, kissed her knuckles. "I'm ready."

CHAPTER TEN

Dusty arrived before anyone else on her team at the hangar where the C-17 cargo planes were fueled, loaded, and ready to go. The transport agents were responsible for securing the presidential limo within the belly of the huge cargo plane along with a second limo—an exact replica of the first that would be used were there any problem with the primary car—the hazmat van, and the SUVs for the Secret Service protection details, presidential staff, press, medical, K9, EOD, counterassault, and communications teams. She liked to inspect the kennels where Atlas and the other dogs would ride before they were loaded, just to be sure everything was secure.

"Okay to check it out?" she asked when Larry Murtaugh, the transport supervisor, appeared in the doorway of the cargo hold. Murtaugh, a burly fifty-year-old with flinty blue eyes and close-cropped red hair peppered with gray, was a stickler for details and always insisted on doing the final checks whenever the presidential vehicles were loaded for long-distance travel.

He waved her up and grunted at her as she climbed aboard with Atlas. "Still don't trust us?"

She grinned and shrugged. "Atlas is a nervous flyer."

"Bullshit."

He was right. Atlas didn't mind flying. It was almost as if he knew a big job was coming when they landed. He had been through this hundreds of times and wasn't bothered by the sounds of the big machines, the air guns driving bolts into metal, the steady background roar of the engines. The smell of gasoline and oil didn't faze him either. She wasn't nervous, but she didn't like securing him in a crate that could break free and go careening around the cavernous space in midflight either. He trusted her to keep him safe, just like she trusted him to alert her to danger before they or anyone else could get blown up. She followed Murtaugh as he walked up and down both sides of the long double rows of vehicles, checking off items on his clipboard. The kennels for the dogs were secured to the floor with clamps and separated by solid barriers, so the dogs could only see out the front. Atlas sat by her side as she looked over the moorings of the crate with his name on it.

"Not just yet, buddy," she murmured at his expectant expression. When she was satisfied all the kennels were securely fixed and there'd be no in-air problems, she dumped her duffel in the back of one of the K9 vehicles and walked him back out into the hangar. Other agents were beginning to arrive, suitcases and travels bags in hand. No one looked particularly happy.

Riding in a C-17 was a miserable way to travel. The massive cargo bay was cold and noisy. The unpadded metal benches along either side were uncomfortable, but better than the jump seats fore and aft that rocked with every dip and roll of the big plane. The roar and rattle of engines and draft made conversation impossible, not that she really went in for small talk most of the time, but a long overseas trip could be deadly boring without a little casual chatter. She always sat where Atlas could see her. And where she could see him. They traveled better that way. She nodded to a couple of guys on her team as they went past with their dogs. She'd wait until the last minute to board. It wasn't as if she had to worry about getting a seat.

She sat on a crate out of the flow of traffic with Atlas at her feet. She was already in uniform—black BDUs, black lace-up boots, and a black cap with USSS above the bill. The back of her nylon jacket read *K9 Division*. Atlas would wear a light vest with similar designations when they disembarked. As soon as they touched down, she and six of the other K9 agents would load into the SUVs, drive directly to the convention center where the president would give his breakfast speech, and do the final sweep on the path he would take inside and in the rooms he would occupy. Once he and his entourage were safely inside, she and Atlas would patrol the inner perimeter and sweep the vehicles before he left to travel to the train.

Until they arrived in Chicago, she had nothing else to do, which was just as well. She was having a little trouble concentrating. Okay, a lot of trouble. Her mind was elsewhere, which probably explained why she'd slept so fitfully, after she'd finally managed to fall asleep. She couldn't stop replaying every minute of the past twenty hours, recalling the conversations she'd had with Viv, dissecting the things she'd said or failed to say, the way Viv had looked at her, laughed with her, touched her. None of it had been expected. All of it was special.

She'd never been able to talk to anyone so easily. She'd never been with anyone who touched so naturally. She'd never gone home wishing she could have had one more minute, one more hour with someone.

She was making too much of it, she knew that. But she couldn't stop herself. Every time she thought of Viv, her stomach tightened and a surge of pleasure rippled down her spine. The sensation was addictive. One she'd never experienced and hoped would never end.

She reached down, scratched between Atlas's ears, stroked his back. Him she knew. Him she trusted, loved, relied on. Uncomplicated feelings he returned a thousandfold. She was totally out of her depth with Viv. Inexperienced didn't begin to cover it.

One of the two phones clipped to her belt vibrated. She glanced down and saw the symbol for a text message on her personal phone. The only texts she ever got on that phone were airline updates or weather alerts. The sky was clear and she wasn't flying commercial. Pulse racing, she thumbed the icon to bring up the message. It was from Viv's number. She already knew it by heart. She'd almost dialed it in the middle of the night just to hear her voice again. Thankfully, sanity had prevailed.

Have you left yet?

Dusty stared. Viv was really texting her. She hadn't expected to hear anything from her until later in the day. Maybe not even then. She tried to type an answer and had to delete the gibberish and press the letters deliberately one at a time. *No, still loading plane.*

Busy?

No. Dusty held her breath, waiting for more.

I woke up thinking about you.

Dusty's heart did a funny thing in her chest, as if it had come loose and dropped a couple of inches. She wet her lips. Her hands were shaking. Carefully, she formed the words. *Didn't sleep much. Yesterday was great.*

:-) For me too.

Dusty stared at the screen for a while. She wasn't sure she should answer. There wasn't a question implied in what Viv just typed. What did she say now? She had to say something. She didn't want to lose the tenuous connection between the two of them. *Atlas says hello.*

Two smiley faces returned. *Tell Atlas hi back for me. Can't wait to see you both later.*

I'm off shift at four.

Dinner again?

On the train? Dusty heard someone call her name. She ignored it. *Anywhere.*

Dining car. 5?

Perfect, Viv texted back. *See you tonight.*

Yes.

Dusty took a minute to collect her scattered thoughts. Viv had texted her. Been thinking about her. She said that. And Viv wanted to see her for dinner. She hadn't imagined any of it. Maybe it was actually real.

"Yo, Nash! You planning on flying or walking?"

"On my way," Dusty yelled to her shift supervisor. She stood, and Atlas rose with her. "Come on, boy. We've got to get to Chicago."

❖

Hooker drove toward the diner thinking about money. He was going to be early for the meeting, but that was fine. He wanted some time to consider his options. If the girl was leaving town and headed toward Colorado Springs, she'd have to take the money with her. She wasn't going to open any kind of bank account or secure the funds electronically somehow. No, she'd have the cash with her.

Chances were she wouldn't bring it in the vehicle when she met him. But it would be close by. Hotel room, probably. Maybe a locker at the bus station. He thought back to the look in her eyes when she'd said there was nothing he could do to make her tell him where it was. He didn't have any experience torturing people, and the idea of torturing a woman turned his stomach. He didn't think it would work with her and was just as glad. He was guaranteed ten grand. She'd come through with that. She looked like Graves, probably more than she knew. And she was likely her father's daughter and righteously honorable too. No, she wouldn't cheat him.

So he could take the money she offered him for providing a contact and that would be the end of it. He'd never see her again. He'd be ten grand richer. Russo would be unhappy that he couldn't retrieve the $250,000, but that had been a gamble and not his decision to begin with. But two hundred thousand plus was hard to walk away from.

If he couldn't intimidate her into telling him where it was, he had to blackmail her. He didn't know her real name, and he couldn't implicate her in the failed attack on the president without putting his own head in the noose. So what mattered to her? She definitely had plans—what he couldn't tell, but if she was after explosives, she wanted to make a big statement. A threat to expose her might do the trick, especially if she was as fanatical as Graves and the rest of that bunch.

He pulled into the all-night diner with its sorry dented metal façade and empty parking lot and sat with the motor running to keep warm. Two pickup trucks were the only other vehicles. She wasn't there yet, but he bet she'd be early too.

She was definitely her father's daughter, he'd bet money on it. He laughed. He was doing just that.

❖

Blair's limo pulled across the tarmac toward Air Force One where a ring of Secret Service agents formed the inner perimeter, assuring that no unauthorized personnel approached the presidential plane. The backup Boeing 747 idled a few hundred yards down the runway in front of the third jet that would carry press and staff who could not be accommodated aboard Air Force One.

Blair glanced at Cam. "Are you ready?"

"You mean to play first daughter-in-law?" Cam grinned. "Can't wait."

Blair laughed and kissed her. "I know you hate it. I'm sorry. We'll keep you out of the spotlight as much as we possibly can."

"Don't worry about me." Cam kissed her as agents jumped out of the follow car and descended upon them. "I'm always happy at your side."

"I love you," Blair murmured just as Stark opened the door.

Cam followed Blair out as the rest of the detail closed in and they crossed toward the stairs at the front of the plane where the presidential suite was located. The rear doors led into the press section. Blair settled in the lounge area adjoining her father's private quarters to wait for him. Lucinda would arrive with him, along with the president's physician and the military aide who carried the briefcase with the nuclear codes.

"I imagine we'll be reviewing his remarks," Blair said.

Cam kissed her. "I'm going to talk to Stark for a while. I'm sure there will be schedule changes once Lucinda boards."

"Undoubtedly."

Cam made her way toward the rear of the forward section, nodding to the PPD shift agents and Blair's detail. She settled into a seat next to Stark. "Anything new in the morning briefing?"

Stark shook her head. "No."

Cam watched Blair rise to give her father a hug. The president looked rested and eager to start his first major offensive of his reelection campaign. Eight days on the road. "Sometimes the quiet bothers me more than anything else."

"Me too."

❖

Viv never got over the excitement of flying on Air Force One. Climbing aboard the most elite aircraft in the world with the president of the United States was one of the premier perks of being part of the White House press pool. She never said it out loud, but every trip thrilled her. Of course, being a witness to history in the making was the greatest honor of all, and every time she boarded Air Force One she was humbled. The thrill was there today, just like always, but as she lined up with her colleagues for coffee and pastries at the small minibar in the rear of the press section, she couldn't totally keep her mind on business.

I'm off shift at four.

She almost couldn't believe she'd texted Dusty at oh-dark-thirty. That was so unlike her! She'd never been one to pursue a woman, not that she had anything against it, it was just that she'd never actually met anyone she'd wanted or needed to pursue. Most of the time an invitation would pop up seemingly out of nowhere for dinner or a show or some other kind of date when she hadn't really been thinking about it—or the woman in question. She'd usually be pleased by the invitation and most of the time happy to accept. She wasn't passive when it came to women, she just wasn't looking.

She hadn't been looking yesterday, either. But she couldn't help but notice. Dusty was hard not to notice. Not just the way she looked, which was hot and sexy and even more so because she clearly didn't have a clue just how hot and sexy she was. More than that, she was a mystery, not dark and foreboding and alienating, but captivating, like the glimmer of something beautiful encased in amber. Viv wanted to crack the smooth shell and free the secret.

"This ought to be fun, huh?" Brad Cooper, every inch the tall, dark, and handsome cliché with eyes so blue they ought to be outlawed, smiled at her sardonically. His tone said he thought the trip would be anything but a good time.

"Oh, hi, Brad." Viv reluctantly deserted her musings about Dusty to be polite. Brad was one of the guys who treated her as a colleague and nothing more, for which she was thankful. She knew there were plenty of other females, attached and unattached, who were interested in catching his attention. Maybe that was why he enjoyed her company. He'd been on the beat a few years longer than her and been one of the more helpful reporters when she'd first joined. While everyone feigned collegiality on the surface, they were all competing for the best angle on the same story. After all, they were all being given the same sound bites from the presidential press office, they were all witnessing the same events, they were all reporting on the same timetable. What it had taken her some time to learn was that they were all secretly working their inside sources, hoping to get a jump on everyone else. She had yet to develop much leverage in that area, partly because of the nature of most of her features, but mostly because it just wasn't her style.

"I've never been on a long train ride," she said with a laugh. "I suspect it's going to be…interesting."

"I suspect after the first night trying to sleep in a bed two feet wide you'll change your mind."

"It's a brilliant media move, though, don't you think?" She waited for him to get his coffee and they sat together. "It will appeal to the public—this grassroots kind of campaign."

He nodded. "He could use a bit of a down-home, common-man image, if he can pull it off."

She was surprised by the flatness in his tone, but then reminded herself that as much as the press sought neutrality, reporters were still individuals, and not everyone was in Powell's camp. She found Andrew Powell to be an energetic, intelligent, and fair president, but that wasn't why she was here.

"I'd prefer a train ride here in the States than an overseas trip anytime," she said, steering away from a flammable topic.

"I agree with you." He laughed. "At least the food will be recognizable."

She smiled, sipped her coffee, and thought that eight days on a train with Dusty Nash sounded like a very fine idea.

Chapter Eleven

O530. The sun wouldn't be up for another hour and a half. By then she'd be ninety miles away, and this town, these mountains, the past wouldn't even be a memory. She'd learned to erase memories that served only to weaken her with longing and loss. All she'd take with her from this place would be anger and determination, and the sound of her father's voice calling her to action. Jane pulled in next to Hooker's black pickup truck, left the engine running, and signaled for him to join her in the Jeep. He frowned but, after a few seconds, climbed out of his truck and slid into the passenger seat.

"Do you have the information?" Jane asked.

"Yeah," Hooker said. "But there's a problem."

His eyes drifted down to her hand in the pocket of her cargo coat. If he made the assumption she had an automatic pointed at his midsection, he'd be right. "What kind of problem?"

"My contact has to bring in a supplier, and they won't deliver unless it's face-to-face."

"I don't have a problem with that, as long as I set the meeting place," Jane said.

"That's the problem. They don't know you. But they know me."

Jane laughed. "Are you suggesting I take you along?"

Hooker grinned, his dark eyes glittering like a fox scanning a henhouse. "That would be the idea."

"No deal. I don't plan on spending the next four days worried about you trying to kill me in my sleep."

"Look, I'm no killer." At her stare, he shrugged. "I'm no cold-blooded killer, let's put it that way. If somebody comes after me, sure I'm going to defend myself. Besides, think about it. You know who

I am, and that's a big risk. If I wanted to kill you, I would've done it already."

"Then we share that much." Jane didn't trust him, but trust was not the issue. Expedience was. Jennifer might not have much more time. And she might never have another chance. She had something Hooker wanted, but he posed a threat. "No deal."

"If you take me with you, I can spell you driving and you'll get there quicker. The buy will go down without a problem, and then we'll part ways."

"What about your boss?"

Hooker grunted. "I'm independent."

Translated as he had no loyalty to anyone but himself. That was in her favor. She wasn't looking for a partner. "How much?"

"Another fifty thousand."

Jane laughed. "Another twenty-five."

"Forty."

"Thirty."

He studied her and seemed to realize she wasn't going to bargain anymore and nodded. "You'll find I'm a pretty handy guide."

"There's one more thing."

He eyed the hand in her pocket again. "What would that be?"

"I want the name of the man who hired you."

Hooker snorted. "Yeah, and then my life won't be worth anything. I can't—"

"What makes you think your life is worth anything now?"

"You're not going to kill me in the parking lot of this diner."

"No, but I might do it a couple miles from here and dump your body in a field. There's a storm coming. They won't find you until summer."

"I don't think you're any more of a killer than I am."

"You're wrong," Jane said softly. "The name."

Something in her voice must have convinced him. He sighed. "Twenty-five thousand."

"A hundred thousand. Ten now as agreed. The rest when I get the explosives…in cash."

"Franklin Russo."

Jane laughed. "Your loyalty is touching."

"Once Russo figures out I'm not coming back with the cash, he'll be pissed. No more job."

"Then why take it?"

Hooker chuckled. "Someday soon he'll decide I'm a liability. When that happens, he'll get rid of me without losing a second's sleep. I consider this my severance pay."

"I'm leaving now."

"I don't live far from here. Follow me back so I can stash my truck and grab some clothes."

"You better pack anything you don't want to do without. You don't know you'll be coming back."

❖

Chicago

The cargo plane taxied to a stop, and a few minutes later the big cargo bay doors opened and the ramp descended. The flashing lights of the police, fire, and emergency response vehicles parked along both sides of the runway lit the landing zone in a wash of red. Blustery winter air flooded the hold, and Dusty hurried to free Atlas from his kennel so he could move around and keep warm. As soon as the K9 SUVs were offloaded, she led him down the gangway and into the rear of the lead car. She climbed into the passenger seat next to the driver.

Dave Ochiba nodded to her. He wasn't even wearing a jacket despite the ten-degree weather. "No time for coffee."

She laughed. "When is there?"

She liked Dave. He was friendly without getting personal. His unlined face, the color of polished walnut, made it impossible to judge his age, but she knew he'd been driving in the K9 unit well before she came on board. He was one of the only people she'd ever let handle Atlas if an emergency arose.

He grinned, started the lights flashing, and pulled out behind a quartet of motorcycle cops who swooped in front of them and led them down the access road to the highway. Two other K9 SUVs and a half dozen support and command vehicles followed as they headed toward downtown Chicago. Three miles out they came to the outer perimeter where local law enforcement had barricaded the road and redirected traffic around the anticipated presidential motorcade route. Dave stopped at a checkpoint and, once cleared, sailed down the now-empty streets. They passed another constellation of local law and

Secret Service vehicles a mile from the convention center at the inner perimeter. Dave pulled around the back of the convention center and she clipped Atlas's leash to his harness.

"Let's go, boy."

In their assigned sector, they checked all the potential sites for ordnance placement—under vehicles, within Dumpsters and trash cans, on loading docks, and along walkways. The other agents and their dogs did the same until all the parking lots and entrances had been cleared. Once inside, the agents and dogs worked a grid pattern on the main floor, basement, and exit. The advance team was already on-site, posted on the stage where the president and his party would gather for the speech, at the exit routes, the restroom that had been cleared for the president's use, the ready room where he could review his notes, and the large banquet hall where the breakfast itself would be served. By the time they finished, the president's motorcade was en route.

Dusty patted Atlas's head. "Good work, boy. Time for a break."

His eyes gleamed. He loved his work. Outside, she put Atlas in the rear of the SUV to wait along with a handful of kibble in a bowl. Once the motorcade arrived, she and the other K9 agents would rotate surveilling the exits and keeping watch on the vehicles while the president was inside.

"How far out are they?" she asked Phil Virtucci, who had just finished talking into a radio.

"Ten minutes."

Dusty jumped into the SUV to warm up, slid her personal phone out of her pants pocket, and texted, *How was your flight?*

Wonderful. Yours?

Bumpy.

Sorry! Is it cold out there?

Dusty laughed. *It's Chicago in January. Balmy.*

LOL. Almost there. Stay warm. C u later.

Warmth flooded her chest. She hadn't let herself think about what she was doing when she'd texted, or she might not have. She was glad now she had. Viv seemed to like hearing from her, and she really liked thinking about her. Usually she spent a lot of her downtime with her mind blank, in that state of ready awareness that marked the mindset of any soldier or law enforcement agent who needed to spring into action in a split second. She hadn't thought about Viv while she and Atlas had been patrolling. That was right. Being able to think about her in these rare free moments felt right too. This feeling of connection that persisted even when she was alone was powerful and amazingly exciting. The only time she'd ever felt anything even close was the always-present link she shared with Atlas. He pushed back the dark corners of loneliness. Viv did more than that—she opened a door to possibility.

She heard the approach of the motorcycle escort leading the motorcade and tucked thoughts of Viv away in a special place to be revisited later. She climbed out, zipped her jacket against the wind, and clipped Atlas's lead to his collar.

"Come on, boy. Back to work."

Atlas grinned.

❖

"Look at him," she murmured to Cam. "He's having fun."

"I think he likes being out in public as much as Bill Clinton," Cam whispered back.

Blair laughed. She and Cam rode in the presidential limo, tagged the Beast by the agents, with her father and Lucinda. Tom Turner occupied the front passenger seat while another PPD agent drove. Only Secret Service agents drove the vehicles with the president aboard. They had the best evasive driving training, recertified every month at the training center, and could whisk POTUS away to a safe house along a preplanned evacuation route in the case of an attack. The rest of the PPD and Stark with her shift rode in the SUVs following them.

Lucinda said, "Do you want your notes?"

"I'll look them over when we get there," Andrew said.

"You won't have much time if you want to stay on schedule. And we'll need to leave by nine."

"Are you trying to remind me I shouldn't talk too long?" He grinned, looking boyish and disgustingly fresh for the early hour.

Blair had consumed two cups of very good coffee on the flight and still felt a little sluggish. Of course, it *was* still dark out.

Lucinda smiled, a fond smile, but her tone was all business. "I was going to suggest you not go off script."

"That's asking a lot, Luce," Blair teased. "You know he likes to ad-lib."

"Much to Adam's chagrin," her father said.

"And the press secretary's," Lucinda added.

"At least you can think fast enough to stay out of trouble," Blair said. "Most of the time."

"I promise to stick to the draft." Andrew squeezed Luce's hand.

The brief gesture might have been simple familiarity, but Blair thought otherwise. They were incredibly discreet, as they would have been under any circumstances. The public and many White House insiders loved to speculate about the relationship between the president and his female chief of staff. There'd never been anything beyond the never-ending speculation to suggest there was anything intimate between them, but Blair had known them both since childhood, and being with Cam had taught her to recognize the look of love. For a while, she'd felt sorry they couldn't be more expressive, that they couldn't own what was between them, but then she realized they were adults and had chosen this path. She suspected they were happy with where the relationship was now. Luce was an incredible asset to the presidency. She was brilliant, decisive, commanding when she had to be, and a peacemaker when called for. She gave the president good counsel and protected him when need be. What the two of them had worked, and Blair suspected eventually there would be more.

She leaned closer to Cam, letting their shoulders touch. She needed the physical contact as much as she loved it. She was the opposite of her father where love was concerned. She never wanted to hide what was between them, even at the risk of creating public controversy. She would've tried if her father had asked, but she doubted she would've been successful. What she shared with Cam was too important, too critical to the core of her existence, to pretend their relationship was other than the center of her life. She slid her hand into Cam's and Cam smiled. That smile and the heat in Cam's eyes was all she needed.

The motorcade turned down the broad avenue leading to the convention center, and surprisingly, she found herself looking forward to the morning. Her father was an excellent speaker, and she was incredibly proud of him.

"Hey, Dad," she said quietly.

Andrew smiled at her. "What, honey?"

"I'm glad you're going for another four years."

"I'm glad I've got you on my side." His eyes sparkled as his gaze took in Lucinda and Cam. "All of you."

❖

Cam mentally reviewed the route they'd walk from the limo into the building. The site team had mapped everything out, and she knew every step Andrew and Blair would take. Large crowds pressed against the barricades lining the path from the parking lot to the convention center's main doors. The rope line was one of the most dangerous places for the protectee since screening individuals outdoors for weapons was an impossible task. Instead, dozens of agents mingled with the crowd—checking faces, looking for individuals dressed inappropriately for the weather or carrying oversized backpacks or satchels, people whose hands were in their pockets. Agents could be heard walking the line uttering, "Hands out of your pockets, please. Hands out of your pockets."

All the same, it only took an instant to grasp a concealed weapon and fire.

As they stepped from the limo, Blair's detail was already waiting and moved in on all sides. The president and Lucinda were ahead of them, similarly sheltered. Blair slid her hand into the crook of Cam's arm. The walk had been shoveled free of ice, but the wind was a force of its own, blustery and fierce, and Cam pulled her close. Reporters and TV crews extended cameras and booms to record the short procession into the building. A few shouted questions, but no one lingered to answer.

Once inside, the lead agents directed the president down a side hallway where he would enter the stage from the rear. Stark indicated a side entrance to the auditorium through which they could reach their front-row seats. As they entered, a handful of reporters from the local and national news surged forward against the inner rope line. For the moment, this was the only story to be had.

"How does the president really feel about having a lesbian daughter?" someone called.

"How do you think your marriage will affect your father's position in conservative states?"

"Will he push for a federa—"

"How do you think God feels about your sin?"

The question cut through the others like a scythe.

A man the size of a linebacker with what appeared to be a press badge around his neck surged out of the crowd, knocking aside the short barricade cordoning off the area in front of the stage.

"Stark!" Cam pushed Blair toward Stark, who grabbed her and

pulled her away. Brock quickly stepped up next to Cam and, shoulder-to-shoulder, they formed a wall between Blair and the charging man. He was even bigger up close, and running full out. He took them both down in a heap. His shoulder hit Cam straight in the solar plexus and air whooshed out of her lungs. Two more agents piled on top of them, and her vision grayed.

An instant later the weight lifted off her chest. A melee of agents wrestled the man facedown onto the floor, yanked his arms behind him, and cuffed him.

Cam coughed and fought the panic of not being able to breathe. It wasn't the first time, and experience kicked in. Consciously stifling the urge to gasp and flail, she took slow, shallow breaths until her diaphragm recovered and her lungs re-expanded. She looked around for Blair and didn't see her. Carefully, still dizzy, she pushed to her knees. Brock lay on his side, red faced and grimacing.

"You okay?" she croaked.

"Will be in a minute."

She glanced down and saw his hand clutched between his legs.

Mac Phillips, the ASAC of Blair's detail, yelled, "Everyone all right?"

"Brock needs to be replaced." Cam pushed the rest of the way to her feet. Pain burned down her injured leg and she winced.

"Are you hurt, Commander?" Mac's usually perfectly groomed blond hair was tousled and his deep blue eyes dark with worry.

"Nothing serious. Where's Blair?"

"The chief has her secured in the back."

"I want to see her. And I want to know how the hell that guy got in here."

Mac grimaced. "We've got him in the command center. We'll know soon."

Cam glanced out over the crowd. Most didn't even know what had happened. Those who were close enough to have seen the brief encounter watched avidly. She was sure some of the reporters had gotten photos.

"I want to see Blair."

Mac took her along a series of halls to a room off the main ballroom. When Cam walked in, Blair was pacing with her arms folded across her chest. Her hands were clenched into tight white fists. Her eyes were furious.

"What did you think you were doing?"

"Are you all right?" Cam asked.

"Me first," Blair snapped, hands on her hips. Stark wisely retreated to the farthest corner of the room and pretended she'd gone deaf. "Let me see you."

Cam held her arms out to her sides. "I'm fine."

Blair stepped closer, eyes narrowed. "You have a bruise on your cheek."

"Probably bumped into Brock. It's nothing."

"What happened to the part where you weren't going to do anything except advise?" Blair feathered a finger over a spot on Cam's cheek and frowned.

"I was right there." Cam carefully did not flinch. The spot was tender—she probably *was* going to have a bruise. "I could hardly step aside and let him bulldoze you."

"That's why I have agents."

"I know." Cam slid her arms around Blair's waist and pulled her tight. "You all right?"

Blair hugged her, her face against Cam's neck. "I'm fine. Pissed, that's all."

"That's good then."

"He could have had a gun."

"He didn't." Cam kissed her cheek. "Besides, the crowd inside is scanned. Metal detectors, remember?"

"You're never going to change, are you?"

Cam leaned back until she could see Blair's face. "Not where you're concerned."

"You have to start wearing a vest."

"That's cruel."

Blair smiled faintly. "Stark wants me to stay back here."

"She's right. He might not be alone."

"My father will look for me. He'll know something's wrong."

"He'll—"

"And I'll look like I'm a coward."

"Blair, no one—"

"Or ashamed."

"Ah." Cam glanced at Stark, who was listening despite her unfocused gaze and expressionless demeanor.

"Chief?"

"You know the protocol."

"I do. But…"

Stark sighed. "Let me get a sit rep. Then we'll go out."

"Thank you," Blair said and took Cam's hand.

CHAPTER TWELVE

Blair sat in the front row of the packed auditorium between Cam and Lucinda, trying to focus on her father's speech. Usually that wasn't difficult. He was a natural orator, not in the words he used so much as in the way he used them. He spoke without referring to his notes, which always made the White House press secretary and his campaign manager nervous. They feared he'd say something he wouldn't be able to retract and they wouldn't be able to spin. But he didn't. Because he spoke what he believed, and his message had always been unswerving. The constituents felt his sincerity precisely because there was no sense of rehearsal. He wasn't reading what someone else had written for him—he was sharing his beliefs, his desire to improve and secure the lives of Americans everywhere.

As much as she loved to hear him speak, today she couldn't fully concentrate. Her body hummed with adrenaline and her muscles roiled with rage. She wasn't afraid, not for herself. She was angry. Being attacked always made her angry, and not being able to fight back herself only heightened her fury. She hated being dragged to safety by a cadre of Secret Service agents, and she hated even more when someone she liked, or loved, was injured because of her. Brock still hadn't returned to his post, although Cam assured her he was all right. Cam was hurt, although of course she pretended otherwise. A purple bruise bloomed on her left cheek. That blow had been glancing, Cam said, but it might not have been. She could have a broken jaw or concussion or worse instead of a scrape. Cam probably thought she didn't notice her limping, either.

And to solidify her outrage, Cam and Stark and the rest of them somehow thought it was perfectly all right that they be injured and not her. She was sick to death of the arguments as to why she should just accept protection with a smile, and tired of trying to rationalize away her reluctance. She understood the concept of representing something larger than herself and the need to keep that image unassailable. She'd given in to Cam and the others because it made sense. But right now she was having a hard time making sense of anything. She would not, *could not*, change who she was or who she loved. Especially not when some idiot claiming to know God's mind attacked her.

Cam slid a hand across the space between their seats and squeezed her hand. Just a second or two of contact, subtle, designed not to be noticed, but Blair felt the message.

It's all right. I love you. We can handle this.

And because she loved Cam more than any amount of anger could diminish, she squeezed her hand back.

When the speeches were over and her father left the stage, Blair, Cam, and Lucinda rose and were quickly surrounded by agents, who escorted them to the banquet hall. They wouldn't be eating with the attendees, although her father would make a brief appearance one more time and thank all his potential benefactors. It was just too difficult to protect him at a sit-down meal with hundreds of people. Even state banquets in other countries were declined if at all possible. The president's food needed to be prepared separately by his own stewards, at the risk of offending the host nation. Here in Chicago food prep wasn't an issue, but every one of his donors would want a moment with him, and that was impossible. Thankfully the train's departure time gave them a reason to escape once breakfast was under way.

The throng of reporters and onlookers waiting outside had grown. Blair noticed a contingent of men and women and a few children waving placards protesting the president's policies on immigration, environmental issues, and the escalating war overseas. And added to the usual mix was a cluster of vocal antigay protesters. Their signs held biblical quotes and clever admonishments such as *God made Adam and Eve, not Adam and Steve*.

She kept her eyes forward, her hand through the curve of Cam's arm, and her teeth tightly clamped. They did not need to start off this campaign tour with a pithy comment from her flooding the airwaves. She climbed into the Beast with a swell of gratitude for its soundproofing and tinted windows.

"Thank God," she muttered. "One down and ten zillion to go."

"Tom told me what happened inside," her father said when he and Lucinda settled into the limo across from Cam and Blair.

"Just a nuisance," Blair said. "A little overeager antigay zealot got a little too close."

"It didn't take them long to home in on you." Her father grimaced, his penetrating gaze studying her and Cam. "It was a little more than a little too close, though. Are you both all right?"

"I'm fine," Blair said. Her father didn't need to be worried about her. Or feeling guilty about his position thrusting her into an unwanted spotlight. Anything or anyone slightly controversial associated with him was fair game for media scrutiny and bigoted attacks—she wasn't alone in that.

"I heard Cam took a few bumps," Andrew persisted.

"It's nothing, sir," Cam said. "Stark's people had everything under control, and Blair was never in danger."

"I don't doubt Stark was on top of it," the president said, "but it shouldn't have happened. I want someone to tell me how it did."

"Dad—"

"I want to know the same thing." Cam saw no point in pretending the near assault didn't bring up the possibility of a breach in security. People rarely became physically confrontational out of the blue. There was almost always a history of violence or radical associations stretching back decades. Somewhere, some background check might have been missed with this guy. If he was actually a member of the press, he should've been vetted and any antigay sentiment or previous history of radicalism uncovered. If something *had* been missed, the after-action debriefing and Stark's investigation would discover it.

"What matters," Blair said, "is that everyone is fine, and you were fabulous."

Andrew loosened his tie and relaxed against the plush leather seat. He glanced at Luce. "What do you think? My daughter's biased. Did I do all right?"

Luce pursed her lips, looking as if she might be searching for the right words to chastise the most powerful man in the world, and then she smiled. "Excellent. Even the improvised bits."

Looking relieved, Andrew chuckled, his voice deep and mellow. He was pleased, and he should be. The crowd had been receptive, even though they were mostly his staunchest supporters. Still, at this point in a campaign, it was important for him to maintain those connections and reward their belief in him. The donors weren't called the faithful for nothing. Their support grew from a deep belief that this man would truly represent them and make a difference.

"And you've got four hours to rest on your laurels before the first stop," Lucinda added.

"Breakfast first," Andrew said, "then we'll go over the script."

They rode in silence as the motorcade turned off the highway onto the arterial circling the rail yard. The train yard, the presidential train, and the rail line along which it would pass were all contained within the secure perimeter. K9 agents with their dogs walked the tracks on either side of the train, counterattack teams with long-range rifles looked down over the route from rooftops, and agents stood post at each of the dozens of train cars. The Beast pulled up alongside the president's private train car, and agents poured out of the SUVs behind them to form a cordon to escort the president into his car.

Blair and Cam, surrounded by Blair's detail, headed for their car. The coach was divided into two parts with a central lounge. Lucinda's quarters occupied the section closest to the president's car and Cam and Blair's sleeping quarters, bathroom, and small private sitting area were at the opposite end. Ellen Marks, a senior agent on Blair's detail, was already stationed in the lounge.

Blair nodded to her and went straight through to their private compartment, found her suitcase, and pulled out a change of clothes. Cam came in and closed the door behind her.

"Would you rather I met you in the dining car?"

Blair pulled on a comfortable red cable-knit sweater, then stepped out of her trousers and into a pair of jeans. She slid into UGG boots and slipped her phone into her pocket. The space wasn't cramped, but when she turned she was only a few feet from Cam. And why did Cam have to look so damn good and sound so damn sensitive when she still wanted to snap and spit and punch that SOB from the convention center?

"It's going to be a long trip," Blair said. "We're not going to have much privacy, but this is what we've got. If I want some alone time, I'll find someplace."

Cam hung her blazer carefully on a hanger in the sliver-sized closet and traded it for a charcoal zip-up sweater over her pale blue shirt. "I can't change my instincts."

"I know that."

"I wouldn't if I could."

Blair blew out an exasperated breath. "I know that too."

"And you can't help feeling the way you feel."

Blair raised a brow. "How do I feel?"

"Angry that you have to accept a situation that makes you feel powerless. Guilty that people you care about could be hurt because of you. And furious that you don't have any say in any of that and never have."

Blair's eyes narrowed. "You do know it tends to piss me off even more when you understand why I'm angry?"

Cam figured smiling was not a good idea at that point. Instead, she slid her arms around Blair's waist, slowly pulled her close, and kissed her. "I know. I apologize."

"Nice try. Very nice, in fact." Blair put her hands flat against Cam's chest, not pushing her away, but signaling she wasn't quite ready to give up her anger. "Have you ever felt so helpless, so terrified for someone—" She stopped. "Sorry. God, that was stupid."

"I was twelve," Cam said quietly. "I didn't understand what was happening at first, when the bomb went off, when the car exploded. Part of me knew it was already too late, but I still had to try to save him. I ran closer, but the bodyguards rushed out of the villa and dragged me back. He was already dead. Had been from the instant the bomb exploded, and when I got old enough to understand that, it helped a little bit. But the guilt never goes away."

Blair pressed her forehead to Cam's chest. "I'm so sorry. I'm such an idiot."

"No, you're not." Cam kissed the top of her head. "If my father had had a choice, I think he would have felt like you do a lot of the time. I'm sure he would have preferred to die and have everyone else live, including the driver and the security guard who died with him. I know he wouldn't have wanted me to be injured."

"I shouldn't have reminded you of it."

"You don't. It's not the same thing. My father was assassinated in front of me. It wasn't my job to protect him, and I couldn't have if I'd wanted to. I know that." Cam cupped Blair's face and kissed her. "You are my wife. You are the woman I love with all my heart. If I weren't trained to protect you, I would anyway. Just like you would protect me if you could."

"It seems like I never can," Blair whispered. "I couldn't do a damn thing when you were captured."

Ah, finally. Here it was.

"Sometimes things like Idaho happen," Cam said. "But street cops are far more likely to be injured in the line of duty than federal agents.

When I headed out there, I really thought it was a fact-finding mission only, or I'd have taken backup. What happened was an anomaly."

"I hate that you're the one that takes the chances."

"I don't know how to be any different. This is my job. I can't do anything else."

"I know. I wouldn't recognize you if you did." Blair pressed her cheek against Cam's shoulder. "And most of the time I'm okay. I know how good you are, all of you. But when I see you put yourself in danger, so instinctively, so naturally, it scares me."

And that was what the anger was all about. Cam understood the fear of losing someone she loved. She cupped the back of Blair's neck, kissed her again. "I'm not going anywhere. Ever."

"Promise?" Blair asked, even though she knew no one could promise. Hearing the words still made a difference.

"I promise," Cam said, because she knew it helped.

❖

Viv found her compartment in the press sleeping car and stowed her bag. She was surprised to find the berth outfitted with a small toilet and shower in addition to her bunk. The accommodations were a little more luxurious than she'd anticipated, although the very narrow bed looked as if she might fall out if she rolled over in her sleep. Measuring it with her eyes, she had the sudden image of her and Dusty trying to fit onto it together. The picture came out of nowhere in absolute clear and vibrant Technicolor. She almost laughed at her adolescent reaction, but the heat that spread through her, making her tingle in some very interesting places, was undeniable. And undeniably pleasant. She couldn't remember a time when she'd had such an intense reaction to a woman. Giving herself a moment to indulge in whimsy, she tried to work out the logistics and decided the only way it would work was if Dusty was on top of her. That thought stoked the flickering embers to an all-out inferno.

Bad idea. She had a story to file on the president's speech and the subsequent fund-raiser, and she wanted to explore the train and hopefully catch a glimpse of Dusty at work. She wasn't going to be able to do any of those things if all she could think about was sex. And what was that all about, anyhow?

Sex was not something that usually intruded into her consciousness during the day. She might be remotely aware of someone being attractive, but not to the extent she'd make mental pictures of the two of them romping naked together. And not to the extent that she could feel herself swell and tighten and throb.

Damn it. She wasn't given to thinking about masturbating in the middle of the day either. The car was suddenly too warm for comfort. She had an hour before they were scheduled to depart, and she needed to take a walk. She slid her recorder from the bag she'd carried that morning into the pocket of her overcoat, grabbed her gloves, and headed back out of the car. Her colleagues filled the aisle, chatting and jostling luggage, and she returned their greetings quickly as she worked her way through to the rear of the car. She stepped onto the short platform between the adjoining cars and paused to button her coat and pull on her gloves. A few minutes of brisk Chicago air would take care of her temperature overload. As the inner door to the sleeper car slid closed, she became aware of someone speaking.

"You know what security is like," a muffled male voice said. "We might as well be talking about breaching the White House…I'll try to work something out. When…"

Viv overheard a hundred personal conversations a day, including people making arrangements for secret assignations that were rarely ever really secret, and tuned out the rest as a handful of her colleagues filled the platform. She stepped back to make room.

"What's it like in there?" Sally Jensen, a super-competitive correspondent from NBC news whose blond hair was perfectly coiffed despite the wind, asked eagerly.

Viv plastered a smile on her face. "Cozy, but I wouldn't plan on doing much entertaining."

A chorus of good-natured groans followed. Gary Williams and Brad Cooper gave her friendly nods. The third man she knew only by sight. She thought he was a veteran White House correspondent, although he looked too young for the role. He sidled by her with barely a glance. The door swished closed again, smothering the chatter and leaving her alone in the cold.

CHAPTER THIRTEEN

Route 84, a diner outside Mountain Home, Idaho

Jane raised the collar on her dark green canvas coat and turned her face away from the wind. The phone booth was little more than a shell, but it was more private than the one hanging on a wall in the back corner of the diner where she and Hooker had stopped for breakfast. He was still inside, nursing a coffee and doughnut. She'd carried her second cup of coffee outside in a Styrofoam container and sipped it between sentences, trying to keep her face warm and her hands from freezing.

"The best chance we'll have is for me to get onto the train," Jane said, "but we can't count on me getting close. I've got other plans."

When she told him about the explosives, she expected his protests. She knew how formidable the task would be. No matter where the president was, inside the White House, in a vehicle, on a stage, or…on a train, he was the best-guarded man in the world. All the same, people had always been able to get close, and not just before the Secret Service had been charged with protecting him. All it took was ingenuity and the unexpected. It was true that Kennedy had been assassinated by a long-range shot by a marksman, but Reagan was nearly killed by a deranged man who had stepped out of a throng at a rope line as Reagan left a hotel and shot him, along with several others, hoping to impress a movie star. Gerald Ford was assaulted by a knife-wielding woman in a crowd and might have been shot by another if she hadn't been apprehended before she could get off a round. Only luck had saved him that second time.

Crowds offered excellent cover for an assailant, especially crowds out-of-doors where individuals couldn't be scanned with metal detectors. And fortunately, Powell had many outdoor events scheduled. But she needed more than to simply kill him. She needed him alive for a while. She knew his scheduled route by heart. She was a little less than 900 miles away from the intersect point. She'd be there well before him. Well before all the roads approaching the train route were closed. And she'd be in Colorado Springs by morning, where Hooker's contacts would provide her with the weapons she needed.

Robbie didn't like the plan.

"I've got an advantage," she said. "I've got you on the inside."

"I'll work on it," Robbie said unhappily.

He wasn't afraid for himself, but for her. She understood that. She'd far rather be in danger herself than endanger him, but they were at a point where risk no longer mattered. This time, the plan had to work.

"I'll call you again according to our schedule. Don't worry."

She hung up the phone, hunched her shoulders against the blowing snow that had started an hour before, and pushed through the smudged, grease-streaked door back into the diner. Hooker was where she'd left him, sprawled in a booth with both big, reddened hands curled around a white ceramic mug of steaming coffee. The doughnut was gone. She slid in across from him and drained her cup. "We should go. Storm coming up. You get the tab."

He half laughed. "Guess that's fair since you're buying the gas."

He acted like they were partners. They weren't. He was a departure from the plan, and she didn't like that. She didn't trust him, but she needed his contacts. She didn't need him to drive, though in this weather a fifteen-hour trip could easily become thirty when drifting snow and white-outs slowed traffic to a crawl. If she let him drive, she'd likely get there faster and be fresher when it counted. There was no percentage in him killing her, not while he didn't know where the money was. Sure, he could dispose of her and tear the Jeep apart looking for it, but he couldn't be certain it was actually *in* the Jeep. For all he knew, she could have sent it anywhere in the country with someone else the night the camp was destroyed. No, he wasn't going to kill her. At least not yet.

"Add on some coffee and sandwiches to go," Jane said.

"I can do that." He leaned back in the booth, looking full and contented, but his eyes were sharp as they roamed over her face. "You gonna tell me what you've got planned?"

"No."

"Why not? It's not like I'm going to turn you in."

"Because you don't need to know."

He shrugged. "Might be I could help."

"Why would you? There's nothing in it for you."

He grinned. "You've still got more money."

"And I can't think of anything you've got I might want to buy."

He laughed and stood up, towering over her. She didn't move.

"Might be after a few days on the road, you'll change your mind."

Dusty and Atlas had spent the afternoon making forty-minute circuits of the train yard—checking along the tracks, the undersurface of the platform, and the undercarriage of each of the cars for signs of disturbance or suspicious scents. After each circuit they took a break to warm up, and then started again. The sky had grayed and was spitting snow mixed with tiny hard pellets of ice. Atlas didn't mind the weather, so she pretended she didn't either. At least she had it better than the Secret Service agents on the protection detail posted outside every car and at the entrances to the train station. Standing still was the fastest way to freeze.

When the motorcade arrived and the president and the rest of the entourage disembarked, she and Atlas swept the limos, the K9, counterattack, and emergency response SUVs, and the command and communication vehicles before they were loaded and trailered. The rest of the support vehicles they'd leave behind and pick up replacements at the next stop.

Once all were aboard and the train signaled its departure with a series of long whistles for the benefit of the press photographing the president standing in the open door of the presidential car, she and Atlas climbed into the K9 car. She gave him a reward and crated him, where he promptly curled up, placed his head on his paws, and after regarding her solemnly for a few seconds, closed his eyes. He knew his shift was over.

Unlike Atlas, who was happy whenever he finished a good day's work, Dusty was usually at loose ends at the end of shift with a few hours to fill before she'd settle in for the night. Most days, she'd return to the crew room and grab a cup of coffee and something from the vending machines to refuel, and then head out to walk in the city. Sometimes she'd stop in a museum or a bookstore, returning at nightfall for Atlas and ending the night at home with a book.

Now she had an hour to wait until she could text Viv about meeting for dinner. Her choices were limited: spend the time chatting aimlessly with the other agents in the crew car or wait it out in her bunk. She patted the eReader in her pocket. No way could she read now. She was totally jazzed, electrified, feeling as if she was about to jump out of her skin. And since she shared her sleeping compartment with another agent who had the night shift, he was likely in there catching some shut-eye. At least they'd staggered the sleeping arrangements so no two people would be trying to sleep at the same time. She'd wait until he'd left to go to bed. That worked unless you were trying to catch a catnap, and then, well, she'd slept in plenty of spaces shared with friends, strangers, and possible enemies over the years.

So, coffee in the crew car it was—at least she'd get warm, and she could always go sit with Atlas for a while after that. She eased open the door to her compartment and quietly slipped inside. Dave Ochiba lay on his back on the right-hand sleeper, eyes closed, mouth open, snoring softly. The train started up with a scarcely perceptible jolt as she slid the zipper on her duffel. She wished for an instant she'd thought to pack a good shirt or two, but all she had were uniforms and casual civilian clothes. She wasn't used to thinking about socializing on her off-time. Dave never moved as she changed from her uniform into jeans and a lightweight navy thermal top. She switched her commission book, badge, and weapon over and pulled on a navy baseball-style jacket to cover her hip holster. She was off-shift, but everyone was technically on-duty for the length of the trip.

The train barely rocked as she made her way to the K9 division dining car. She pushed through the door, still picturing dinner with Viv, and stopped short, thinking for a split second her imagination had distorted her vision. Because Viv was sitting at one of the bench tables along the side of the car surrounded by four K9 Secret Service agents. She was laughing at something one of them had said.

Dusty almost turned and left. Viv was working, maybe, and it looked like she had plenty of people to talk to. The guys certainly looked like they were enjoying the conversation. Every K9 agent was an expert at reading body language. Without that special sensitivity to the slightest flicker of a dog's ear or nose or tail, a subtle sign of something wrong could be missed. And reading men was no different than reading dogs. Even from the end of the car, their body language was easy to read. They were bumping shoulders ever so subtly, jockeying for position, trying to catch Viv's attention.

A familiar sensation of rivalry flared in her chest—she'd competed all her life professionally, so she recognized it—but the quick surge of possessiveness that rushed through her when she looked at Viv was new. She wasn't quite sure what to make of that, but one thing was for sure. She wasn't leaving. She started down the aisle, and Viv was all she saw.

Viv looked up and smiled. Dusty could read that smile too, at least she hoped she could, because it seemed to say *I'm glad to see you.*

She couldn't stop her answering smile. *I'm really glad you're here. I couldn't wait.*

"Hi," Viv said.

"Hi." Dusty didn't care that four guys were trying to catch Viv's attention. She had a date for dinner with Viv in an hour. No, forty-nine minutes now, and that's what mattered. And Viv had smiled at her, a smile that said she was glad to see her.

She leaned against the booth across from Viv. "Working?"

"Just finishing," Viv said. "You done for the day?"

The guys turned as one and gave Dusty curious looks.

She just grinned. "So far, but you never can tell."

"You got that right," Joe Aiello, one of the drivers, said importantly. "You never know when you might get called in."

"It's been great talking to you guys. I really appreciate all the information." Viv rose, gave the men a smile, and nodded to Phil Virtucci. "And thanks again for being so generous in giving me access to your crew."

"No problem," Phil said.

Dusty felt them all watching as Viv moved next to her. "Maybe we can fill in some of the blanks from the interview this morning."

"Great idea," Viv said. "Dining car?"

"Absolutely." Dusty couldn't take her eyes away from Viv. Little sparkles of light kept bursting and swirling in Viv's dark eyes, like they were dancing. Her face glowed too, and her lips turned up at the corners, just a little bit of a smile that seemed to say *Come with me.* And that was exactly what Dusty wanted to do. Follow her anywhere. She swallowed because her throat was suddenly dry. "I'm at your service."

The little lights in Viv's eyes danced even faster.

❖

Cam nodded to the steward who appeared silently beside their table to take their plates away. The train had been under way for thirty minutes, and the view out the window was one of a cold, blustery winter day with a light snowfall softening the harsh sky. Blair was quiet, drinking her coffee, reading a newspaper. Cam was content to watch her, always astounded by the many facets of her beauty. Blair was most beautiful when she was painting, when her passion and enthusiasm and intelligence all sparked together. But she was beautiful in moments like this too, when she was relaxed and unconcerned about what was happening around her. Blair almost never truly relaxed, probably because she almost never felt safe. Cam's jaw tightened with the frustration that had plagued her since the first time she'd seen Blair. She wished for the impossible—to change the circumstances of Blair's life—and she could no more do that than Blair could change hers.

"I can feel you watching me," Blair said quietly.

"I like watching you."

"I'm not doing anything."

"I know. That's why I like watching you."

Blair put the paper down beside her plate and studied Cam from beneath narrowed brows. "Want to tell me why?"

"I like seeing you with your guard down. Your edges get soft."

"Really. Are you trying to say most of the time I'm prickly and unapproachable?"

Cam grinned. "You mean like now? No."

Blair suppressed a smile. One of the things she loved about Cam was the way Cam never feared her temper—in fact, she sometimes seemed to enjoy goading her. Maybe that was because they always had such great makeup sex. Maybe that was why she was never afraid to let her temper show, even though, now that she thought of it, her temper *had* cooled since they'd been together. "You know, all you have to do is ask."

"Ask what?" Cam said.

Blair leaned forward over the table, glancing around the car to see how close the agents were. Ellen and Mac were at a table just inside the door. Lucinda sat at the far end of the presidential dining car drinking a cup of tea and reading a stack of briefs. No one close by. "If you want to get laid, all you need to do is say so."

"I might be able to manage it even without asking." Cam leaned too. "I'm good with my hands."

Blair grinned. "That's a possibility."

"It doesn't look like Lucinda is going anywhere for a while," Cam said. "We'll have the entire car to ourselves."

"Even if we didn't, I'm pretty sure all of the berths are soundproof." Blair pushed back her chair. "Want to test it out?"

"Yes." Cam dropped her napkin on the table and rose. "Ready?"

Blair stood and slipped her phone into her back pocket. "Absolutely."

Cam's phone went off just as Blair opened their door. She glanced at it and grimaced. "I'm going to have to take this. Sorry."

Blair turned to face her, kicked off her boots, and unzipped her jeans. "Go ahead. I'll wait."

Cam watched her as she took the call. "Roberts."

Blair pushed her jeans down and off, taking her underwear with it. Cam slid a hand behind her and locked the cabin door. She leaned against it as Blair slowly undressed.

"I think I've got something for you," Loren McElroy said.

"Go ahead."

"Turns out one of the deputies in the local sheriff's department has been feeding information to the bikers around here for almost ten years. We've got somebody in the department too, and he reports this good old boy likes to talk a little bit. Seems he got word that the militia was about to pull a double cross and there was likely to be a lot of firepower involved. He tipped the bikers, who came in shooting."

"What was his source?" Cam shrugged out of her sweater. Blair smiled, pulled back the blanket and sheet on the bunk, and lay down on her side. Cam held up one finger and shot her a look begging for mercy.

"It's a guy by the name of Hooker, could be an alias, probably is. But he's been feeding this deputy—and probably pumping him for plenty too—for quite a while. That suggests he's operating local."

"A merc?"

"Seems like it. Anyhow, we're digging. We've got some of the militia in lock-up. They may have had dealings with him. If we don't get anywhere, we'll pull in the deputy. We'll get an ID."

"Push it." Cam stepped over to the bed. "And good work."

"No problem. I'll be in touch."

Cam cut the call and tossed the phone onto the pint-sized dresser. Blair reached for her belt. "My turn."

Chapter Fourteen

Idaho

Russo stabbed the off button on the remote, and the eighty-inch plasma screen above the fieldstone fireplace went black. He'd seen enough of Andrew Powell in twelve hours to last the rest of the year. Every national and local news channel had been covering the first day of Powell's Greet the People trip through the heartland, as it was cleverly being called, nonstop since six a.m. Powell's campaign strategists had made a smart move getting the smug bastard out of the cloistered halls of Washington and into people's front yards. Into the heart of conservative, traditional, God-fearing America. *His* territory.

And while he and his rivals for the national nomination were traipsing back and forth across the country from Boca Raton to Palm Springs, Vegas, and every other winter getaway where conservative donors gathered to flaunt their money and force the candidates to prance around like whores soliciting favors, Powell was out glad-handing the constituents like some old-time, friend-of-the-common-man politician. As if he didn't know political offices were bought, not won at the ballot box.

And of course people, sheep-like, flocked to the media circus. Large crowds congregated at points along the train route, standing in the arctic cold for hours, for a chance to see the historic passage. Sure, many of them were pro-Powell standard bearers, but just as many were merely curious to see the spectacle. Who they supported didn't matter now. All those citizens gathered to see him gave an impression of popularity Powell didn't deserve, and he was savvy enough to capitalize on the lie. The goddamned train slowed even at the places it wasn't scheduled to stop—Franklin had seen the schedule, as had everyone else with an Internet connection—and Powell emerged from his car to stand in the blowing wind and snow, hatless in just a suit, waving to the crowds, looking young and vigorous and accessible. As if the weather that would freeze an ordinary man's balls had no effect on him at all. Must have given his security fits, being exposed like that.

The speeches at the scheduled stops were all more of the same rhetoric he'd been spouting since his inauguration—getting Americans back to work, ensuring a strong America in the global market, protecting our shores and our interests abroad, safeguarding the rights of all Americans. That last was where he tripped up, of course. Because what Powell considered *rights* others considered sacrilege. That was one of his many weaknesses Franklin planned to make clear to the voters, no matter what it took. All the same, the entire train trip was a brilliant political move that couldn't go unanswered.

Derek handed him a scotch. "The novelty will wear off in a day or two."

"I doubt it. Americans love a spectacle, and he's certainly making one." Franklin wasn't in the mood to be placated. For once, he found Derek's earnest faith annoying and naïve. Could his aide still be as much a Boy Scout as he appeared in his khaki pants and button-down shirt and pale blue cashmere sweater? Hadn't the past four years with Franklin taught him anything?

"We need a rebuttal then—" Derek began, his tone half-soothing, half-belligerent.

"Damn right. Get Nora for me. We need to be making some news of our own right now."

"Certainly." Derek's expression didn't change at the mention of Franklin's campaign manager and lover, but his voice chilled. "What should I tell her?"

"What do you think?" Franklin slugged down the scotch and rapped the glass down onto a gleaming polished walnut table, where a ring of condensation immediately formed. "Tell her I want to see her. Now. She knows where."

"Of course, sir." Derek lifted the glass and slid a linen cocktail napkin under it to absorb the moisture.

"And try Hooker again. I want an update on the investigation into that mess up in the mountains. The last thing we need is a bunch of feds snooping around here for weeks."

"I'm still getting direct to voice mail when I call him, sir," Derek said stiffly.

"Then keep trying and text me when you get him."

"Of course."

Franklin stalked toward the door, then recognized the chill in the room and turned back. He put on a conciliatory grin and squeezed Derek's shoulder. "Sorry. Hypocrisy always enrages me, but I shouldn't take my anger at Powell's betrayal of his office out on you." He let his eyes and smile soften and swept a hand down Derek's arm, gripping his hand for a long second before he let go. "Certainly not you."

Derek's lips parted and his body swayed ever so slightly in Franklin's direction. Franklin noticed and congratulated himself on settling the waters.

"Of course, Senator."

"Franklin," Franklin said. "When we're alone."

"Of course...Franklin."

❖

The press dining car doors slid open with barely a whisper, and Viv quickly took stock of its occupants. They were early for the dinner service, and she was hoping it wouldn't be too crowded. Several reporters sat alone with laptops and tablets, and a group of four occupied a table in the center of the car. She knew them by sight and nodded when they glanced up. When they went back to their conversation almost immediately, she breathed an inward sigh of relief.

"Is that table back there okay?" She pointed to a small table tucked into the corner of the rear of the car.

"Looks great," Dusty said.

Once they were seated at the white-linen-covered table, Viv felt almost as if they were alone. No one paid them any attention, and she indulged her urge to just stare. She'd been thinking about this meeting—might as well call it what it was, *date*—all afternoon, and Dusty didn't disappoint. She looked different out of uniform. Still with that easy, rugged air of confidence and physical grace all the agents exuded, but her plain navy waffle-knit hugged her body in a way her BDU shirt hadn't, revealing the swell of her breasts and tapering torso. Her sandy hair was just a little disordered, as if she'd been running a hand through it, and her eyes when she met Viv's held a suggestion of heat that hadn't been there earlier. Or maybe that was just wishful thinking. Because Viv's temperature was definitely soaring. God, but Dusty pushed every button she had, and some she hadn't even known about. And she really did have the most fascinating mouth…

A steward appeared at her elbow, making her jump.

"Would you like to see menus?" The slender blond steward, immaculate in black pants, a short white tux jacket, white shirt, and black tie, looked both friendly and discreetly distant, like all the White House staff.

Viv hoped Dusty hadn't been reading her mind and asked as calmly as she could while looking into Dusty's amused eyes, "A drink first?"

"Sure." Dusty grinned and turned to the steward. "I don't suppose you have beer?"

"Actually, ma'am, we have both bottled and on tap."

"Agent will do," Dusty said in a friendly tone. "Dark ale?"

He nodded and reeled off the names of several brews unfamiliar to Viv. "And of course, a farmhouse ale that the president prefers."

"That's the one, then," Dusty replied.

"And you, ma'am?" the steward asked of Viv.

"Wine?"

"Of course. Glass or bottle? I can bring you a list."

"That won't be necessary. I think I'll start with a glass. White burgundy?"

He smiled. "Very good."

He disappeared, and Viv sighed. "I could get used to this kind of service."

"Don't you get that, powering around on Angel?"

Viv frowned. "Sorry?"

"Air Force One."

"Oh!" Viv laughed. "Not back in the cattle car. I mean, it's luxurious compared to commercial, but we pretty much look after ourselves in the press area except when meals are served. That is definitely nice."

"Well, this pretty much beats cargo planes all to hell."

"I can imagine." Viv frowned. "Or maybe not. Do you think Phil would let me fly back with you all?"

Dusty snorted. "Trust me, you do not want to do that."

"No, really, I do. I'll ask him."

"I hope you brought long underwear."

"Uh," Viv said, "I don't actually own any."

"Then you're going to freeze your a—" Dusty flushed. "Sorry."

Viv smiled. "I've heard the word, and I think I actually have one."

"You do. I noticed."

A little shower of sparks trickled down Viv's spine. "Did you?"

Dusty just nodded, her expression completely serious. Did she know how sexy it was when she acted like everything about Viv was important, even her ass? She didn't. No one could pull off that unstudied charm so effortlessly. She was just *that* sexy.

"I bet it won't be much worse than today, at least weather-wise." Viv tried to get her mind off Dusty and her ass—either of their asses. Of course, Dusty's was mighty fine in those blue jeans, a bit more than two handfuls, firmly packed. And that image wasn't helping. At all.

"What was it like today?" Dusty asked.

"I didn't think it was possible for things to be more hectic than his normal trips, but it was. Between his scheduled appearances and then the unscheduled stops along the way, I was running for most of it. But it's exciting. No president has done this in so long." Viv nodded her thanks when the steward slipped her glass of wine onto the table. She grabbed it and tried not to gulp. Her throat was so damn dry. "Does it make it more difficult for you—the train, I mean?"

"Not really. Whenever POTUS travels, our job is the same whether it's a train or a building or a plaza. Atlas is always scenting for explosives. And I need to make sure he gets to check all the potentially dangerous places." Dusty laughed, and small crinkles Viv hadn't noticed before appeared at the corners of her eyes. "I'd rather be doing this in SoCal, though."

"I know, and more snow is coming."

"Atlas at least won't mind."

Viv frowned. "Where is he?"

"In the kennel car in his crate."

"Alone?" Viv didn't see how she could miss him after only knowing him a few hours, but she did. "Is he all right? Is it warm enough in there?"

"He's probably snoozing right now, but he won't be happy if I leave him for long. He's used to being with me."

"It must be very special, living with him and working with him, the bond between the two of you."

"We're partners," Dusty said. "No different than any other partners."

"Tell me how you knew this was what you wanted to do."

Dusty grasped the glass of beer and seemed to be studying it.

Maybe the question had touched a nerve. Viv hadn't intended for this meeting to be about work, and she really hadn't meant to bring up anything uncomfortable. Dusty had been clear earlier in the day she was most comfortable talking about Atlas's role, not hers. Viv reached across the table and rested her fingertips gently on the top of Dusty's hand. "This is off the record, but if you don't want to tell me, it's okay too. I really just wanted to know about how you knew this... partnership...was for you."

Dusty looked up, her green eyes hazy, as if seeing something, or someplace, far away. "Most of the guys would probably say they like the chance to work solo in the field pretty much all the time, just them and their dogs. You're moving around, searching out potential threats, rather than waiting passively for something to happen."

"But not you?"

"Oh, me too. We like to poke fun at the guys standing post hour after hour by a door or a car." Dusty laughed softly, but her expression remained distant. "All those things make the job really great. But for me, it's more about him. He makes everything—my job, my life— work."

"Atlas."

Dusty nodded. "He gets me. I've always been able to connect with animals. I know that sounds kind of crazy, but growing up on a farm, I was always the one that could get a nervous mare to settle down or an aggressive buck to mind his manners."

Charmed, Viv murmured, "Like the Dog Whisperer."

Dusty blushed. "I was just more comfortable with them than anyone else."

"Any idea why?" Viv had no intention of putting any of this in her article. This was about Dusty, and she wanted to know her. "Just between us."

"When I was young, I stuttered," Dusty said.

"Really? You'd never know that now."

"It went away by the time I was ten or so, but it made me pretty shy in school."

Viv squeezed Dusty's hand. "I'm sorry. It's tough being different at any age, but worse for kids."

"It's okay. Long time ago." Dusty shook herself, just as Atlas had, shedding snow from his coat earlier. "So how about you? I bet you were the most popular girl in your class."

Startled, Viv shook her head self-consciously. "I wasn't."

"I bet you were. Wait—cheerleader?"

Viv felt heat rush to her face. "Yes, but—"

"Prom queen?"

Viv groaned. "Listen, it was—"

Dusty's eyes narrowed. "Let's see, I bet you went to…Vassar."

"You're scary. Stop."

"President of student union? And—"

"Okay, that's it." Viv narrowed her eyes. "You Googled me."

Dusty laughed again, and the clouds in her eyes disappeared. "I did not. Although that's a good idea."

"I can't believe you were ever shy."

"Why?"

"Because you're so good at reading people…well, me at least."

"You think so?" Dusty said quietly.

"You were embarrassingly correct just now."

"I was guessing, because of what you do and how you carry yourself. You're confident, intelligent, and…beautiful."

"Now you're really embarrassing me." Viv realized they were still almost holding hands and the dining car was filling up. She didn't care what anyone thought about her, but they were in a work situation. Reluctantly she broke the contact and drew her fingers away. "If those were guesses, what are you thinking about me now?"

"I'm wondering how I got so lucky to be having dinner with you."

"I was thinking something similar. Because I can't imagine how you've managed to stay single so long."

"I don't bump into beautiful, intelligent, confident women very often. At least, not ones who have ever had any interest in talking to me."

"Then you must bump into a lot of foolish women."

"What about you?" Dusty asked. "Is there someone?"

"If there were, I wouldn't be having dinner with you right now," Viv said. "Oh, I might be having dinner, but not quite like this."

"Like this?"

"Like personal, not business. Like I could sit here for the rest of the night with you because I want to find out everything about you."

"I don't think it would take that long."

"Oh, I think it would take a lot longer."

"I wish…" Dusty looked away, then directly into Viv's eyes. "I wish we weren't on this train right now. Because I'd really like to be alone with you."

Viv's heart thudded. "Would you? Why?"

"So I could keep holding your hand while we talked."

"Well," Viv said, as breathless as she'd been the first time she'd been alone with a girl and realized they were about to become more than just friends. She suddenly very, very much wanted to hold Dusty Nash's hand. "Why don't we have the steward bring us some sandwiches, and we can get Atlas and have a picnic somewhere."

"You want to get Atlas?" Dusty's startled expression morphed into something dark and intense and so compelling Viv leaned closer until their thighs touched beneath the white linen cloth.

"I don't want him to be alone and wondering where you are," Viv said softly. Her leg trembled. *She* trembled everywhere. "Do you mind?"

"No. I don't mind at all." Dusty's long golden lashes flickered as her lids dropped lazily and her gaze skated over Viv's face. "My room should be free now. It'll be a little crowded, but cozy."

"Sounds perfect."

Dusty pushed back her chair. "I'll tell the steward to rush the sandwiches."

Chapter Fifteen

On the Rails

Blair grabbed the safety handle above the berth with one hand and the back of Cam's head with the other, steadying her shaking legs. She twisted the thick dark locks between her fingers, pulling her lower lip between her teeth while trying valiantly to hold back a moan. Another stroke of Cam's tongue broke her will.

"God," she groaned, "stop. I think I hear someone—"

"There's no one," Cam murmured, rubbing her cheek over the soft valley between Blair's thigh and her lower abdomen. "And even if there was, the train noise is louder than you are."

Blair tossed her head back as Cam's mouth closed over her again. "I think…you're wrong there."

She thought she heard Cam chuckle, but her mind was melting. A blazing sunburst wiped out thought, replacing awareness with glorious sensation. She didn't remember falling, and maybe she didn't, but the next thing she knew she was lying on the bunk with Cam beside her, leaning on an elbow and watching her with a self-satisfied grin.

"Proud of yourself?" Blair gasped.

"Supremely," Cam said, her voice low and husky.

Blair hooked a finger in the waistband of Cam's pants and tugged. "Why are you still wearing these?"

"I was overcome."

Blair laughed. "Well, overcome some more and get undressed. I want skin."

Cam kissed her and hurried to sit up. "Anything you say."

Blair blinked some of the haze from her brain to watch Cam undress. Seeing her get naked was a pleasure that never got old, and one that somehow managed to stir the fires where she would've sworn she was completely reduced to ash. When Cam stripped off her shirt, Blair's brain crashed back online. "What the hell?"

Cam frowned. "What?"

Blair jumped up and flicked on the small light over the tiny dresser sandwiched between the two miniature closets. "Turn this way."

Brow creased, Cam obeyed, pulling her shirt the rest of the way off. "Let's get back in—"

"Hush." Blair gently brushed her fingers over a bruise roughly the shape and size of Texas on Cam's side. "Cam, look at this. Don't tell me you can't feel that."

Cam glanced down. "Huh. Must've gotten that when Brock and I got tangled up this morning. I didn't feel it."

"Take a deep breath. Does it hurt?"

"Hey." Cam grasped Blair's shoulders, pulling Blair's attention to her face. "It's nothing. It's a bruise. I'm fine."

"Take off your pants. I want to see your leg."

"Blair, we can do all that later."

Blair poked a finger at Cam's chest. "No. We'll do it now. If you're hurt, I want you to see Wes."

Cam laughed. "I'm not going to have the first doctor take a look at me because I've got a little black-and-blue mark."

"You will if I say you will."

"Actually, you're right, so promise you won't overreact."

"Overreact?" Blair took a slow breath. "Am I the sort of person that overreacts? Next you're going to say I'm a hysterical female."

Cam shook her head, unbuttoned her pants, and slid them off. Below her briefs, the bandage on her injured calf was tinged with red. Thankfully, it wasn't soaked, and the rest of her leg looked fine.

"It's really all right?" Blair said quietly.

"I swear to you, I would tell you if it wasn't." Cam slid her arm around Blair's waist and led her back to the bunk. "Can we lie down? It's a little chilly in here, in case you hadn't noticed."

"I had other things taking up my attention."

Cam grinned. "Oh yes, I remember that now."

Cam pulled back the covers and when Blair slid in, she got in beside her and covered them both. She settled Blair into the crook of her arm with Blair's head against her shoulder and stroked her hair. "I know it's been a bad week. I'm sorry I put you through that whole business out in Idaho. This morning was another unhappy surprise. But it's done now, and your father's okay and I'm okay and you're okay. We're likely to get some verbal sticks and stones tossed at us this week, if not something more. But that will be okay because we'll handle it. You and me, together."

"I don't know why I'm so edgy." Blair kissed Cam's throat and settled her cheek back against Cam's chest. "I just get the feeling it's not over. I don't mean the bigots on the rope line—I mean with my dad. We don't know who else was part of Jennifer's plan, but for anyone to get that close to my father, they're likely someone we know. That makes me so angry, and it makes me afraid. I hate that feeling."

Cam just nodded. Now was not the time for reassurance, and she couldn't give any when Blair was right. All she could do was listen.

"Do you know anything more yet?" Blair leaned back to search Cam's face.

"A little." And then, because Blair deserved the truth, she added, "But not enough. I've got some pieces but I can't quite get them lined up to fit together yet. I know Jennifer is related to this group out in Idaho, but we can't track any of them back far enough to know who else might be a part of this. The woman who took Skylar and me prisoner is almost certainly related to Jennifer—I'm guessing part of the larger plan."

"And she's loose somewhere," Blair said, her tone hollow.

"We've got a task force looking for her—people I trust." Cam wished she didn't have to tell her how little she knew and how little she could do. She wished she didn't have to tell her the worst of it. "I killed the militia commander. I don't think our Jane Doe is going to forget that."

"You think she'll come after you?" Blair asked in a surprisingly calm voice.

"I don't know." Cam rubbed Blair's back. "She's hundreds of miles away, and I'm not an easy target to get to, so I think the odds are against it. But I can't know for sure."

"You'll be careful," Blair said sharply.

Cam cupped her jaw and kissed her. "I swear."

Blair slipped above her and settled a thigh between Cam's legs. "When this train trip is done, we're going away somewhere, just the two of us."

"On my honor," Cam murmured.

"Yes." Blair kissed her, ending the soft slide of her mouth with a tiny tug of her teeth. Cam arched beneath her and groaned.

"Don't move." Blair kissed her way down Cam's torso.

Cam let her fingers trail over the tight muscles in Blair's shoulders as Blair moved lower. Her hips rose of their own accord.

"I said don't move," Blair whispered in the semi-dark.

"Not my doing." Cam gasped. "It's all you, baby."

"Just remember that," Blair murmured as she took Cam slowly into her mouth.

❖

"Are you sure you're all right with this?" Dusty asked as she keyed in the code to the door of the K9 kennel car. "We could eat first, and—"

"No, I want to see Atlas. And I don't want him missing you." Viv took in the row of crates and the watchful dogs, all of whom seemed perfectly content. The car was warm and smelled like fur and coffee. An agent sat in a booth at the rear of the car with his feet up, reading a magazine. He put it down when they came in, his eyes lighting with interest. She recognized him from the crew car. Joe Aiello. Thirty, dark and handsome, and he knew it.

"Hey," Joe said, rising. "What's happening?"

"Nothing." Dusty crouched in front of Atlas's crate. "Just came to get the boy."

"You on shift?" Joe joined them, talking to Dusty but focused on Viv. "I don't have you on the duty roster for tonight."

"Nope." Dusty attached Atlas's short walking lead and stood up. Atlas bounded out and nosed her hand. "Just taking him to my cabin for the night."

Joe glanced at Viv. "How's the article coming?"

She smiled. He was a nice guy, not exactly pushy, but he'd let his interest be known earlier. "It's great. You've all been super helpful."

"I'm off in a few hours," he said in what she was sure he thought was a casual tone.

"Maybe I'll catch up to you and the other guys tomorrow," Viv said. "I still want to hear about how you ended up in this division."

Disappointment flickered across his face for a second and then he grinned. "Sure. Why don't I give you my number, you can text me?"

"I think I'll know where to find you." Viv laughed and gestured to the car. "We're kind of in our own little world here."

Dusty thought about that as she walked Viv back to her cabin. They *were* in their own little world, on a train speeding through the dark in the middle of one of the least populated per capita areas in the country. If she was permanently transported from her life in DC to this train, nothing much would change for her. Other than her parents missing her weekly call, no one would even know she was gone. Her friends, more colleagues really, were mostly here on the train. Atlas was here. And now Viv. When she thought of Viv, though, she didn't think of her the way she thought about friends. Friends were people you greeted, had casual words with, maybe even a beer. Friends weren't people you told about growing up in a small town, where everyone knew you, and everyone formed expectations based on who your parents were and things like whether you stuttered or not. She'd already told Viv more about herself than she'd ever told a single person in her life. She'd never told her parents about the misery and humiliation at school, before she mastered the shyness that led to the stuttering, or maybe it was the other way around. Maybe when she'd gotten to the point where she didn't care if other people liked her, the stuttering had started to go away. It didn't matter now, at least not so much.

"Are you all right?" Viv asked quietly.

Dusty jumped a little, chagrined. "Yeah, I'm sorry. I was just thinking."

Viv slid her hand around Dusty's forearm. "Hey, you know, he was just being friendly."

"Funny, I was just thinking about friends. I don't think he was being friendly. I think he was trying to ask you for, you know, a date or something."

"Maybe. Probably." Viv squeezed her arm. "Being friendly is usually the first step in that direction. But I'm not interested."

Dusty unlocked her cabin and let Atlas enter first. Dave had left the night-light on above the dresser when he'd left, and the small room was dimly lit in a soft yellow glow. When she took Atlas off his lead, he immediately toured the room, sniffing under the bunk and in the corners and even putting his paws up onto the dresser to check out the top where Dave had stowed his shaving kit.

"What's he doing?" Viv asked.

"Making sure we're secure. That we have a safe den."

Viv laughed, delighted. "He thinks of you like pack, right?"

Dusty nodded. "You meant it when you said you knew dogs."

"Thanks, but actually I was thinking about wolves. I'm fascinated by their social structure. Have you ever seen that documentary about the guy who lived with wolves for two and a half years, eating and sleeping with them, like he was a wolf? Left his family—or maybe they left him."

"I've seen it. Maybe a little extreme."

"Oh, totally," Viv said. "But fascinating just the same. I love how they work out who's responsible for rearing their young and hunting for food. How they're a family."

Atlas lay down in front of the berth and watched them. Dusty scratched behind his ears and he sighed.

"You don't think it's weird, that I think of him like family?"

"Not at all."

"You know," Dusty said, "I don't think about you like a friend."

"No?" Viv's tone was curious, not critical or upset. "How do you think of me, then?"

"As something special, something I don't have a category for."

"All right, no labels. But how about descriptions?"

Dusty pointed to the bag of food the steward had given Viv. "Any chance we could eat while I tell you?"

"Oh." Viv laughed and passed the bag to Dusty. "I almost forgot about it." She glanced down at Atlas. "What about him? Will he be upset if we eat in front of him?"

Dusty shook her head. "He knows he doesn't eat people food. It's important for his safety and his work that he only eats what I or one of the handlers feed him, and never food from the hand, the table, or anywhere else. He'd starve before he'd take food from a stranger."

"God, I can't even think about that. I understand why it's necessary, but what if he got separated from you?"

"Then he'd find me, or one of us would find him. If I go down out there, I know the guys will rescue him, no matter what."

Viv's heart seized. Until now, she'd thought of her article as a sure-win popular piece, because everyone loved dogs. Well, everyone who wasn't a cat person, at least. Maybe because attacks on the president were so rare as to be unthinkable, she'd never really considered the life-and-death nature of what Dusty and those like her did every day. How shallow of her. To Dusty, something that horrible was all in a day's work. The thought of Dusty being injured left her feeling superficial and a little naïve. And beyond that, frightened. "Would you mind not saying that again?"

Dusty paused in the midst of taking the food from the bag. "What?"

"About you being hurt. When I think about it, it hurts me."

"Hey, I'm sorry. You know, it's not very likely."

"I'm glad. Very glad." Viv brushed Dusty's cheek with her fingertips. "But I'd just as soon not think about it all the same."

Dusty would have stood in that spot until she perished just so Viv would never move her fingers. She swallowed around the lump that developed out of nowhere in her throat. No one had ever looked at her the way Viv looked at her, as if she meant more than anything in the world. "Atlas isn't going to let anything happen to me. He can tell a long time before me when there's danger. So you don't have to worry."

Viv's eyes glistened as she slowly nodded. "Fair enough." She glanced down at Atlas. "And I expect you to look after her every day, all right?"

His ears flickered and he raised his muzzle, his jaws opening in a perfect approximation of a doggie grin. Her heart lightened at the sight, and she shook off the melancholy. "Hey, let's eat. And you can tell me about why we're not friends."

"Deal." Dusty handed Viv one of the plastic plates the steward had placed in the big bag along with containers filled with what looked like the makings of a gourmet dinner. He'd even included real silverware and linen napkins. A chilled bottle of white burgundy, a couple of sweating ales in a thermal sleeve, and a corkscrew completed the assembly. "Some picnic."

Viv sat beside her, opened the bottle of wine, and filled her plastic wineglass while Dusty removed the cap on the ale with the bottle opener she found in the bag. Viv tapped her glass to Dusty's bottle. "To our first picnic."

"To spring and a real picnic on the grass."

"And it can't come too soon." Viv sipped her wine thinking about spring, and how her emotions always veered from a little sad she wasn't sharing the joy of fresh blossoms and new life everywhere with anyone special to the heady anticipation of possibilities yet to come. Maybe this year would be different. If Dusty was there to share it with her, she was certain it would be. She was likely making plans when she shouldn't, but it felt so right she couldn't deny herself the pleasure. "To spring."

Dusty sipped her ale. She wasn't the least bit hungry. All she really cared about was being near Viv, watching her smile, talking to her, sharing in her enthusiasm and energy. "You know what you were saying about Joe earlier?"

"About him being friendly?"

"Yeah. I didn't mean that I didn't want to be friends with you, but

I don't feel casual. I haven't since the very beginning. Being with you feels a lot more than casual. I don't think about my friends when I'm not with them…but I think about you."

Viv swallowed hard. "Do you?"

"Pretty much all the time, except, you know, when I'm working."

"I don't want you thinking about me when you're working. But the rest of the time, that would be just fine. In fact, I'd pretty much like it if you thought about me *all* the time when we're not together." Viv set her food aside and sipped her wine again. They were sitting close and her thigh brushed Dusty's. She edged a little closer until the contact joined them from hip to knee. The pressure was more erotic than when she'd been naked in bed with some women. She literally trembled inside. She hadn't thought that possible. "I've been thinking about you too."

Dusty drained her ale and set it aside along with her plate of untouched gourmet food. She turned so just her knee was against Viv's and she could look directly into her face. "What do you think about?"

In the hazy light of the cabin, Viv's face seemed to glow. For an instant she looked very young and a little embarrassed. She laughed lightly. "I don't know if I know you well enough to tell you that."

Dusty frowned, trying to decipher that. "Tell me anyways."

"I thought about kissing you," Viv said after an instant.

Dusty's stomach tightened, a feeling something like she got in the middle of a requal run with Atlas, adrenaline, excitement, anxiety. But something different too. A ripple of pleasure shot into her thighs and heated the base of her spine. "Kissing me. Is that it?"

"I think we better stop there for now."

"Isn't it more like that's where we should start?"

"You know, at first I thought you were kind of inexperienced," Viv said, her tone light and teasing. "But I'm changing my mind. You are very smooth."

"Does it matter? If I'm inexperienced?"

"Not in the least, and I wasn't asking."

"I'm not, entirely." Dusty slid both hands onto Viv's waist and leaned forward. "But I might need some practice."

CHAPTER SIXTEEN

Dusty didn't think. She just went by instinct. Viv's eyes were so bright, so intent, eclipsing every other thought in Dusty's mind, in her memory. Viv's mouth was curved into a faint welcoming smile, her lips parted a breath, looking full and soft. They *were* soft, when Dusty's mouth touched hers. Moist, warm, silky lips that tasted like fruit and spring breezes. For an instant, she froze, absorbing the sensation like sunlight on her skin after coming out of a cold dark place. She shuddered from the heat.

Viv's hands cupped her face, holding her there as if she might retreat, but she wasn't going to. She wanted more. She tilted her head, let her mouth glide over Viv's, and the tip of her tongue skimmed the inside of Viv's lip, skated over her tongue. Taste exploded down her throat, a fireworks of light and color. Her chest tightened and her breath caught as if a fist had landed in her middle, but she didn't care. She would gladly go without drawing another breath as long as the honeyed touch of Viv's mouth remained.

Viv played with the hair at the back of Dusty's neck, sending a cascade of shivers down her spine. She moaned, a sound she'd never made before and had no control over.

"Oh yes," Viv whispered against her mouth, and pressed close until their bodies touched.

The swell of Viv's breast against hers was mesmerizing, at once soothing and exciting. Dusty stroked Viv's side, feeling the cool satiny shirt slide beneath her fingers. She couldn't stop exploring, captivated by the wonder of Viv's body. She ventured higher and found her palm cradling the undersurface of Viv's breast. Even through the layers of satin and silk, she sensed the elegant curve of her flesh and molded her fingers to the contours. Viv moaned and Dusty stilled. She hadn't meant…but she had.

"Did I—"

"You have a beautiful mouth. Beautiful hands," Viv whispered. "Don't stop."

"I don't want to." Dusty kissed her again, deeper, trying to go slow, trying to savor every moment of exploration. They still sat side by side, food forgotten. The kisses were endless and not nearly enough to sate the hunger surging through her belly. Her arm was trembling, she didn't know why.

Viv drew back, her breath coming fast. She stroked Dusty's face, cupped her jaw. "I'm about to melt."

"Is that bad?"

Viv shook her head. "No, it's very, very good." She pressed her hand to Dusty's chest, her fingers fanning out over Dusty's collarbone, brushing lower over the top of her breast. "Another few seconds and I'm going to start tearing your clothes off. I need a minute."

"As long as you want," Dusty said. "But I don't think I'd mind."

"I might." Viv laughed shakily. She didn't want to stop any of it. She wanted Dusty's mouth on her again. The kisses were more than kisses, they were invitations to open herself to something she'd never experienced, to take and give and fly. "I've never felt quite so out of control before."

"I've never felt anything like any of this before."

Viv fought a moment of panic. Dusty's words cut through to her core. What was she doing? All she could think of was being naked with Dusty on top of her, inside her, driving her up and over. She'd never been so consumed by need before. Never been so lost in a woman. Dusty was tender and totally commanding without even realizing it. The combination was thrilling and terrifying. Dusty's hands on her skin took her out of the fetters of everyday life and into some place of light and color and passion, and oh God, she wanted to come.

She shivered.

"Are you cold?" Dusty lifted her into her lap as effortlessly as if she were a feather and kissed the side of her neck.

"Anything but." Viv wrapped her arms around Dusty's neck and slid her tongue into her mouth, seeking the heat and safety and wild place that only Dusty had ever taken her. Dusty's palms spread over her back possessively, and she was gone again, lost to the pleasure.

When she came back to herself, her hand was under Dusty's shirt, her fingers stroking Dusty's bare stomach. Hot flesh and hard muscles glided beneath her skin. She didn't remember tugging Dusty's shirt from her pants. She jerked and pulled away, but Dusty caught her wrist and pushed her hand back against her belly.

"Leave it." Dusty's voice was gravelly, her stomach rigid beneath Viv's fingertips.

"Sorry. I just needed to touch you." Viv feathered her fingers up and down the faint ridge in the center of Dusty's abdomen. She wanted to see her naked so bad. Wanted to touch every inch of her. She groaned. "I'm not usually so crazy."

"I like it."

"Oh, me too," Viv whispered. "Me too. Only…"

"Only?"

"I want everything all at once," Viv said. "But I don't want it to be fast either. I don't want to miss a single thing."

"Then we should have supper," Dusty said. "I don't want this to be over too fast, either. I don't think I want it to be over at all."

Viv pressed her forehead to Dusty's. "You do realize you're the sexiest woman in the world?"

Dusty laughed. She knew some things about herself. She was tough, she was good at her job, she wasn't afraid to die. She also knew she didn't stand out, didn't impress, didn't catch anyone's eye. "I don't think so. I know sexy when I see it. I've been looking at it since the second I saw you."

"Where did you learn to say the things that make a woman want to surrender?" Viv's tone was playful and just a little serious too.

"I never said anything like this to anyone." Dusty kissed her again because her mouth looked so damn delicious. "You taste so sweet." She wanted the soft fullness of Viv's breast back in her hand again, in both hands, but if she did that she'd want more and Viv might let her, and then they wouldn't have the slow. And the slow was important. "I'm going to think about you naked every second I can until it happens."

"Will it?" Viv's eyes were searching, her tone a little uncertain. "Happen?"

"If I have anything to do about it."

"Then I'll think about your hands on me, your mouth on me, every second until it does." Viv pushed her fingers into Dusty's hair and kissed her again, and again and again and again. So hungry, so damn hungry. When she couldn't breathe anymore, she slumped against Dusty's chest and pressed her face into Dusty's neck. "God, you destroy me. I think I could come from kissing you alone."

"That would be unbelievably awesome," Dusty whispered. "Do you want to try?"

Viv chuckled weakly. "You'd probably have to carry me back to my cabin."

"I could do that."

Viv raised her head, dropped a line of kisses along Dusty's jaw to the corner of her mouth, to her lips. "I believe you, and the thought is incredibly sexy. I'd just as soon keep you to myself for a while, though."

"A secret?" Dusty asked, a cautious note in her voice. "You don't want anyone to see us together?"

Viv pulled back until she could look into Dusty's eyes. "No, not that. I don't care who knows that we're dating. But the special part, the private part"—she took Dusty's hand and carried it to her breast—"this part, that's mine. Ours."

Dusty moved her hand down to Viv's side again. "If you want to go slow, you can't do that."

"Really? Are you so weak?"

"Yes," Dusty said instantly.

Viv laughed. "Mm. Good."

"Are we dating?"

"We damn well better be, after this." All the same, Viv waited breathlessly.

"Yes," Dusty said firmly. "I might need some practice at that too."

"If you're as good at it as you are at kissing, you don't need any practice."

Dusty kept one arm around Viv's waist, picked Viv's wineglass up from the floor, and handed it to her. "I've never actually dated anyone."

Viv sipped her wine, taking her time sorting the millions of questions she had. Dusty was like a closed flower, holding its secrets in the heart of its bloom. She didn't want to damage the beauty of her, pushing and probing. "Why not?"

"When I was a teenager, I didn't know how to go about it. Then later I never met anyone…any woman…who made me want to figure out how. Until you."

"Does that make me the first?" Viv rather liked that idea, even though it wouldn't have mattered. She'd had lovers, and she felt like a virgin in Dusty's arms.

"Once," Dusty said, "on an away trip—overseas—after the principal had left and the detail was waiting for transport home, I was sharing a room with another agent. Everybody tends to party pretty hard after an assignment's over. She'd been partying a little more than usual, and when we got back to the room, she kind of..." Dusty lifted a shoulder.

"Put the make on you."

"That's a good word for it."

"So, you went to bed with her." Viv wasn't jealous, she really wasn't. Much.

"No. She was a little too drunk. After things kind of got a little out of hand, I left and slept with Atlas."

Atlas's tail thumped at the sound of his name.

Viv stared. "In his *crate*?"

Dusty laughed. "No, in the kennel shed next to his crate. At the airfield."

"If you ever feel like you need to go sleep with Atlas when we're together, just tell me." Viv kissed her. "And *I'll* go sleep with him."

Dusty took Viv's empty wineglass and set it aside. "That's never going to happen."

"How do you—"

Dusty's mouth on hers told her everything she needed to know.

Sweat streamed down Franklin Russo's face. His heart jackhammered in his ears. Nora rode him like he was a goddamn mechanical bull in some redneck barroom. She braced her hands on his chest and drove her hips up and down in a fury, pounding his dick and beating his balls into stones.

"I'm gonna come," he groaned.

Nora bared her teeth, her hair flailing around her face as she threw her head back and glared at him. "Don't you fucking dare."

He grabbed her ass, tried to slow her down, but nothing would stop her now. She closed her eyes, chanting *yes, yes, yes.*

He gritted his teeth when the explosion churning in his balls let loose. "Oh fuck. Oh fucking Christ."

She came with a high, keening wail, her nails scoring his chest. A hoarse cry tore from his throat.

Thank God. Franklin panted, the ache in his loins slowly easing.

She kept going, even after he grew soft and started to slip out. She reached back, tried to get him up again, but he was done. Finally she dropped beside him on the bed and let out a long sigh. "God, I needed that."

"Yes," he said, feeling as if he'd been run over by a steamroller. She reached for his cock, but he covered her hand and drew it to his chest. "You're the sexiest woman I've ever known."

She laughed. "You mean I'm the only woman that ever wore you out."

"I'm not worn out yet." He was lying and she probably knew it, but she was smart enough not to say it.

She kissed him briefly. "So, what's the emergency?"

"Maybe I just wanted some time with you."

"You don't need to sweet-talk me, Franklin." She pulled her hand free, slid it down his stomach, and wrapped her fist around him. He didn't get hard. "I know what I want. And I know what you want."

"I want the White House," he said. "And I want you there with me."

"We're on track for that."

"Powell is going to gain a lot of mileage with voters with this goddamn train trip of his. We need to do something to counteract it."

"I agree. We keep working the donors behind the scenes, but we need some grassroots appearances to offset what he's doing."

She stroked him as she talked and goddamn, if his cock didn't start to get hard. His heart banged against his ribs. "Such as?"

"Let me review his talking points today. We'll start by countering some of those with infomercials. But I want you out and visible very soon. No more thousand-a-head dinners for a while."

"Good. Wherever you need me to be."

She straddled him and slid down onto his dick, even though he was only half hard. "Right now, this is where I need you to be."

He stifled a groan. He was tired and a little sore, but he gripped her hips and started to thrust. "Just get me where we both want to be."

CHAPTER SEVENTEEN

Cam lay awake with Blair's head on her shoulder, faintly aware of the rhythm of the train moving nearly soundlessly through the night, reviewing everything she knew about Jennifer Pattee's failed attempt to infect the president with a lethal virus and the subsequent trail that led to Idaho and ended in a bloody battle where she'd killed a man whose true identity she still didn't know. Who was Jane Doe, the fierce woman who had kidnapped her and Skylar Dunbar and tried to ransom them to free Jennifer? That one move—the attempted prisoner exchange—was the fissure in the stone façade of the case, the tiny crack she had to break open. Jane Doe's actions, presumably sanctioned by Augustus Graves, were strategic suicide. Paramilitary groups were founded on fanatical loyalty to a cause greater than any individual. Sacrifice was expected and lauded. Jane Doe's plan risked the entire organization for a single person. Why? Why would they do that?

The reason had to be a personal one. Jennifer Pattee was personally important to Jane Doe. Possibly even to Graves. That was the only thing that really made sense. Because otherwise, soldiers were expendable and everyone accepted that.

Cam worked the other side of the equation, playing devil's advocate. Maybe she was wrong and Jennifer Pattee had acted alone when she'd attempted to secrete a vial of contagion into the White House. Cam's instincts disagreed, and she couldn't take the chance of overlooking another inside person close to the president. Jennifer was deeply embedded, and that degree of penetration into the highest echelons of the government had taken years. This was a long-range plan, one Cam believed reached far back into Jennifer's life, and probably that of Jane Doe as well. How many other sleepers were there? How close had they gotten?

She was riding on a train filled with hundreds of people, all of whom had been thoroughly screened and were assumed to be trustworthy. Just as Jennifer had been carefully screened. And yet Jennifer had been part of the medical team that cared for the president of the United States. She could just as easily have shot him when he walked into an examining room, and she might not be alone. Jennifer, Jane, and Graves held the answers if she could just ask the right questions.

Blair stirred, stroking Cam's abdomen. "Working?"

Cam kissed her temple. "Thinking. Am I keeping you awake?"

"You're thinking pretty loudly."

"Would you mind if I stepped out to make a phone call?"

"As long as you're not gone too long. It gets chilly when you're not next to me, remember?"

Cam had a vision of getting naked while Blair watched. A pulse of desire stirred in her depths. "I promise to return and keep you warm."

"Go ahead. I'll be here."

Cam made no move to get up. She wrapped Blair closer in both arms. "You know that makes all the difference in my life."

Blair kissed her. "Mine too. I count on you being here, understanding me, loving me. More than I ever imagined I could. It's downright scary."

"I know the feeling. Mostly, though, I just feel lucky."

Blair raised herself on an elbow. "Keep it up and I'm not going to let you go anywhere."

Cam grinned. "You know, you're pretty easy. A little sweet talk and—"

Blair slapped her stomach. "And you are altogether too arrogant. Actually, I noticed that about you the very first day."

"Me? As I recall, you're the one who tried to lure me with your charms into… Come to think of it, you *did* lure me with your charms."

Laughing, Blair kissed her again. "Go, so you can come back and I can lure you some more."

Cam slid from bed, pulled on jeans and a navy blue sweatshirt with a Homeland logo on the chest, stepped into a pair of boots, and ambled out into the lounge area. Stark sat at a small dining table in the center of the right side of the car, flipping cards onto a series of rows in front of her. She'd folded her black blazer neatly over a nearby chair. Her powder-gray shirt looked fresh, the starch still evident in the sharply creased sleeves. When she saw Cam, she started to rise.

Cam waved her down. "Solitaire?"

"Evening, Commander. Yes."

Cam craned her neck, studied the layout. "Red two on the black three in the second to last row."

Frowning, Stark checked the cards, nodded, and moved one. "Thanks." Setting the cards aside in a neat, squared-off pile, she went to the small kitchenette tucked into one corner and poured coffee from a pot that sat atop a hotplate next to a pile of bagels and a few tubs of cream cheese. "Get you anything?"

"Coffee would be good."

Stark handed her a cup. "I've got some preliminaries on the guy from this morning. I thought you might be asleep and figured it could wait."

Cam settled on a bench opposite the table. "Fill me in."

"Not much to say." Stark broke off a piece of bagel, added some cream cheese, and took a bite. "His press credentials were legit until three months ago, when he was fired from a local syndicated newspaper. Apparently he'd been acting a little oddly and had fallen behind on deadlines, turned in scattered copy, and generally underperformed."

"History of violence?"

"Not that we could find, other than some run-ins from his college days that were chalked up to fraternity shenanigans." Stark put the word *shenanigans* in air quotes and shook her head. "The kind of thing that gets pushed under the rug, but I bet if we dig we'll find out there was some racial or other bias behind it all."

"Easy to overlook until there's a reason to dig." Cam sipped the very good coffee. Traveling with the president always guaranteed excellent food and drink. "How did he get through into the hall?"

Stark winced. "His press pass had never been deactivated. We didn't check back far enough."

Cam nodded. Stark was shouldering part of the blame, although it hadn't been her job to screen individuals with potential access to the principals. Her protectee had been targeted, and that made the fault at least partly hers. Cam would have felt the same way. All the same, these were the kinds of things you prepared for, but could never completely eliminate. Anywhere along the line something might have popped up to raise suspicion about this guy, but it all could just as easily happen as it did—a string of coincidences that allowed a deranged individual to get too close. At least the metal detectors had prevented him from entering with a gun. She didn't bother saying that. They both knew weapons could be fashioned from substances that would not trip a metal detector, including ceramic guns and knives. He could have had a knife in his hand when he lunged at Blair. He could have shot her from point-blank range.

"He never would've touched her," Stark said as if reading her mind.

Cam met her eyes across the width of the car. "He already did."

"I'm sorry."

"She'll be fine."

"I'm still sorry."

Cam shook her head. "Not your call. You did what needed to be done. How is Brock?"

"He says he's good to go." Stark grinned a little bit. "But I made him go see the medic."

"Ah. Good call."

Stark studied her coffee. Sighed. "Do you dislike this trip as much as I do?"

"Probably more. At least you're not on camera."

Stark laughed. "That's a point." She tossed her paper plate and bagel remains into a nearby waste can. "To make things even more pleasant, communications tells me we're headed right into a big storm. Ought to hit by morning. Our schedule is likely to go to hell."

"Par for the course," Cam said. "Keep me updated, though, will you?"

"You'll be at the briefing in the morning?"

Cam nodded. "I was about to call Renée." She glanced at her watch. "I didn't think about the time difference."

"I just talked to her. She's working," Stark said. "Everybody's going twenty-four seven on this one. You want me to give you some space?"

"Not necessary. You've been read in on all of this." Cam pulled up Renée Savard's number and tapped it in. Two rings and Renée answered.

"Savard, FBI."

"Renée, it's Cam Roberts."

"Director," Renée said briskly. "What can I do for you?"

"Help me follow a hunch."

Renée laughed, a bright, brittle sound laced with frustration. "A hunch would be more than what I've got right now. Jennifer Pattee appears to have sprung full-grown from a mushroom patch. We can't find any trace of her before college. The deep background info was completely fabricated, but really well done. Standard checks turned up nothing. That took some money and a hell of a lot of advance planning."

"That's why I'm calling. I want you to look into military records. Augustus Graves has to be ex-military, and he's in the Armed Forces database somewhere. We've got a face, we've got a general locale. My guess is Idaho is his home territory. Men like him always go back to their roots, where they have connections within the local population and know the terrain. He might have purchased the land for his camp decades ago under another name. Track the land purchases back as far as they go, search facial ID in all the military and civilian databases, and filter for men of his age in special-ops units. Vietnam and the Gulf Wars."

"You think he's the key?"

"I think he's one of them. Someone else was providing the money, but he was providing the soldiers."

"We've already started some of those checks, but you know what the military's like. Even for us, getting redacted records is tough and slow-going."

"Then use my name and squeeze."

She laughed again, this time sounding truly happy. "I'm on it."

"And, Renée, when you find something, call me anytime. Just me."

"Understood. How's everybody handling the train ride?"

Cam glanced across the car. Stark had gone back to flipping cards onto her solitaire game. "We're loving it."

Jane pulled into a Motel 6 outside Colorado Springs a little before two a.m. The snow had thickened into a solid wall of white as she'd been driving, and a subzero wind sent swirls of flakes blowing against the windows like mini-tornadoes. She cut the engine and looked at Hooker. "I'll get rooms."

"We could share."

"If for some reason there's only one, you can sleep in the Jeep."

He laughed good-naturedly. "It'd be smarter for the two of us to be in the same place. Maybe nobody's looking for you, but maybe they are. Maybe they got a photo by now. Maybe your ID's out on the airwaves. We can sleep in shifts. And if we have to clear out quickly, it'll be better if we were together."

She thought it over. He was right. The Homeland Security and FBI agents had seen her face. If one or both were still alive, they could be circulating sketches to local law enforcement. Some of the weaker militia who'd been captured might even have given her up in exchange for a lighter sentence. They wouldn't know her true identity, but they might have photos. And they'd know whose daughter she was. She hated being forced into accepting Hooker as a partner, but he'd done nothing threatening. Her father had worked with him, which meant he trusted him to some degree, at least as far as anyone could trust a mercenary who owed no allegiance to anyone or anything. She didn't for a second think he would risk himself for her, but they both wanted to stay alive and out of custody. "All right."

She climbed out of the truck, pulled her collar up against the icy blast, and tramped through foot-deep snow to the only light she could see in any of the rows of rooms. The lighted sign announcing *Office* over the door flickered valiantly against the snowy dark. Inside, a skinny clerk in his twenties wearing a T-shirt with a band logo she didn't recognize regarded her with flat, bored eyes. "Help you?"

"I need a room."

"Eighty-nine dollars."

She counted out the cash and pushed it over to him.

"Sign here." He handed her a clipboard with a form to fill out. She made up a name for herself and fabricated the model and license number for her vehicle. She left Hooker out completely. The clerk would never check in this weather. She passed the form back to him, and he gave her a plastic key. "Ice machine's outside." He laughed sharply. "Course, it's probably frozen and won't work."

"Is there a convenience store somewhere nearby?"

"Gas and snacks a quarter mile out the driveway to the right." He looked at the plain-faced, dirt-streaked clock on the wall. "They won't open until six, though."

"Thanks."

She'd just reached the door when he called, "There's a vending machine down the other end of the building. You get to it from the hall outside your room."

She nodded and went out without answering. Hunched against the snow, she rapped on the front of the Jeep to signal Hooker to follow and let them into a twelve-by-twelve room that smelled of cleaning disinfectant, old smoke, and stale food. Two twin beds with worn gold covers stood on a stained gray carpet along with a dresser and a fifties-style yellow vinyl chair with cigarette burns on the arms. A closet standing open with a few hangers dangling at odd angles and a bathroom tucked into one corner with a shower stall, a minuscule sink, and a toilet completed the picture. Only one door in and out. One window with drapes and blinds, closed. Warm and dry. It would do.

She took off her jacket and put it on the chair by the door. She transferred her gun from the pocket to the waistband of her pants. She turned, saw Hooker watching her. "When do we meet your contact?"

"I'll call in the morning, set something up. What's your timetable?"

She smiled. From here she had another three-hundred-mile drive. But first, she needed to go to the FedEx office and pick up a package due in the morning delivery. Hooker didn't need to know any of that. "I want to be on the road tomorrow night."

"I can't guarantee that."

"I've got thirty thousand reasons that say you should."

"I might be more inclined to be helpful with a little more incentive."

She shook her head. "I promised you the rest on delivery. And you'll get it. I keep my word."

"I'm going with you when you leave here."

"I don't think so."

Hooker shed his jacket and tossed it on the end of the bed nearest the door, somehow knowing she'd want the one against the wall with the best sightline to the door if anyone were to come through. He sat on the side and started unlacing his boots. "Let's face it, whatever you're planning, you'll need a little help. Like you said, I'm for hire."

"Don't you mean you're for sale?"

Hooker grinned. "Is there a difference?"

"That's why you're not coming with me." Jane stretched out on the bed with all her clothes on. She didn't expect to sleep. They'd never turned the lights on and the dense snow outside blocked the weak glow from the parking lot and office lights. In the dark she could hear Hooker's faint, raspy laughter.

CHAPTER EIGHTEEN

Close to dawn, Blair lay alone in the berth after Cam quietly left the room while it was still dark. She'd gotten used to the rhythm of the train, kind of like swinging in a hammock as she used to do light-years ago when her mother was still alive and they'd escaped the big house—the governor's mansion—for her mother's family home in the Adirondacks every July. The log-cabin-style lodge overlooked Lake George north of the village, with a rolling lawn that ended in a dock where they'd kept an outboard motorboat and a canoe. She'd been eleven, she remembered, that last July, and she spent hours in the hammock strung between two pines reading, swimming when the heat finally drove her from her nest, and still believing life was an endless summer.

She hadn't yet realized freedom was an illusion and life was often far shorter than she imagined. Her mother hadn't been sick then, or if she had been, it'd been a secret. There'd still been guards around, but they were always in her father's shadow and only distantly in hers. She wasn't bothered by their presence when she went to school, and she only realized years later how much her mother had shielded her from the press and the public scrutiny that even a governor and his family attracted. Especially a young, handsome, dynamic governor from a political dynasty, who everyone assumed would soon be headed to the White House. That last, long summer might have been the happiest time of her life, until now.

She smoothed the sheets in the spot where Cam had slept, imagining she could still feel her warmth. Heat lingered, but that might be more the connection she felt in her heart than anything real. But then, the warmth and certainty Cam stirred in her heart was perhaps the realest thing in her life.

With a sigh, she swung her legs from beneath the covers. She wasn't going to go back to sleep, and Cam would be gone for the briefing with Stark and Tom Turner for hours. They might be on a train, but the work continued.

She pulled on sweats, scuffed into her UGGs, and dragged on an old woolen sweater. Having some of her favorite clothes around when traveling helped dispel the feeling she was a bit of a performing seal. And on that cranky note, she decided coffee was definitely in order.

Luce was alone in the staff lounge, dressed as always for the day's work in a crisp emerald green suit with a champagne-colored shirt, a gold necklace with a few discreet dark green stones, and earrings and bracelet to match. A cup of coffee sat by her right hand and half a muffin by her left. She glanced over at Blair and smiled. "Good morning."

"I'll grant you the good part," Blair muttered, "but morning it isn't."

Lucinda laughed. "You never were much of a morning person."

"That's not true." Blair poured herself a cup of steaming black coffee and shook her head when a steward appeared and offered her a menu. She snagged a bagel, scooped peanut butter onto a china plate, and carried everything over to Luce's table. "I'm very good in the morning, as long as morning starts at nine a.m."

"Fair enough." Lucinda fixed her with that piercing blue-eyed stare of hers that never failed to make Blair squirm just a little.

"What?" Blair asked.

"Tom Turner filled your father and me in on the follow-up to the incident yesterday morning. Everyone agrees it was a one-off. It won't be repeated."

Blair carefully divided her bagel and spread a layer of peanut butter over one half. "You don't know that. None of us do."

"Well, let's put it this way," Lucinda said. "If it does, someone's ass will be in the fire around here."

"I'm not angry at any of our people. You know as well as I do it's not possible to predict everything." Blair took a bite of bagel and tried the coffee. "But I am supremely pissed."

"Is that all?" Lucinda's query held an undercurrent of concern and a subtler invitation to talk.

"I'm fine, Luce. Really. That was nothing compared to Cam practically being killed a week ago."

"Neither is a situation I want to see repeated," Lucinda said.

"So," Blair said, injecting a light note into her voice. "Are we still on for the dual appearances this morning?"

Lucinda nodded. "You'll be at the hospital while your father is at the luncheon. If the snow doesn't delay local transport, the entire thing should take four hours."

"And then the dinner engagement and we're done?"

"That should be it for the day."

"All except for the unscheduled stops between here and Trinidad."

Lucinda smiled wryly. "I'm working on him."

"Well, you're the only one who seems to be able to curtail his enthusiasm." Blair grinned. "If I didn't know better, I'd think you had some secret hold over him." Astonishingly, Lucinda blushed. Blair didn't think she'd ever seen her do that before. "You know, I'm good at keeping secrets."

"You're his daughter," Lucinda said. "I'm certainly not going to discuss…" She frowned. "Such things with you."

Blair laughed, the melancholy of the predawn moments sliding away. Childhood was a miraculous time for many, and it had been for her. Idyllic, safe, innocent. But she'd been wrong a few moments ago when she'd recalled those times. The happiest moments of her life were now, knowing she was loved, loving in return. Luce was a big part of that picture. And her father. And Cam, above all, Cam. "You really want another five years of all of this?"

"Of course," Lucinda said without the slightest hesitation. "Your father is the right man for the office. And the office is right for him."

"And you?" Blair knew she was pushing, but she remembered what it was like to want something and not be able to have it, to long for things she couldn't speak of. She hated the idea that Lucinda might feel that way.

"Me too," Lucinda said. "I know you think on some level I've sacrificed, but I don't feel that way. I wouldn't want your father's seat, but I very much like the one I have."

"You know, you're right and I apologize. What you do is amazing. You are the president's chief of staff, and I shouldn't forget that." Blair sighed. "I have trouble separating my worry from my pride sometimes. And I am proud of both of you."

Lucinda's smile was soft. "Blair, you don't think of your father as the president, and it doesn't bother me that you don't think of me in terms of my office. But I do enjoy my job very much."

"The two of you remind me of Cam. Driven. Needing to be part of something bigger."

"And you don't think you are?"

"By default, maybe."

Lucinda shook her head. "I'm not talking about being the first daughter, and in most senses, the first lady. I'm talking about your art. You think the lives you touch with that aren't bigger than you?"

"Sometimes that part of me seems very far away."

"Then you need to get further away from all of this."

"About that"—Blair took another bite of bagel—"when we get back, I'm taking Cam away somewhere secret and private."

"I think that's an excellent idea." Lucinda got up to pour herself another cup of coffee. "Assuming the timing is…right."

Blair narrowed her eyes, hearing the big unspoken *but*. She was very used to the nuances of Lucinda's voice and posture. "What? You know something I don't know?"

Lucinda returned and sat across from her. "No. I wish I did. But once we get back from this trip, your father will be in Washington for at least a few weeks. Once I thought that was where he was as protected as he could possibly be. That may no longer be true."

"You know Cam won't leave if there's any question of a threat to Dad."

"I'm afraid I wouldn't let her," Lucinda said. "I'm sorry that puts us at odds sometimes."

"No," Blair said. "The things you ask of Cam sometimes put her in danger, and I hate that. But I don't hate you for asking and I don't hate her for needing to do it. That's my issue to deal with."

Lucinda reached across the table and took her hand, a gesture made all the more significant for its rarity. "If I could spare you any of this, I would."

"I'm fine," Blair said, meaning it. Part of loving Cam, and her father and Lucinda too, was loving who they were and what they needed to do. She couldn't resent that without resenting loving them, and that was as impossible for her as to stop her own heart.

❖

Viv showered in the tiny stall in her cabin and dressed in clothes suitable for the weather and a day of running after the Secret Service agents and the president. She prayed the black wool trousers would cut down some on the biting wind and paired them with a charcoal cashmere sweater over a gray open-collared shirt, and boots that came up to midcalf. With luck she'd be able to keep snow out of these as she waded through the ever-present drifts around the train. She checked her bag to make sure she had the extra battery for her phone, the little portable charger, and her recorder. With all the photographs she was taking, she couldn't afford to have a dead phone by dinner, and she had no idea when she'd get back to her cabin. She slipped on her watch, something she'd noticed most people had given up wearing. For her it was an item of jewelry as much as functional. The gold watch with the antique ivory face had been her grandmother's, and she cherished it along with the memories. As a final touch, she applied a little light makeup, enough to cover the circles under her eyes. She hadn't slept much. Her mind had been racing and her body right along with it.

She'd finally gotten back to her own cabin around one with Dusty's kisses still alive on her skin. She had Dusty's schedule for the article and knew she had the morning shift. She had a packed day ahead too. All the same, neither of them had wanted to part the night before. Thank heavens, reason had finally gotten the better of her, and she'd reluctantly said good night. Dusty had been gallant, of course, and offered to walk her back to her cabin. As if she needed protection for a trek through a few cars on the presidential train. She'd smiled all the way back to her cabin thinking about it. And then she'd collapsed into her berth and thought about everything some more.

The amazing intensity of her feelings, the way her body hummed, more alive than she'd ever felt in her life, left her aching for more of Dusty's kisses. More of all that Dusty's kisses promised. God. Dusty was like a force of nature, blowing into her world like a hurricane, bending her will like saplings in a gale force. She'd never in her life been overpowered by anything or anyone, until now. And somehow Dusty managed it with tenderness and the gentlest of touches. She couldn't wait to see her again, and even though she was early, she headed for the K9 crew car, telling herself she could get in some early morning interviews. Maybe, if she was lucky, a little conversation would take her mind off the insane desire to be in bed with Dusty. Every time her mind skipped back to the two of them on that skinny little bunk, kissing for hours with all their clothes on, her insides heated and threatened to burst into flame. She needed to be very, very careful or she was going to find herself in way over her head. As if she wasn't already. The problem was, she didn't want to be very, very careful. She wanted to burn.

She pulled open her cabin door and barely caught it before it slammed into the wall and woke the whole car. She had an hour before the daily press briefing, and she needed to get her head back in the game before then. There was a reason she didn't have much of a love life—who had time with a few dozen competitors breathing down her neck?

Joe Aiello and Larry Murtaugh slouched in a booth in the K9 crew car, nursing coffees and looking half-asleep. They both perked up when they saw her.

"Morning," she said. "Mind some company?"

Joe jumped up. "Hey. Morning. Get you some coffee?"

She smiled. "I can get it. You fellows mind talking a little bit about the job?"

"Nope. Come on ahead." Larry waved her to the booth as she approached with her coffee. "Have a seat."

Fifteen minutes later, the door slid open and Viv glanced up. The question she'd been about to ask died on her lips. Dusty sauntered in, her sandy hair damp and darker than normal, still wet and clinging to her neck in places. The very same lean, tanned neck Viv had tasted just a few short hours before. Instantly, Viv pictured Dusty naked in a tiny shower like the one she'd just been in, only this time the two of them were there together, pressed close, skin slick and flushed and hot. Heat rose to her cheeks, she felt them burning. Dusty strolled toward her, her lazy-lidded gaze taking in Larry and then Joe and then sliding into Viv's. Her green eyes were hot, dark, and anything but lazy. "Morning."

"Hi." Viv tried for casual but the word came out husky and a little choked. Joe narrowed his eyes and frowned. Viv groaned inwardly. *Telegraph how you feel to everyone, why don't you?*

The merest hint of a grin flickered across Dusty's mouth. That mouth. That amazing mouth that created the most incredible kisses. Hot and firm and so surprisingly demanding. How was it possible that no one had claimed those kisses yet? Viv's nipples tightened and she pressed her lips together. She would not embarrass herself any further. But she couldn't help looking as Dusty walked by, appreciating the fit of her black cargo pants, the short leash clipped to her belt where Atlas would be in a few minutes, the black lace-up boots, the shirt with the insignia on the shoulder.

God, could she be any hotter? Viv hoped not. She would likely melt in place if she was.

Dusty poured coffee, returned, and leaned against the booth across the aisle. She bit into a jelly doughnut and a few flakes of sugar clung to the corner of her mouth. "Snowing pretty good out there."

Viv wanted to lick the sugar off. She wanted to taste the raspberry sweetness on her tongue. Oh, she was well and truly gone.

Larry stood. "Command called with an update not long ago. The roads are a mess and traffic is slowing down the escorts. We'll probably be half an hour late."

Dusty stared at Joe as Larry squeezed past. He looked as if he planned on sitting there with Viv till it was time to roll. She and Atlas were with Egret's detail, and Viv was supposed to be with Egret too. Joe was driving one of the SUVs in the president's motorcade. Joe. She didn't blame him for wanting Viv's attention. She wasn't even jealous of that. Made perfect sense to her. Viv was amazing. And she didn't think Viv was interested in Joe. Viv had kissed *her*, after all. A lot. She grinned and polished off her doughnut. Viv was watching her eat. She liked that. Not as much as kissing, but she liked it. She would've kept kissing Viv all night if Viv had wanted to stay. She didn't care if she had to work eighteen hours after no sleep. She'd done it plenty of times.

After Viv had left, she'd been happy to finish her beer lying on her bunk, replaying the moments, savoring the sensations. Viv wanted slow. She did too. Sort of. Except part of her wanted to rush over the edge of the cliff that seemed to loom right in front of her whenever she was near Viv, and feel the rush of air around her body as she fell, exhilarated and free. The thought of what that rush would be like, losing herself in Viv, started a heavy pounding between her thighs, an ache that was new and damn distracting.

Joe said something to Viv and Dusty's attention snapped back. She wanted to tell Joe to back off, Viv was hers. That was new too. She didn't even have words for the kind of possessiveness Viv stirred in her. She thought she might be like one of the wolves who fascinated Viv, but not for the reasons Viv liked them. She and Atlas were part of a pack, true enough. But if Viv were hers, she'd be sure no one ever came near her. She felt like growling right now.

"Thanks, Joe. Have a good one." Viv stood up and grabbed Dusty's arm. "Let's get some photos of you gearing Atlas up for work."

"Sure," Dusty said with a last look at Joe, who followed them with his eyes. She let Viv lead the way out of the car, still thinking about wolves.

Viv stopped as the door to the crew car slid closed behind them, leaving them alone in the narrow passageway between cars. "You looked like you were about to bite his head off."

"I was thinking about it," Dusty said.

"You know there's nothing going on there, right?"

Dusty glanced over her shoulder to make sure they were alone. She kissed Viv, giving vent to the possessive urge still simmering in her middle. "Doesn't matter. He doesn't know that."

Viv moaned softly. "I probably shouldn't tell you this," she said, her mouth against Dusty's ear, "but the look in your eyes back there turned me on."

Dusty kissed her again, the pulse in her belly getting harder and brighter. "Good."

"It's going to be a very, very long day."

"You don't mind?" Dusty caressed her neck, slid her fingers into soft silky hair. "That I want you so crazy bad?"

"I don't think...no, I *know*...I've never seen that look in another woman's eyes because of me. I definitely don't mind."

"I don't think I could change it. It's kind of instinct."

"I like your instincts. I like them a lot. But..." Viv brushed her hand over Dusty's chest and pushed her back an inch. Somehow they'd ended up pressed chest to chest with Viv's back against one of the compartments. "I've got to be at the morning press meeting in half an hour. And if you want to get to work on time, you're going to need to take your instincts and back up a little bit."

Dusty braced both hands on the wall on either side of Viv's shoulders and kissed her neck. "Whatever you say."

Viv closed her eyes. *Yes, I say yes. Right here. Right now.* "How do you feel about another picnic tonight?"

"I'll bring the wine."

Chapter Nineteen

Jane's internal clock woke her at 0530. She'd slept four solid hours, more than she'd gotten when she'd been twelve on her first training mission with her father. They'd been in the woods then for seventy-two hours, and he'd never let her sleep. Telling her she had to stand guard, and every time she'd start to doze, he'd waken her with a shot in the air. She'd learned to anticipate that sharp blast every time her mind would start to shut down until it became second nature for her to control her sleep along with all her other bodily needs. She could go without food, she could go without water, she could go without sleep and function efficiently up until the moment her body quit, and then it wouldn't matter anymore. She'd be dead.

Across from her, Hooker breathed lightly, regularly. He was awake too. She wasn't surprised. For all he looked and acted like an Idaho redneck, he hadn't survived as a mercenary by being lazy or sloppy. He'd probably opened his eyes at the instant she had.

She'd slept in her clothes, including her boots, so she only had to stand and take three steps to be at the bathroom door. Turning, she caught him watching her, his eyes glittering points in the gloom. "I'm going to take a shower. The door will be locked. If you try to open it, I'll shoot you."

"I can wait to take mine," Hooker said agreeably. "Unless you think you'd like company?"

Jane flicked on the room light, illuminating Hooker, as she quickly stepped into the small, dark bathroom and closed the door. She set her gun on the toilet tank and twisted the shower dial all the way to hot without turning on the lights. Her night vision was good, and she didn't want to impair it. If Hooker decided to come in, she'd have the dark on her side. The dark, she had learned a long time ago, was her friend. She methodically piled her clothes on the floor in order: boots, pants next to them, shirt next to that, so she could get dressed quickly if she had to. She showered quickly too, the hot water easing some of the aches from long hours in the vehicle and the tension she carried between her shoulders. When she was dressed again, five minutes later, she returned to the outer room and picked up her coat.

"One of those bagel-with-eggs things and ham would be good," Hooker said. He was sitting on the side of the bed, the light still on, a day's worth of beard blunting his heavy jaw.

"What makes you think I'm going for food?"

He grinned. "Because you gotta be as hungry as I am, and you're not going to let me drive the Jeep to go get us something, because you figure I'll be looking for the money."

"You know it won't do you any good." He was right, of course.

"Still have to try." He lifted a shoulder. "Force of habit."

Hooker reminded her of her father in some ways, although he was nowhere near the man her father had been. But he thought like a soldier. He understood tactics and logistics. That at least was comfortable and familiar, and in some weird way, he understood her because they thought the same. The idea of him knowing even a little of what drove her was unsettling, and she couldn't afford to be unsettled. So she put Hooker out of her mind for now. She had a busy day ahead and needed a clear mind.

She turned right out of the lot and drove a quarter of a mile over empty, snow-covered roads to the convenience store. She arrived at 0559. Hers was the only car in the lot. Someone had plowed it at least an hour ago, and a fresh inch of snow lay over the surface. The storm hadn't lost any of its power, and at this rate, they'd have another foot by midmorning. She needed to be downtown and out again by then. At six exactly all the lights came on and a teenage boy, tall and skinny and moving slowly, unlocked the door.

The store smelled of burnt coffee and microwaved food. Her boots left muddy tracks on a still-damp floor. The sandwiches in the hot case were probably a day old, but neither she nor Hooker would care about that. Food was fuel, and as long as it wouldn't make her sick, she'd eat what was available. She picked up half a dozen egg-and-meat sandwiches and four large cups of coffee. She didn't have anything to say to the boy behind the counter, and he didn't speak to her either.

Behind the wheel, she started the motor, cranked up the heat, and opened the plastic lid on one of the coffees. She added a creamer and dug out her phone. Robbie answered before it rang a second time.

"Hey," he said. "Where are you? You good?"

His voice, so familiar, vibrating with warmth and concern, put a lump in her throat. "Less than a day away. You on schedule?"

"More or less. We haven't briefed today but I'm guessing by tonight we'll be behind."

"Remember what Dad used to say about surprise and diversion being two of our most important weapons?"

"Yeah?" Rob sounded uneasy. "What's going on?"

"If the train stops suddenly, get away from the front."

"Jesus."

"And it's better if you don't know. I'll be expecting you to pull into Trinidad tomorrow morning. If that changes, call me. But be careful."

"Okay. Are you su—"

"It's going to be fine. Don't worry."

She was back at the motel in fifteen minutes. She brought her duffel in along with the coffee and food to change into clean clothes. Hooker must have showered. His stubble was gone, and he'd even put on a clean red-and-black checked flannel shirt.

"Did you call your contact?" She put the food and coffee down on the dull brown metal dresser between the two beds. Hooker picked up a coffee, took off the plastic lid, and shook two packets of sugar into it. He added three of the dozen creamers she'd grabbed and put the lid back on. "Bit early for that. My friends tend to be late sleepers."

"Wake them up."

Hooker laughed. "Yes, ma'am. In an hour or two, I'll do that."

"Checkout here's eleven thirty. I'm going to be on the road by then. We need to arrange the meet for this afternoon."

"I'll do what I can, but—"

"Five-thousand-dollar bonus. Make it happen."

Hooker sighed and reached for a sandwich. "Women officers are always a pain in the ass."

"It's a volunteer army. You know where the door is."

Hooker grinned. "No, ma'am. I love my job."

❖

Viv typed in changes to her schedule as the White House deputy press secretary updated the reporters on the day's events. Par for the course, the morning had been scrambled due to unavoidable changes in the motorcade routes for both POTUS and the first daughter due to weather. The motorcades couldn't leave the train station until local police finished rerouting traffic and setting up the barricades and perimeter blocks. The station squatted on a river plain on the outskirts of a small rural community with nothing nearby except a few gas stations, a Denny's, and a Dunkin' Donuts. Nothing worth braving the storm for. The only good part of the delay was she'd get to spend more time with Dusty before Dusty and Atlas headed out with the advance team. According to the duty roster Phil Virtucci had given her, Dusty and Atlas were assigned to the detail working the underground parking garage where Blair Powell's motorcade would enter the hospital for Blair's tour of the children's ward.

As soon as the briefing was finished, Viv gathered her things and worked her way through the departing throng toward the rear of the train. The only way to get anywhere was to go through the intervening cars, but fortunately, the press section was only a few cars away from the kennel cars. She intercepted Dusty and Atlas as they were climbing back into the car. They both had snow in their hair. Atlas gave a brisk shake and sparkling drops of melting snow flew from his thick, dark coat. Dusty shook her head quickly too, and a halo of flakes hung in the air for a second. They both looked happy.

"Been for a walk?" Viv asked, the sight of them warming her with delight.

"He was getting a little cabin fever in here."

"How is it out there?"

"Visibility is pretty bad, but the wind's died down. Could be worse."

Dusty rested her hand on Atlas's head, and Viv had an instant of wishing she was the one being petted. Okay, enough of that. The day would be a damn long one if she didn't get her mind off sex.

Dusty said, "There's a little coffee kiosk over in the station. It looks like they have pretty decent Danish. You hungry?"

Oh yes, she was, she definitely was. If she couldn't get Dusty alone in a cabin, at least she could grab a few minutes with her away from curious eyes.

"That sounds great."

Dusty held out her hand and drew Viv toward the ramp leading down from the car. "Watch it, it's slippery."

Viv followed her out and onto the train platform. Local law enforcement and Secret Service agents kept the station clear of pedestrian and vehicular traffic, and all the other trains had been rerouted. The area was deserted except for the agents posted on the platform and along the train. The old-fashioned train station was a long, low green building with high-backed wooden benches in front. A Secret Service agent stood post outside the station, her topcoat collar turned up against the wind and a hat with ear flaps pulled down to practically obscure her face. She didn't move as they passed.

Inside, more benches filled the tiled waiting area. The ticket area at the end of the large, high-ceilinged room consisted of individual windows lined up side by side behind a red-velvet rope line. Two ticket sellers waited at the windows with nothing to do. Another Secret Service agent stood just inside the main entrance. Sepia photographs on all four walls displayed scenes of old cars, a bus and train station, and a town with board sidewalks. The light fixtures dangling from chains overhead were wrought iron and looked to be a hundred years old. Everything about the place was old, but genuinely old, not reproductions.

Three round tables with wooden slat-back chairs were tucked into one corner in front of a coffee kiosk. A cold case and a small barista bar offered hot and cold drinks, fruit, yogurt, ubiquitous doughnuts, and some excellent-looking Danish. Viv ordered a cinnamon roll and coffee, and Dusty did the same. They sat at one of the small round tables, almost alone.

"It's kind of eerie with no one else here," Viv said into the hushed silence.

"Kind of nice." Dusty looked completely at home in the rustic setting in her black nylon windbreaker and boots and black pants. She had the windblown look of someone who lived and worked outdoors. Rugged and strong and sturdy.

Viv had never really gone for earthy and dependable before. Most of the women she met and consequently dated were urban sophisticates. Dusty was completely different, but definitely not simple. Nothing was simple about Dusty, except that she was genuine. Viv was finding genuine to be decidedly sexy. She dragged her mind back to work. "Can I follow you on your rounds this morning?"

"If Phil says it's okay, I don't see why not."

"It won't bother you or Atlas?"

"Nope. There's always a few spectators around. People like to watch us."

"I'm not surprised. You're kind of exciting."

Dusty laughed. "You're putting me on, right?"

"No, really. People think your job is glamorous. To travel with the president and his family. You guard the most important man in the world. And of course, there are the super powers."

Dusty narrowed her eyes. "You know, I can tell when you're making fun."

Viv grinned. "Only just a little. I happen to think you're pretty glamorous, and I know you have super powers."

"Is that right?"

She nodded solemnly. "I've kissed you, remember."

Dusty's eyes darkened and her grin turned into a hungry smile. "I remember very well. Every single one."

Viv's heart fluttered in her throat. She was hopeless—she just couldn't stop flirting with her. Hell, she wasn't trying to flirt with her, she just wanted to seduce her. And she wanted to know that Dusty was as crazy out of her mind as she was. "I remember every one too. Especially the last one this morning. I'm still recovering."

Dusty glanced at her watch. "In about twenty-five minutes I'll go to work, and I'm not gonna think about kissing you until we're back on the train and Atlas is in his crate taking a snooze."

"Good, I don't want you to."

"I'm not quite finished," Dusty said in a tone of voice Viv hadn't heard before.

Strong and certain. Commanding. The fluttering in Viv's chest flamed into her throat.

"The minute he's squared away, I'm going to find you, and the next minute I want more kisses...more of everything."

More of everything. Yes. So did she. Viv grasped at reason. "I know this sounds completely ridiculous seeing how I've been thinking of nothing else myself, but I don't usually move so fast."

"Is that a no?"

"No! It's not. No. I mean, most definitely a yes." Viv's face heated. "I just want you to know this is different...I'm not usually like this with women."

"I don't care about before or other women," Dusty said. "I don't just think about seeing you tonight, I think about seeing you tomorrow, and tomorrow after that."

"Dusty," Viv said softly.

"I know. I know it's not supposed to be that way and that's okay, I'm just telling you how I feel."

"You're making me very, very crazy."

"And that's bad, right?"

Viv laughed. "Oh no. It's really, really good."

❖

A Stop along the Way

Hospitals were the hardest. She did them all the time, because hospitals were part of larger organizations, often with patrons who were big donors, and because the patients loved the visits. The children's hospitals were the hardest. So much sadness mixed in with the triumphs. Her heart broke a little every time. Thankfully, this was the only hospital visit on the schedule, and she was almost through. Having Cam with her helped.

She'd been reading a story to a dozen children in the pediatric oncology ward for the last twenty minutes, while Cam sat nearby with a couple of kids balanced on her knee and the rest scattered around them on big pillows and little chairs with their IV poles and their plastic bags filled with poisons designed to kill the killer inside them. She finished the story and closed the book.

Several children cheered, and those who could clapped.

"You've all been terrific. My best audience ever!" Blair handed the book to one of the nurses and rose. "Thank you so much for letting me visit."

The children waved, a few touched her hand, and they all called good-bye. She slid her hand through the curve of Cam's arm. "Thank you."

"Anytime."

The hospital administrator, a husky blond with a too-tight suit shiny at the knees, walked them out as Stark and Mac Phillips fell in behind them. He made the usual platitudes about how happy he was they had visited and how sure he was that the board would remember her father's generosity in sponsoring the fund-raiser designed to help build a new wing, and all the usual politically appropriate things.

Blair shook his hand. "Thank you for having me. Please tell your board my father supports the kind of health care reform that allows our hospitals to grow and provide the best care possible."

"Of course. Wonderful to have you and your...uh..." He glanced at Cam and flushed.

"Spouse," Blair said helpfully.

He cleared his throat. "Yes, well, we're very glad to have you."

"Our pleasure." Blair turned to the elevator where Secret Service Agent Felicia Adams, tall and elegant as an Egyptian queen come to life, held the door open. As soon as she was inside and the door slid closed, she let out a long sigh. "I am ready for two hours of absolute silence."

Cam laughed and squeezed her hand. "They were a bit vociferous."

"I guess that's better than them being too sick to enjoy it." She leaned back and closed her eyes. Hospitals. She hated them. She had since those last months when her mother had spent more time in one than out, and finally had entered never to return.

The elevator bumped to a stop and Felicia straightened, squinting at the numbers above the door. They were between the first floor and the garage level and not moving.

"We've got a situation in the elevator," Felicia said into her wrist com. "Stopped between floors. Brock?"

Cam looked up at the ceiling, frowning.

"What?" Blair asked.

"Nothing," Cam said. "I just wanted to make sure I couldn't hear anything above us. Probably the electronics misreading the sensors. It'll probably start up again in a second."

"Brock's downstairs," Felicia said. "Everything's clear there. Just hold on." She opened the control box, inserted a key, and punched *G*. After a second the elevator started up again, and a minute later they settled and the doors opened.

"Just wait a moment," Cam murmured, sliding her hand inside her topcoat.

Brock appeared in front of the door. "Everything all right?"

"Yes," Felicia said. "Just a little glitch with the electronics."

"This way, then." He gestured for Blair and Cam to follow him, and three more agents converged on their small party, heading for their

SUV. A K9 agent with a gorgeous dog wearing a vest with the USSS K9 emblem on it walked along beside the line of SUVs, accompanied by a brunette Blair recognized. One of the reporters, but she couldn't recall her name.

When the reporter saw them coming, she stopped and smiled warmly as Blair passed. "Congratulations, Ms. Powell, Director Roberts. I missed the wedding, but I heard it was wonderful."

Blair paused. She was used to reporters calling questions to her about the marriage, but she couldn't think of one who'd congratulated her. "Thank you." She nodded toward the agent with the dog. "Interviewing for a new job?"

"Not just yet," the brunette said. "Research. An article on the K9 division."

"Terrific idea. They're amazing—the dogs and the people."

"I know. I'm Vivian Elliott. *Washington Gazette*."

"Nice to meet you, Vivian. You'll have to let me know when it's coming out. I'd love to read it."

"Actually, would you mind talking with me a few minutes about it?" Viv asked quickly. "Ten minutes, whenever you've got a chance. Your view of the division would be a great addition."

"Of course. We'll have plenty of time between now and the end of the line."

"Great," Viv said. "Who should I contact to schedule?"

Blair laughed. "That would be me. Give me your number and I'll text you."

Blair handed over her phone, and Viv punched in her number, then handed it back.

"Thank you so much," Viv said, stepping back. "Looking forward to it."

Mac opened the rear door of the SUV, and Blair waved. "I'll be in touch. Thanks again."

The SUV pulled out and Cam said quietly, "How are you doing?"

"How much longer is this trip?" Blair asked.

"You were great. It will be over soon."

Blair counted the days in her head. Less than a week to go, and only a dozen appearances. She'd survive. She took Cam's hand. "I'm so glad you're here."

Cam slipped an arm around her shoulders. "Where else would I be?"

CHAPTER TWENTY

Outside Colorado Springs

"Well?" Jane asked as Hooker slid into the front seat, bringing a gust of cold air and blowing snow with him. She'd spent the last ten minutes sitting outside a gas station with pumps that didn't look like they'd been updated in thirty years while Hooker used one of those pay phones clamped to a metal pole, the kind she hadn't seen anywhere since she was a kid, at the side of a squat building with no lights showing. She couldn't argue with him not using a cell phone, especially when she didn't know anything about his contacts. For all she knew, Hooker's friends could be under surveillance by local law enforcement or even the feds. But she didn't have a choice. She had to use what she had, and right now, that was Hooker.

"We're all set," Hooker said, stomping snow off his boots onto the rubber mat in the wheel well. "Fourteen hundred hours."

"Where?"

"A warehouse just outside the city limits. I've got directions."

"Who owns it?"

"Nobody. It's abandoned, but my friends have liberated it and given it a new life."

Jane snorted and punched the FedEx address into her nav con.

Hooker frowned at the screen. "Expecting something?"

She didn't bother to answer and they rode in silence through the snow. By the time she navigated across town, it was after noon. She pulled into the small lot in front of the FedEx office, turned off the ignition, and left him sitting in the front seat. She showed ID, collected her packages, stowed them carefully in the cargo area, and pulled out again in under five minutes.

"So?" Hooker asked. "You gonna tell me what's in there?"

Jane laughed. "No."

"I can see it's from Amazon. What'd you order? New clothes?"

She said nothing.

"You know, if you let me in on your plans, I could be more useful."

"I already told you. I don't need a partner."

"Sure you do. Didn't your father teach you the importance of backup on a risky op?"

Fury rose through her, swift and hot as a knife plunged into her belly. "Don't pretend you know anything about my father."

"Lucky guess, then, but I'm right, aren't I? This is all about your sister, right? You think you can spring her?"

"You don't know anything about me. And you're never going to."

"Look," Hooker said reasonably. "We're out here in the ass-end of nowhere in the middle of winter. Not exactly a great time for an operation. Targets are scarce. Except that right about now, the presidential train is headed our way. It doesn't take a college education to do the math."

Jane pulled into the drive-thru at McDonald's and slowed at the kiosk. She ordered enough for two meals for each of them in case dinner wasn't on the horizon.

Hooker kept talking as if she'd actually answered him. "Getting to him isn't impossible, but almost. You need inside help and a lot of planning. Flying by the seat of your pants can get you ki—"

Jane rolled down her window to hand over the money and collect their food. Hooker actually shut up for one minute. She pulled into a space across from the drive-thru, put the vehicle in park, and kept the heater running. Damn, she was tired of being cold. She reached into the bag and pulled out a hamburger and fries. "You can eat or not eat. Your choice. Once the deal is done this afternoon, we part ways."

"You'll need backup." Hooker stuck a hand into the bag and pulled out a red cardboard box of fries. "I already know enough to guess what you're doing, so why not take advantage?"

"Because I don't trust you."

Hooker munched a french fry. "Why not? Because I'm a merc?"

"That, and because you're working for Russo."

"*Did* work for him." He pulled out a cheeseburger and unwrapped it. "I'm not gonna have a job after this. Russo sent me after the money, and since you're busy spending it and I'm getting a cut, that's not gonna happen."

"That's my point," Jane said. "You have no loyalty."

"Not strictly true." Hooker lifted a shoulder. "I'm loyal until the job is done. And to prove it"—he took a bite of his cheeseburger, took his time chewing, and swallowed—"I'll let you in on something you don't know."

Jane sighed and put her wrappers into the bag. "I'm all ears."

"Russo tipped off one of the deputies in the sheriff's department about your meet with the Renegades. Only he screwed with the details a bit. The Renegades thought you were gonna try to take them out. That's what started the whole firefight that ended up getting your old man killed."

The fury burning in Jane's chest exploded behind her eyes. Her vision went red until she blinked it clear. "Russo. He double-crossed us."

"And that's loyalty for you." Hooker reached into the bag for another cheeseburger. "Fifty-fifty split and I'm yours till the job is done."

"Let's go see your friends," Jane said. "Then we'll talk."

❖

Franklin paced restlessly in front of the french doors leading onto the deck outside the cabin's great room while Nora disconnected her call and made notes on her tablet. A fire burned in the huge stone fireplace. Snow fell, obscuring the road up the mountainside, isolating them in his mountain retreat. Any other time he would have welcomed the time away from prying eyes, but he couldn't relax.

He'd have to go home soon or fabricate some excuse for his wife. Maintaining the charade of his marriage was important. Preserving some semblance of her happiness was insurance. He doubted that she'd ever think of leaving him. She didn't have the spine for it, and the pills and alcohol kept her mind too clouded to conceive of any other life. But her family still controlled a large part of her wealth, and he couldn't afford to lose that pipeline if they decided she was better off without him. Derek would chafe at his absence as well. And if he stayed another night here with Nora, he wasn't sure he could keep up with the physical demands. His cock barely twitched at the idea of fucking her anytime soon. Her appetites were fed by challenge, and going head-to-head with Powell was a big challenge. He turned when he felt her behind him. "Well?"

"I've got you lined up for a town meeting, a banquet with the Midwest Farm Consortium, and giving the keynote speech at the United Cattlemen's annual meeting." Nora stretched, showing her teeth in a satisfied smile. If she'd been a big cat, she'd have blood on her canines. Her breasts, unfettered by a bra, pressed against her silk blouse, her nipples puckered beneath the material. Her eyes glinted, feral and hungry. "Satisfied?"

"Of course. You always satisfy."

She laughed and stroked his stomach. "I haven't told you the best part yet."

He tensed when she reached for his belt. "What would that be?"

"The kickoff for the cattlemen will be an outdoor auction opposite Powell's grandstand final stop in Flagstaff." She loosened his belt. "He's got a parade and a speech planned in the plaza."

"Head-to-head with him." Franklin laughed, and damn if his cock didn't start to get hard. "You're perfect."

She opened his pants, reached inside, and knelt in front of him. "Aren't I."

❖

Jane pulled around behind the warehouse and parked. A black Hummer was the only other vehicle in sight. She glanced at Hooker. "Really? Couldn't they be less obvious?"

"Hey." He spread his hands. "You didn't give me a lot of time to set things up. What you're looking for isn't exactly common street merchandise."

"If this is a trap, you'll be the first to go down."

"Why would I do that?"

"How do you know the DEA or ATF isn't on to these people and just waiting for the meet to take us all at once?"

"I don't."

Jane studied him for a long moment. "That might be the first truthful thing you've ever said to me."

He shook his head. "I told you about Russo. There was no percentage in that for me."

He wasn't lying about that either. She pulled her Glock out of her coat pocket, checked the magazine, and jacked a cartridge into the chamber. "Let's go. We're here. We're doing it."

Hooker pulled his automatic from his waistband, checked it, and slid it into the front pocket of his coat. "You have the thirty grand they want?"

"Yes, and I plan to give it to them. A straightforward exchange and we're out of there. Ten minutes and then I'm gone."

"Nice and smooth," Hooker agreed.

The hairs on the back of Jane's neck stood up as they walked toward the gray metal door leading into the warehouse. If this was a trap, she was making it easy for whoever waited inside. She didn't have a choice. If she couldn't get the explosives, her last best chance at forcing Andrew Powell to free her sister was gone. If Hooker had double-crossed her, she'd probably die before the next ten minutes were up. If federal agents had these people under surveillance and a firefight broke out, she wouldn't let herself be taken. Either way, this might be the end of the road. Strangely, she felt nothing. Only the kind of wariness she always felt going into a fight. The fear of death was something she'd lost along with her childhood. Hooker looked relaxed, and she wondered if he thought about death. "Do you feel anything?"

"No." He hesitated. "Actually, that's not true. Times like this are the only time I *do* feel anything."

Another truth. "Keep your eyes open. I'm not in the mood to die today."

He grinned. "Yes, ma'am."

The interior of the warehouse was dark and dank and lit only by a few bare bulbs high up in the rafters. Jane and Hooker walked slowly forward on a cracked, grease-stained concrete floor. Two people stepped out of the shadows. One was a woman, tall and blocky in a heavy winter coat, tight jeans, and combat boots. Her blond hair was layered to collar length, her eyes sharp and appraising. A man stood just behind her left shoulder: the muscle. Brutish looking, with a broad boxer's face that was scarred and pitted, close-cropped black hair, and a heavy merciless jaw. He held an assault rifle across his chest.

"I thought this was a friendly meet," Jane said flatly, stopping at the edge of the faint circle of light.

The woman smiled, but her eyes didn't. "Precautions. I don't know you."

"I don't know you either," Jane said, "but I didn't step in here planning to kill you."

The woman glanced at Hooker. "That's good to know. Let's get this done."

"Let's see the merchandise," Jane said.

"Let's see the money," the woman answered casually.

Jane reached for the flap of her jacket and the muscle lowered his rifle in her direction. She paused, fingers an inch from the jacket. "Friendly exchange, remember?"

"We just want to make sure it stays that way," the woman said. "So take your time."

Jane opened her coat with her left hand to show the square package outlined in the zippered lining of her jacket. "I have to reach in here. If you shoot me, Hooker will shoot you."

The blonde flicked a look at Hooker. "Is that right?"

Hooker shrugged, pulled his hand from his jacket pocket, and pointed his Glock at her. "That's right."

The blonde sighed. "Jay."

The muscle moved the rifle back to rest position.

Jane unzipped her jacket pocket and pulled the flap back enough to reveal the stack of bills inside. "Your turn."

"Jay," the blonde said again.

The man backed away into the shadows and returned a second later with a black nylon gym bag. He set it down in the middle of the circle, unzipped it, and peeled back the top to reveal a row of thin clay-colored rectangles lined up inside.

Jane said, "I need to look at it."

"Go ahead," the blonde said.

Jane stepped forward, careful not to block Hooker's line of fire, and crouched down across from Jay. She reached in, extracted a rectangle at random, and sniffed it. She nodded, put it back, and checked two more. If they'd substituted some other material for the explosives, she should have hit a dummy package by now. "All right."

She took out the money with one hand, grabbed the handles of the duffel with the other, and passed the cash to Jay. He riffled through the bills and grunted.

"Okay."

They both backed away at the same time until she was beside Hooker and Jay was back at the blonde's elbow.

"Nice doing business with you," the blonde said, disappearing into the shadows.

Jane and Hooker backed toward the door. An instant later they were outside and back in the Jeep.

"Satisfied now?" Hooker said.

Jane let out a breath and the tension eased from her chest. She tossed the duffel into the backseat. "I will be, once we're out of this parking lot."

"You gonna tell me the plan then?"

Jane glanced at him. "No, but I'll show you."

CHAPTER TWENTY-ONE

Two hundred miles southeast of Colorado Springs, Jane pulled off the highway into a small town whose main street was already closed and shuttered for the night. She cruised the snowy streets until she found the public library and pulled into the parking lot. After hours, the library lot was dark and deserted. Everyone still out was in a hurry to get home. No one would remember them, even if they happened to notice them.

Hooker looked at her. "Got the sudden urge for a book?"

"Sit rep."

Hooker laughed and dug around on the floor for the fast-food bag.

Jane swiveled, pulled the duffel from behind the backseat, and slid out her laptop. She plugged the car charger into the dash and logged on to the free Wi-Fi. Nine times out of ten, she could find an Internet connection at a library. A minute later, she had a live update from the White House feed on the progress of the president's train. The White House communications department did a great job of keeping everyone informed of the president's activities and general schedule on a daily basis. As Robbie had predicted, the train was behind schedule due to weather-related problems, but so was she. All things considered, her intersect point was just about where she'd anticipated.

She enlarged the map and studied the fine lines representing county roads. Before railroads were usurped by planes and trucks for hauling freight around the country, wagon trails ran alongside the tracks so farmers and merchants could pick up and deliver goods. Eventually those old wagon lines had become paved roads, and as time progressed, they too were replaced by faster highways farther from the tracks. But the roads remained, little used now as drivers favored the multi-lanes for speed. In many places, the back roads were in sight of the tracks or an easy hike. She switched to Google Maps and laid out a new route running parallel to the train, set her nav con, and logged off.

"I don't suppose you're going to tell me what the plan is?" Hooker pulled out one of the cold hamburgers, unwrapped it, and took a bite.

"Need-to-know." Jane slid the laptop back into her duffel and stowed it away. The snow had let up a little, but the weather predicted more on the way. She'd have to drive all night to get ahead of the train and wait. Never rush a plan based on opportunity. Luckily, she'd learned patience along with endurance on those early training missions in the mountains. After checking that they were still alone, she pushed open the door and stepped out. Hustling through the snow, she climbed the steps to the library's small porch, hunched under the overhang, and hoped for a signal. Luck was with her. Robbie answered a minute later.

"It's me," he said.

"I'm on schedule. Enjoying the ride?"

His laughter sounded grim. "Let's just say I'll be glad when it's over."

"Me too." She was weary, physically and emotionally. Somehow hearing his voice always reminded her of the feelings she could usually shunt aside—long-ago memories of being surrounded by family. Happy times with the three of them and their father. When she was alone, nothing really mattered except the mission. Then she forgot about everything else. Loneliness, hunger, even fear, drifted away. Maybe one day, when all this was over... She caught herself angrily. Thoughts like that only made her weak.

"Give me the order of the cars," Jane said.

"There's a lot of them."

"I have a good memory, remember? Go."

He recited them, his memory as good as hers, and she fixed them in her mind. They'd all been trained to be able to do that—to survey a hillside, a city street, a plaza, and recount in detail the location of civilians, targets, entrances, and exits. It was a game when they were young, and a mission when they were older.

"Keep your distance from the front the next twenty-four hours," she said when he was done.

"I'll be expected to cover anything that happens," he said. "If I disappear, I'll be suspect."

"Fine, just don't be in the front line." Jane watched Hooker in the front seat, checking to see he wasn't rummaging in her gear. "Besides, maybe you won't need that cover much longer."

"What are we going to do about rebuilding the forces?"

Jane clenched her jaw. The compound was in ruins, and the feds would be scouring the area looking for anyone with information about them. They couldn't go back there. They couldn't contact their old militia. But she had to give him something to hope for. "Dad had contacts in Montana. We can go there. Once we have Jenn."

"I've been checking with my contacts back in DC," he said. "Word is they're going to move her soon."

"We expected that," she said, forcing a calmness she didn't feel into her voice. Of the three of them, Robbie was always the weakest soldier. He wanted to please, but he was never as disciplined as her or Jenn. He hated the wilderness missions, didn't revel in the physical challenges, and preferred indoor duty over range work. "It won't be much longer, and then we can all decide."

"Okay." He paused. "I love you."

Jane tensed. Personal attachments couldn't be allowed to intrude in the midst of a mission. Losses were always expected. Loyalty, commitment, those were acceptable emotions that made a soldier stronger. "Soon we'll be talking face-to-face."

"Right," he echoed, "soon."

Jane disconnected and bent her head into the wind. Soon.

❖

The train started up again a little before seven p.m. and pulled out into the night. Viv shed her work clothes, showered, and chose a soft light blue V-neck cashmere sweater and jeans. She slipped into flats, considered makeup, and finally settled for a little lip gloss. She studied herself in the mirror, her skin buzzing with anticipation, like a teenager getting ready for a date. She laughed and the thrill spread deeper. When the knock came on her cabin door, her stomach did an honest-to-God flip. Wetting her lips, she turned the light down low and opened the door.

Dusty carried a small wicker basket and wore jeans, a white button-down shirt, and a big smile. She looked so sexy Viv's knees went a little weak.

"Hi," Dusty said. "Too early?"

"You're perfect. The timing, I mean—perfect." Viv stepped back to let her in. "Where in the world did you get a picnic hamper?"

"I asked the steward." Dusty set the basket on the floor by the bunk. "You can almost always get anything on a trip like this. You'd be amazed what they carry."

"I commend you on your hunting abilities."

Dusty gave a little bow. "Thank you. I hope sandwiches will—"

Viv wrapped her arms around Dusty's neck and kissed her. She was hungry, but the sandwiches be damned. She wanted kisses. And heat and sweetness and relief from the burn in the pit of her stomach that had simmered all day.

Dusty groaned and pulled Viv close, forgetting everything except the lush contours of Viv's body and the urgency that poured through her at the first press of Viv's mouth. The kiss started low and soft and quiet, like birdsong at dawn, just a single refrain at first, delicately building as the sky lightened and more voices joined. Soon her head was filled with sound and light and wonder. She slipped her hand underneath the incredibly soft sweater and found even softer skin, stroking lower to the hollow at the base of Viv's spine, pressing a palm to the mesmerizing curve of muscle and flesh. She could spend a lifetime exploring every amazing dip and swell, if only she wasn't so damn crazy for more. More kisses, more touches, more of everything that made those little cries escape Viv's throat. She skimmed upward and feathered her fingers over Viv's side, just grazing the edge of her breast.

"Viv," Dusty gasped. "Can I?"

"Yes, God yes," Viv whispered against Dusty's mouth. She clasped Dusty's wrist, pulled Dusty's hand around her body, and pressed it to her breast. Electricity sparked, tendrils of pleasure twisted in her depths, and her back arched. "Oh, that feels so good. God, I've wanted your hands on me."

Dusty backed up and guided Viv down to the narrow bunk and somehow got them both on without breaking their kiss. She braced herself above Viv on one elbow, brushed her fingers lightly over Viv's nipple and down the inner curve of her breast.

Viv slipped her legs around Dusty's narrow hips and pulled her tight between her thighs. The pressure was agonizing and exquisite. "Your mouth…"

"What?" Dusty gasped, her eyes dark and deep, searching Viv's. "Tell me what."

"Your mouth on me…my breasts. God. Please."

Dusty's lips parted in a feral grin and she pushed Viv's sweater up in one swift sweep. Her mouth closed around Viv's nipple, firm and sure.

Viv bucked, a white-hot arrow streaking low, unerring in its target. Her clit tightened and she gasped. "Oh yes. Like that."

Time stopped. Thought fled. Dusty's awareness became only the sensation in her mouth. Incredible softness. Heat. Breathless awe. The pounding of her own heart, wild and urgent. Her teeth grazed the firm peak and Viv gave a tiny mewling cry. Dusty bit gently and the sound came again, making her blood thrum in her veins.

"No, no, no," Viv chanted, her fingers fluttering at Dusty's nape. "No more, you'll make me come."

Viv's cries made everything inside Dusty pulse, and she did it again. She replaced her mouth with her hand and moved to the other breast, sucking gently at first and then harder until Viv's cries were constant. Dusty raised her head, afraid she was hurting her.

Viv stared at her with sightless eyes. "No, you're good. So good. Don't stop, I'm so close."

Dusty followed the movement of Viv's hips with hers, pressing down rhythmically, and played her nipples again and again and again. Viv's fingers bored into her shoulders, and she screamed. A muffled cry, her face buried in Dusty's shoulder. Dusty'd never heard a sound like that before, part triumph, part surrender. She wanted to hear it endlessly.

❖

Cam balanced her reader on her chest, advancing the pages with her thumb while Blair dozed beside her with her head pillowed against her shoulder. She kept her close as much for her own sake as Blair's. The morning had been rough on Blair emotionally, and then standing by her father's side while he'd given yet another speech and fielding more questions about their relationship had finally worn her down. Cam hadn't been able to do anything except stand by, feeling alternately helpless and angry. She wasn't looking forward to another year of the additional security risk, with Blair's constant public exposure, or the toll the public scrutiny took on Blair. But it had to be done, and all she could do was give Blair a safe place to rest. She kissed her temple and settled her closer into the curve of her body.

Blair stirred, slid a hand under Cam's shirt, and caressed her stomach. "I think I could sleep anywhere as long as you were next to me."

"It's a good thing. Because you'll probably have to."

Blair laughed softly. "Thanks for keeping me from falling off while I slept."

Cam kissed her. "No problem."

"I needed this."

"Me too. I love you."

"Mm, good." Blair rubbed her cheek against Cam's chest. "I think I'm hungry."

"Feel like dinner?"

"Maybe my father and Lucinda are fre—"

Cam's cell rang.

"Damn it," Blair said.

"Sorry."

Blair sat up. "It's okay. Take it."

Cam fished her cell out of her pocket and checked the readout. "It's Renée." She took the call. "Roberts."

"I've got something for you, Director."

"Go ahead."

"You were right about Graves. It took some doing and calling in a lot of favors, but we got into the right database finally. No surprise, really. Army Special Forces. Black ops, Major Augustus Gary."

"Background?" Cam's focus crystallized, sharp and cold. Finally her quarry was in sight, and every predatory instinct kicked in. Until now she'd been chasing phantoms, but at last the mists were rising and she could see the fight ahead. One she welcomed.

"Just like you expected. Idaho native, career military until voluntary retirement eight years ago. A lot of his service record is redacted, and it will take some time to work through it, but we got the personnel file. His original enlistment forms are in there."

"Children?"

"Three, two daughters and a son."

"One unaccounted for," Cam said softly, the burn of the hunt churning in her depths. "Find them."

"No hits on any of the names."

"I'm not surprised. If he's black ops, chances are parts of his personnel file were modified." Cam bit back her frustration. Stay on the trail, keep the prey in sight. "Work the timelines in reverse and search a five-year window on either side of the probable birth dates—court records, school registers, hospital and local police reports."

"Yes, ma'am."

"And, Renée, start vetting every single person on this train. Check every transcript, reference, and clearance report."

"We'll need more people."

"I'll make the calls. You'll have more bodies within the hour."

"We'll find him," Renée said.

"Good work. Keep me updated."

"Roger that, Director."

Cam disconnected and looked at Blair. "There's a third."

"I heard."

"Dinner will have to wait. I need to talk to Tom Turner and Stark."

"You think he's here?"

"Probably not, but we can't take that chance." Cam pulled on trousers and a fresh shirt, slid her shoulder rig into place, and took a blazer off its hanger. Blair watched her with a closed, flat expression. "I can't not do this."

"I know. I'll see you after the briefing."

Cam kissed her. "I'll leave it to them. If I can."

Blair framed her face, kissing her back. "Just keep your head in the game. And find the bastard."

CHAPTER TWENTY-TWO

Off! Off, off, off," Viv said.

Dusty sat up so quickly the room swirled. "What? What happened?"

"Nothing. Everything." Viv grabbed the bottom of Dusty's shirt and tugged on it. "I want you naked. Now. Off."

Laughing, relief bursting like sunshine in a cloudy sky, Dusty yanked the shirt over her head and sent the top button careening across the floor. "I thought I'd done something wrong."

"Wrong? God. If you'd done anything more right I'd be comatose." Viv trailed a finger down Dusty's midsection. "Mm. Stay just like that. I want to look at you."

Dusty knelt astride her, her stomach in knots. She wanted her hands on Viv again, wanted Viv's hands in her. The press of her jeans between her thighs was torture. "Viv, I'm on the edge here."

"Perfect. My turn." Viv gripped her own sweater, arched her back, and lifted it over her head. Her breasts rose, firm and full.

Dusty groaned, her fingers aching.

"You like?" Viv asked softly.

"You're so beautiful," Dusty gasped. She cradled Viv's breasts and rubbed her thumbs over the taut nipples. Her head threatened to explode, and she groaned again.

"Don't...distract...me." Viv drew an unsteady breath, covered Dusty's hands, and gently pulled them away. Hurriedly, she unzipped her trousers, pushed them down, and kicked them away with one bare foot. Rearing up, she wrapped her arms around Dusty's hips, gripped her butt, and pressed her mouth to Dusty's stomach. "I knew you'd look like this. All hard and sleek and sexy."

Dusty closed her eyes. Viv's mouth was so hot she couldn't breathe. Her thighs trembled, and she fought to keep herself upright.

"Your pants." Viv licked the center of Dusty's stomach. "Off. Off, off, off."

"You have to...let me go, then." Dusty looked down. The sight of Viv's mouth against her sent a jolt of pleasure down her thighs. A warning. A promise. "Viv. I'm going to die here."

"Mm. Not yet you aren't." Viv pressed her open mouth to Dusty's belly again, this time with her teeth grazing skin.

Dusty jerked. A heavy pounding started in her loins. Another few seconds and she'd explode. "Viv. Come on. I can't stand it."

Viv laughed, a wild triumphant sound, and Dusty shivered. She felt conquered. Owned. She liked it. Way more than liked.

"Please," Dusty whispered.

"Soon, I promise."

Viv's fingers curled around the waistband of Dusty's jeans and yanked them down. Dusty half tumbled off the bunk and caught herself before she fell on the floor. She danced from one leg to the other and finally got her pants off. She stood, suddenly naked and uncertain. Viv made a little cooing sound in her throat and sat up with her legs on the floor, her knees between Dusty's. Her face was level with Dusty's belly again and she looked up, a strange fierce light burning in her eyes.

"Am I the first?"

Dusty nodded.

Viv's face, her skin flushed and damp, glowed like she'd just won a battle on some unsettled plain a few centuries before. Her hair lay in an untamed tangle on her throat. She smiled greedily. "Good. All mine, then."

"Yes." Dusty slipped her hand around the back of Viv's neck by instinct. Viv's mouth closed over her. Wet, hot, piercing pleasure. Her back arched. Her stomach convulsed. Blinded, she gripped Viv's head in both hands. "Wait, fuck, no."

"Oh yes." Viv licked her.

"I can't. I can't...Viv, I can't..."

Viv traced her tongue through the valley between Dusty's thighs and sealed her lips around her clitoris. Dusty twitched, clenched her fist in Viv's hair, and came in a shudder of wild, white light and sweet surrender.

Viv held on until Dusty softened between her lips and her breathing steadied. She leaned back. "Good?"

Dusty gripped Viv's shoulders so she didn't collapse and make a fool of herself. "Incredible."

"It was. You are." Viv smiled and rubbed her cheek against Dusty's thigh. "Lie down with me. I want you all over me."

"Hell, yeah." Dusty stumbled when she took her first step, but finally caught her balance and stretched out on the bunk. Viv rested her head on her shoulder and their legs entwined.

"You're amazing." Viv kissed Dusty's throat, straddling Dusty's thigh, sensuous and thrilling. "You drive me crazy. I can't believe I want to come again already."

Dusty kissed her, caressed her breasts, the soft curve of her belly, between her legs.

Viv tensed, her hips lifting, and moaned.

Dusty stroked in smaller and smaller circles. "I love the way you sound when I touch you."

"Keep doing that and I'll come," Viv murmured into Dusty's neck. "So, so good."

Dusty caressed her until Viv tensed and thrust against her fingers, her wordless cries stopping Dusty's heart in her chest.

"I'm shameless," Viv gasped, collapsing against Dusty. "I've never been this responsive in my life."

Dusty rested her chin against the top of Viv's head. "I think you're amazing. I can't stop touching you."

"You do amazing things to me." Viv rubbed her cheek against Dusty's chest. "I just have to look at you and I get hot."

Dusty chuckled. "I have no idea why, but I'm really glad."

Viv tilted her head, studying Dusty through heavy lids. "You really don't know, do you?"

"What?"

"How damn sexy you are. How beautiful." Viv stroked Dusty's face. "How special."

"I'm pretty simple," Dusty said.

"No, anything but." Viv smiled and kissed her. "What you are is real. And I like it."

Dusty rested her forehead against Viv's. "I'm really, really glad. I can't stop thinking about you, and now I'm never going to stop wanting you."

"I'll hold you to that if you're not careful. Last chance to tell me you're not serious."

"I'm very serious." Dusty clasped Viv's hand and entwined their fingers. "I want you to hold me to it."

Viv settled on top of her and kissed her. "Easiest assignment I ever had."

❖

Cam gritted her teeth. Arguing with the president of the United States was just not done, especially when he also happened to be her father-in-law. Never mind that she'd awakened him and his chief of staff after midnight to inform them she recommended terminating their much-publicized and so far very successful reelection expedition. "Sir, I've conferred with Tom Turner and Evyn Daniels and we're in complete agreement. The threat level is unacceptable, given what we know now."

"I can't see how this changes anything," Andrew said. "You've made good progress, Cam, better than anyone could hope at this stage, and I predict you'll get to the bottom of this mess by the time we reach the end of the trip. But we can't cut this excursion short, especially when we can't supply a reasonable explanation."

"I appreciate your faith in me, sir, but ID'ing an UNSUB who's been part of a sleeper cell for decades is a long and often fruitless process." Cam glanced at Lucinda, looking for an ally. This was when she hated politics the most, when reason fell before appearances. Her job was to keep the country, and especially the president, safe. That was the charge she'd been tasked with, presumably because they believed she was the best person for the job, but no one seemed to like her doing it.

"Andrew," Lucinda said evenly, "in this case, I have to agree with Cam. The facts support our suspicions that at least one other person was involved in the aborted attempt on your life, and given the possibility of a deeply buried operative, you're much too exposed here."

Andrew, despite his casual khakis and hunter-green pullover sweater, looked as presidential as ever, his expression one Cam had seen many times before in all kinds of crisis situations: determined, decided, unswayable. She knew his answer before he spoke.

"I'm even more protected here than in DC," Andrew said. "Physical access to my location is limited, we have excellent security in and around the train, and everyone aboard has sound security clearance." He smiled at Lucinda, a smile that held a hint of apology that Cam had never seen in public, but one she recognized. She probably looked a lot like that herself when she disagreed with Blair and knew it would make her unhappy.

"It's not as if I can stop making public appearances," Andrew said, still facing Lucinda. "The risk factors are no worse here than anywhere." He turned to Cam. "No. The trip continues."

Lucinda sighed. "I can't disagree with his logic, at least about the degree of security here. Is there any more we can do until this trip is over?"

"Yes, ma'am," Cam said. "Tom will move all the security teams into high-alert status. We'll rerun probabilities and make sure everyone is ready to deal with the unexpected."

"Well, then," Andrew said. "That's settled."

Cam waited for the president to rise and then stood. "Good night, sir."

"Cam," Andrew said. "Be sure Blair doesn't take any chances. She's as much a target as I am. And you too. Everyone I love is a target."

"Blair will be fine, sir. I'll see to that."

Andrew nodded. "I'm sure of it. Good night."

Cam joined Tom in the adjoining lounge, shaking her head as he looked up. "What we expected. The show goes on. We need another briefing update. Thirty minutes."

"I'll gather the crew chiefs."

"Good. I'll meet you in the command car." Cam made her way back to her cabin and let herself in.

Blair sat propped up on the bunk in a T-shirt and panties, a blanket over her bare thighs. She put her reader aside. "Are we going to get off this blasted train?"

"How did you know that's what I'd recommend?" Cam shrugged out of her blazer but kept her weapon harness on. She opened a bottle of water and drained half of it. The cool liquid did nothing to quench the rage burning in the back of her throat.

"Even if you don't think the third sibling is on this train, the smallest possibility would be enough for you to want my father off it. I take it he didn't agree."

Cam blew out a breath and scrubbed a hand over her face. "Of course he didn't. When have any of the Powells ever been reasonable when it comes to security?"

Blair smiled, pushed the blanket aside, and stood. She threaded her arms behind Cam's neck and rubbed the tense muscles in her shoulders. "I know we're a terrible chore."

Cam groaned and pulled her close. "The worst."

Blair pressed her cheek to Cam's chest and worked her fingers into the knots along Cam's spine. "How serious do you think it is?"

"I don't know, and that really bothers me. It's just a feeling that something's off. I've had it the whole time. Stark and Tom too."

"Your feelings have always been deadly accurate. Trust them. I always have."

Cam sifted the soft strands of Blair's golden hair through her fingers. Just holding her close steadied her, and most of her frustration drained away. "We'll have every possibility covered, I promise you that."

"Then no one could do more." Blair tugged Cam's head down and kissed her. "Don't stay up all night. We've still got a long trip ahead, and you need to be sharp."

"I'll be back as soon as the briefing is done."

"I'll be awake."

"Blair, make sure you don't go anywhere without your security detail."

"You don't have to worry about me. I'll be careful. I want you focused on taking care of my father."

"I will be, I swear." Cam brushed her fingers through Blair's hair and kissed her again. "I need you to be safe."

"Ditto for me. So we'll be careful for each other, all right?"

Cam held her tightly. "That's a deal, baby."

CHAPTER TWENTY-THREE

An hour before dawn, Jane turned off the narrow county road and onto the highway that had once been the old Santa Fe Trail. She drove for another hour, heading southeast toward Trinidad, passing a lone eighteen-wheeler whose lights appeared like UFOs out of the white curtain of snow, bearing down on them and then disappearing into the storm. The latest weather report said a break in the snowfall was expected near dawn, and already the visibility was improving. By daybreak, she'd have enough light for the mission.

Hooker dozed with his head leaning against the window. He'd spelled her for four hours, and she'd napped long enough to feel alert and sharp now. Pre-mission adrenaline pulsed through her blood. This time tomorrow it would all be over. Hooker was right, but she'd never tell him that. The mission was likely a suicide run, but every soldier needed to be prepared for death every time they deployed. She wasn't afraid of dying, only of failing. Jenn depended on her, and Robbie was at risk. And she was head of the family now.

Following the route she'd mapped out on the nav con, she left the highway on a single track and climbed into the low foothills of the Rockies. During tourist season the winding road was heavily traveled, but only the few locals living in scattered pockets in the foothills risked it now. She shook open a topo map, laid it across her lap, and flicked on the map light. When she stopped at an overlook, she left the headlights on and looked down at the train tracks a mile below with a swell of satisfaction.

Hooker leaned forward, his elbows on his knees, and grunted. "I didn't think Amazon was selling surface-to-surface missiles. And unless you've got an SSM in those boxes back there, you'll never hit a train from up here."

"I don't want to hit it," Jane said. "I want to stop it."

Between their position and the tracks, rocky snow-covered outcroppings littered the terrain. The hike down would be a challenge, but anything would be better than being cooped up in the vehicle for much longer. The welcome frisson of excitement in her belly burned brighter. After hours of driving, days of planning, she was finally going to be able to act.

"What about me?" Hooker asked.

"Your job is to secure the vehicle. All you need to know is the time and location of the rendezvous point." She wasn't convinced he'd wait for her to show up, but trusting him was a better option than her original plan of abandoning the Jeep up some snowed-in ravine. She couldn't drive out of here. The feds would have birds in the air if the storm held off, and roadblocks everywhere.

"I could be more useful if you gave me a few more details." He looked over his shoulder. "Like what you've got in the boxes."

"First we brief the op."

Jane climbed out, opened the back of the Jeep, and pulled out one of her knapsacks. She returned to the driver's seat, opened it, and passed Hooker a radio.

"We'll be on Channel One."

"Where are you going to be?"

"About a hundred yards down the slope." Jane gestured down the mountainside. She handed him a handful of MREs, broke one open for herself, and stuffed half a dozen in her jacket. She wasn't hungry, but she'd need fuel for what was coming.

"How do you plan on getting at the train?"

Jane pulled out her SAT phone from the bag, powered it up, and searched for a signal. When she had it, she linked into her cell phone and searched for the train's location. The White House website hadn't been updated for a couple of hours, but the last blinking red dot indicating the train's progress put her two hours ahead of the train's arrival. Two hours would be plenty of time.

"I'm going to call them on the phone," she said.

"And you think they're gonna slow down if you make a threat?" Hooker grunted again. "You think they're not prepared for that? They'll blast through here so fast you won't have a chance to hit them, no matter what kind of firepower you got."

"I told you, I don't plan on hitting them. I plan on talking to the president and making a deal." Jane reached behind her and pulled forward one of the boxes she'd picked up at the FedEx office. She slid her utility knife off her belt, cut the tape, and opened the flaps.

Hooker peered in. "What the hell is that?"

Jane smiled. "That is our negotiating power."

❖

Dusty dozed in Viv's cabin, naked beneath the light blanket, Viv curled around her. She didn't sleep deeply under most circumstances, and she hadn't wanted to, especially tonight. The newness of sleeping with another person would have been enough to keep her awake, but lying next to Viv kept her too excited to want to sleep. Their bodies fit in a way she'd never imagined possible. Viv's hand rested between her breasts, a gentle, possessive weight that made her feel like she belonged in this place, with this woman, in a way she'd never belonged anywhere before. Viv's leg rested across her thighs, Viv's breath wafted across her throat, warm and sweet. Dusty stroked Viv's hair, mesmerized by the softness. If she could stay here, just like this forever, she'd be happy. All she needed was Atlas snoozing by the door to make the picture complete. She laughed, hardly recognizing herself. Foolish fantasies were never part of her imaginings.

Viv murmured, a low contented sound, and her mouth brushed Dusty's throat. "Did you sleep at all?"

"Some," Dusty whispered. "Not tired."

"Are you okay?"

"Better than I've ever been."

Viv snuggled closer. "Oh, good. Because I feel incredible and I'd hate it if you didn't too. I don't think I ever want to move."

"I wish I didn't have to. I've got the morning shift, though. Another couple hours and I'll have to get up."

"I know. Later this morning we'll be in Trinidad, and the president has meetings with three or four of the state's biggest donors and then a town meeting. More speeches, more banquet food."

"Can I ask you a question?"

"Of course."

"When we're all done with this train ride and your article is finished, and everything, what then?"

Viv raised her head, immediately captivated. The night-light in the corner cast just enough faint glow to see by, and she'd never get tired of looking at Dusty naked. She was the perfect image of female strength, sleek and honed and graceful in all the right places. Just now a frown line marred the space between her brows. Viv traced the line of her jaw and kissed her. The immediate surge of desire caught her off guard. She would have sworn she hadn't an ounce of energy left in that area, but she was wrong. Dusty had taught her more about herself in a few days than she'd learned in a lifetime. "You know, you constantly surprise me."

"Why?"

"Because you don't play games, and apparently you've never learned to protect yourself. You're not afraid of being hurt, or you wouldn't ask questions like that."

"I'd rather know the truth."

"Well, I'm going to do my best to be as brave as you are and answer your question, even though it scares me a little bit."

"You don't have to, if you don't want to."

"You know, I want to. You make me feel brave." Viv made sure Dusty could see her face before she answered. She wanted her to know she meant every word, from the heart. "I want to see you when we get back from this trip. I want us to spend time together, and I want us to be together like this again." She laughed, feeling the desire rise swift and hard. "I want that a lot. And I would be very, very sad if you didn't want the same thing."

Dusty tightened her arms around Viv. "I want that too, more than anything. I should've told you that first, shouldn't I? Before I asked?"

Viv kissed her, her heart so full she had trouble finding her voice. "Dusty, honey, you're doing everything exactly right. Don't change a thing. Please, not ever."

"I won't." Dusty rolled them over, somehow managing the turn so Viv was on her back without dumping them on the floor. "I think I want to try something else."

"By all means," Viv said, gripping Dusty's ass and pulling her tight between her thighs. Dusty's weight gently pinning her down ignited tendrils of pleasure between her legs. "Anything you want."

"I want all of you."

Dusty kissed her way down between Viv's breasts and onto her stomach. Viv spread her fingers into Dusty's hair, needing to be grounded as her body threatened to fly away. She arched as Dusty stroked her hips and along the inner curve of her thighs toward her center. "Dusty, you feel so good."

"I can't wait any longer," Dusty murmured.

"Don't. I can't wait either." Viv tugged Dusty's head closer, aching for the silky heat of her mouth. "Please."

Guided by instinct and the memory of how Viv had made her feel, Dusty kissed her lightly. When Viv jerked and pressed closer, she covered her with her mouth, letting Viv's soft cries set the pace, calling the rhythm.

"Inside me," Viv gasped suddenly. "Fill me up, and you'll make me come."

Dusty obeyed, and Viv came against her mouth. When Viv quieted, she gathered her into her arms again and cradled Viv's head against her chest.

"Don't move." Viv stroked the back of Dusty's neck. "I love listening to your heart. I've never imagined being so close to anyone like this."

"Neither have I." Dusty closed her eyes, wanting to capture the rightness of the moment in her memory.

"Give me a min—"

Dusty's cell rang in the pocket of her cargo pants.

"Sorry," Dusty said.

"Damn," Viv echoed.

Dusty grabbed her pants and found her cell. "Nash…Yes, sir. On my way." She closed the phone and eased Viv to the side. "Sorry. Gotta go."

Viv stroked her back as she swung out of bed. "I understand. Is everything all right?"

"I don't know," Dusty said, jerking on her shirt. "Could be just a change in the schedule." She paused at the door. "Be careful, okay?"

"Of course. You too," Viv whispered as the cabin door swung closed.

❖

Hooker hunched in the wind next to the open rear of the Jeep, watching Jane work. The drones didn't take much to assemble, the pair of them looking like oversized toys. Guess that was because they were. "Can you really direct those things?"

"The electronics are very sophisticated. You can set GPS coordinates and they'll find their target without any other direction." Jane carefully taped the payloads in place, balancing the weights so the aeronautics would not be compromised. She'd need to test them to be sure the guide paths were still accurate, but she had time. "Or you can direct fly them visually."

"As long as they don't come flying home and blow us up."

Jane smiled grimly. "Don't worry. I've had plenty of practice with these." She ignored the cold wind, laced with the tapering snow, blowing through her hair and double-checked all the mechanics. After activating both and checking the camera feeds to her phone, she shut them down to conserve battery power. She'd been flying them in remote areas of the mountains in South Carolina for the past six months, ever since her father had decided these were weapons of opportunity. Opportunity once owned, he always said, was a powerful weapon, and this was a sweet one. She loved flying them.

She packed her rucksack with ammo, food, and backup batteries for her phones, radio, and drones and shouldered the forty-pound load. After sliding her sniper rifle from its case, she turned to Hooker. "There's a little town twenty miles away. La Veta. Head back to the main road, find a diner in town, and wait for me until twelve hundred hours. If I haven't checked in by then, you're on your own."

"How are you gonna get to me?"

"I'm going to hike."

"Jesus, they'll be looking everywhere for you."

"Not off-road—not right away, and even if they do, they won't find me."

"They don't have any reason to think I'm with you."

"Then you have nothing to worry about."

Hooker frowned. "You're letting me take the Jeep."

"I can't use it. You'll have plenty of time to get there before any roadblocks go up. They don't know the vehicle. They don't know my face. Hopefully, they don't know yours either."

"What about the money?" Hooker peered into the back of the Jeep. "It's not in here, is it?"

She smiled. "No."

"Did you ever plan to pay me?"

"Of course. I just never said when." Jane shouldered her rifle. "If you want it, you'll have to wait for me."

"Good luck," Hooker muttered.

Jane set off down the slope in the semi-dark. Luck was for gamblers, not soldiers, but today she hoped for a little luck on her side.

CHAPTER TWENTY-FOUR

With Dusty gone, the berth felt cooler even though Viv doubted the temperature had actually changed. Dusty's presence simply changed everything, heightening every sensation and painting the moments with possibility. She wasn't sure when she would see her again. The morning press briefing was still a couple of hours away, but she could make use of the time to firm up the article. She hadn't really been thinking about work much beyond the essentials in the last twenty-four hours. Thinking about anything was hard with thoughts of Dusty intruding at unexpected moments. She hadn't been so distracted, so completely diverted from everything that usually defined her life, in years. Possibly in forever. She'd always been so grounded, so focused, so goal-directed. Although she supposed she was just as goal-directed now, only her goal was more of Dusty and the incredible excitement of being with her.

Determined to at least earn her daily wages, she stepped into the shower, smiling at the aches in places she didn't usually ache, reminded that she hadn't had hours of abandoned sex since she'd been a teenager. And back then, she hadn't known what she was doing, so the aches didn't always translate into mind-blowing sex. She knew what she was doing now, though, and so, miraculously, did Dusty. Her instincts were incredible, and her hands and mouth were even more phenomenal. How had she gotten so lucky? Honest, bold, sexy as hell, and incredible in bed. If she didn't stop thinking about Dusty, she wasn't going to get out of the shower or the cabin anytime soon.

Turning her face up into the spray, she reveled for another minute in just feeling wonderful. Drying and dressing quickly, she grabbed her shoulder bag, double-checked her equipment, and headed forward toward the dining car. Now that she was moving, she realized she was starving. They'd eaten a few nibbles of the picnic dinner Dusty had brought, but that seemed like a week ago. All of the physical exercise had left her ravenous. The press dining car was empty but the coffee urn was hot and full. She poured a cup and wandered forward to the main communications car in search of the White House press staffers, none of whom ever seemed to sleep. They were great sources of info, and it paid to foster their friendship. The car was empty except for Blair Powell, Lucinda Washburn, and Ian Wilcox, the presidential press secretary, sitting around a table in one corner.

"Oh," Viv said, "I'm sorry. I didn't mean to barge in on a meeting."

Ian gave her a wave. "It's all right, we were just comparing notes on the schedule. You're up early. Cabin fever?"

At the mention of cabin and fever, Viv immediately pictured her and Dusty naked and sweaty, unable to get enough of each other. Her face heated and she prayed no one noticed. "Not exactly, just a little restless. I'll leave you to it, then."

"Vivian!" Blair called. "You free for a while?"

Viv paused. "Sure. Just wandering."

"Me too." Blair rose. "Do you want to discuss the article now?"

"That would be great." Viv joined her.

"This place is likely to get crowded before too long," Blair said. "Why don't we walk back to my car where we'll have some privacy."

"Of course." Viv followed the first daughter forward, wishing she'd dressed for the workday already instead of having pulled on casual pants and a clean if somewhat wrinkled cotton shirt. Blair managed to look elegant in a tailored white-and-blue-striped boyfriend shirt worn loose over slim-cut jeans and plain dark loafers. "I really appreciate this. It's these kinds of personal touches that readers really relate to, and of course, they're fascinated with you and anything you have to say."

"That is truly frightening," Blair said with a rueful smile.

"I imagine that it is a bit of a burden."

"Most people think that it's glamorous."

Viv shook her head. "I suppose sometimes it must be. I kind of feel that way about being in the press corps. The places we go, the dignitaries we meet, the history we witness. But it's a bit of a fishbowl too, isn't it? And for you, so much worse."

"It has its good and bad moments." Blair nodded to an agent standing post by the door to one of the private cars. She opened the door and led Viv into an expansive lounge with furnishings far more plush and elegant than what she'd seen previously in the rest of the train.

"Ms. Powell," Viv said, suddenly realizing that the first daughter was probably very aware she was speaking to a reporter, and Viv hadn't been thinking like one. Blair was far more approachable than she'd expected of someone in her position, and Viv had been speaking her mind as casually as she might to a new friend. "None of this is on the record, just so you know."

"I appreciate that." Blair smiled and gestured to a seating area with side tables next to upholstered chairs. "We've got some breakfast staples, if you're hungry."

"Coffee is good for now."

"Sit anywhere. I'll grab us coffee."

Blair handed Viv a cup of coffee and sat down across from her.

"Thanks." Viv took out her recorder and tablet. "If it's all right with you, I thought we'd just chat a little bit. I'll tell you about the article, and what I've seen so far. Anything you might want to add from a personal perspective would be terrific. If you'd like, you can read the transcript of our discussion, and I'll be happy to redact anything you don't want included."

"You haven't been on the White House beat very long, have you?" Blair asked.

"No, but I've been a reporter for quite a long time."

"An unusual one. It usually takes reporters a long time to discover they'll learn a lot more if they start a conversation rather than an inquisition."

Viv laughed, understanding exactly why the country loved the first daughter. She was beautiful and charming and perceptive. "I totally agree. Let's talk."

❖

Jane built a tripod out of rocks and packed ice and snow around the base for extra stability. She set up her rifle and sighted on the tracks. The rails jumped into view within the circle of the scope. Mid-distance shot. No challenge.

She pulled out the battery packs she'd kept warm inside her jacket, close to her body, and inserted them into the drones. The electronics came to life at the push of a button. The remotes checked out. Her cell phone was edging into the low power zone—probably dying from the cold—but the burn phone battery was full. Fifteen minutes and the train should be within range. Visibility had improved over the past hour as the sky lightened and the blowing snow relented. Her window of opportunity would be short, but she didn't need long. She didn't believe in fate, but like all soldiers, she was superstitious. So far that morning, luck had been on her side. Her father would disagree, she knew, and point out her success, or failure, was due to planning or lack of it. That was one of the differences between them. Jenn had planned the bio-attack for years, had sacrificed her personal life to work her way inside the White House, and in the end, she'd fallen victim to someone else's shoddy performance.

Jane set aside thoughts of Jenn and her father and focused on the terrain below. This was her op, and hers alone. She'd selected a blind 500 yards up the snowy escarpment from the tracks and dug in beneath a rocky overhang where she'd be invisible from the air. A pair of helicopters had flown over forty-five minutes before, the advance security teams checking the train tracks to be sure there was no obstruction. They would've been watching the roads for suspicious vehicles parked along the train route or shadowing the train's progress too, but Hooker should be long gone by now. Her thermal winter BDUs and the small snow cave she'd scooped out beneath the overhang helped conserve her body heat. She wasn't cold. Her blood raced too hot and fast for her to be cold or nervous.

A distant rumble traveled through the shallow valley and her pulse jumped for an instant before she settled into battle mode. Calm settled over her, her heart rate slowed, her vision cleared, and her mind went crystal sharp. The train was coming. Now timing was everything. Like always, the battle came down to a matter of minutes, minutes in which she would win or fail, live or die. She scanned the length of the track with the long-range binoculars and saw the first glimmer of flashing steel in the gray distance. Judging the intercept, she released the first drone. As it flew, she punched in the number she had programmed into the burn phone.

❖

Cam, Evyn Daniels, Tom Turner, and Stark sat opposite the president's campaign manager, Adam Eisley, and two White House staffers under his direction in the USSS command car. The president had been clear about continuing his campaign trek, but he might be convinced to modify his plan if a viable alternative could be provided.

"Our recommendation," Cam said, "is to terminate the train excursion at Trinidad. The president can continue with his planned itinerary by motorcade and plane. That way, we can isolate him to a far greater extent than we can here, and decrease the threat level."

"Absolutely not," Adam said. "Have you looked at the ratings lately? They're climbing every hour. We're getting great press coverage. TV networks are running maps of his route morning and night. All his personal appearances are pulling prime-time coverage. He's the biggest show in town during a long, cold winter. This has been the shot in the arm he's needed. Hell no, he's not getting off this train."

"You've got plenty of time to bolster his ratings," Cam said, not bothering to point out to someone like Adam, who lived and breathed poll reports, that Andrew Powell's ratings were the least of her concerns. "His security is far more important than a ten-second TV spot."

"Twenty second. What you fail to understand," Adam said dismissively, "is the impact of appearances. If you did, you and the first daughter wouldn't have started the circus show by getting marr—"

"Be very careful," Cam said quietly. "You don't want to bring Blair into this."

A few uncomfortable coughs and clearing throats followed and the campaign manager shrugged. "What's done is done. But the president hired me to manage his reelection campaign because I'm the best there is. I know what I'm doing." He glanced at Tom Turner. "Unless, of course, you feel that your people aren't adequately prepared to protect the president—"

"Look," Tom snapped, "this isn't about who has the most power here. This is about securing—" Tom broke off and jumped up, his hand to the receiver in his ear. "The president just signaled a code red."

As Cam bolted to her feet, her phone rang, and she grabbed it. "Roberts."

"Cam," Lucinda said, her voice vibrating with urgency, "we have a situa—"

An ear-shattering screech filled the car and the train decelerated rapidly, throwing everyone off balance. Cam caught herself on the edge of the table, trying to stay upright. "Where? Lucinda, where?"

"Stand down," Lucinda ordered. "No one is to approach the private cars. Tell Tom—no one is to try to come forward."

Cam's gut clenched. Blair was somewhere forward in the train.

She motioned to Tom and switched her phone to speaker. "What is the president's status?"

"We're…he's fine." Lucinda drew a breath. "But, Cam, we've got someone claiming there's a bomb on the tracks."

Tom said, "I'll alert the—"

"No," Lucinda said, "you can't. She says anyone trying to clear the tracks will be shot. And Tom—she says there's another bomb. On the roof of one of our private cars."

CHAPTER TWENTY-FIVE

Blair managed to avoid the coffee sloshing across the table as the train jerked to a halt. She regained her balance, righted the coffee mug, and pushed to her feet. Across from her, Vivian grabbed onto the chair beside her, her eyes wide. "Are you all right?"

"Yes," Viv said, swiping her recorder from the floor. "What do you think it is?"

"I don't know, but I'll find out." Blair hurried toward her father's cars. When she tried to slide the door open, it wouldn't budge. An icy chill slid down her spine. The train was no ordinary train, and like all her father's transportation, it was equipped with multiple layers of enhanced security, including mechanical. Something had probably triggered the lockdown system on his private cars when the train made an unscheduled stop. She'd been through things like this before. She thought about the elevator ride the day before. Probably just another glitch in some electronics somewhere. Just a precaution. She pushed the kernel of panic back down where it belonged. The train was filled with dozens of highly trained Secret Service agents. They were as safe here as they were in the White House. She turned back and met Vivian's concerned eyes.

"Locked?" Viv asked.

Blair nodded and slipped her phone from her pocket. "It appears so for the moment. Cam will know what's happening. Just hold on a sec."

"Of course," Viv said calmly. She walked to the window and pushed the button to roll up the shades that had come down when the train stopped. Nothing happened.

"Blackout shades," Blair said flatly. "The power must be off to them too."

Cam's phone went straight to voice mail. She tried Lucinda, the same thing happened. "Damn it."

Now Blair was getting worried. If Cam and Lucinda were both out of reach, something was happening. She spun around at the sound of the rear door sliding open. Her heart leapt when Paula entered, partly from relief at seeing a face she knew, partly with a growing sense of uneasiness. The grim expression on Paula's usually easygoing face didn't help. She gripped the back of a chair to have something to divert her attention from the bubble of panic growing in her midsection. "What is it? Why are we stopped?"

"I'm not sure yet," Stark said. "I've been advised that someone has made a credible threat to detonate a bomb if we try to move the train."

"A bomb? On the train?" Blair said. "How can that be? Where?"

Stark shook her head. "I don't know. Orders are everyone needs to stay exactly where they are until the location of the ordnance is pinpointed and the threat neutralized."

"Neutralized," Viv said. "What does that mean?"

Stark regarded her with a frown. "Who are you?"

"Vivian Elliott, the *Washington Gazette*." Viv held out her press pass. "Have you any word on who's making the threats?"

A muscle in Stark's jaw throbbed. "No comment. And anything that happens in this room is off the record."

Vivian straightened. "I'm afraid that's not possible. *I'm* in this room, and I don't require permission to report anything I witness."

"I wouldn't want to have to declare you a threat to national security, confiscate your recorder, and impose a gag order on you," Stark said in an unemotional tone of voice that was all the more unnerving for its quiet certainty.

"I assure you, Agent," Viv replied just as calmly, "as long as you're reasonable in your requests for confidentiality, I won't report anything I see or hear without clearance from you or Ms. Powell."

"Stark, what about my father?" Blair couldn't care less about what Vivian might or might not report. Once the crisis passed, the spin doctors would take over.

"He's in communication with us."

The icy tendrils reached into her marrow. "What do you mean, he's *in communication*? Where's Cam? Stop being evasive."

"I wish I didn't have to be," Stark said darkly. "I don't know much more than what I've told you. All of us are getting our orders by com link from Tom and Cam in the command car. We've been told to restrict our movement and to see that no one leaves their car."

"I want to talk to Cam."

"She's been assured you're safe."

"But what about her? Is she?"

"Of course," Stark said.

Blair knew that game. All the agents played it—danger was normal, so of course everything was fine. She tamped down her temper. "How long do you think they intend to keep us in here in the dark?"

Stark looked as unhappy as Blair felt. "For now, we wait."

Blair wanted to snarl, but Stark was only doing what she had to do. Just as somewhere, so was Cam.

The command car was crowded with Cam, Tom, communication techs, and the K9 and ERT chiefs crowded around a speaker they'd programmed to broadcast incoming calls.

"Cam," Lucinda said via the speaker, "the first call was routed through the White House switchboard. The caller told the operator she needed to be connected to the president immediately or the train would be attacked. The president was notified, and he took the call. Any further incoming communications will be direct to him, so you and Tom can hear…wait…it's ringing now."

"Go," Cam said. "We've got it."

"This is Andrew Powell," the president said an instant later. He sounded calm and confident.

"Let me clarify your instructions so we have no misunderstanding that could lead to a tragedy none of us want," a woman said. Her voice was distant but clear.

Cam leaned closer, fighting to keep her anger from clouding her senses. Blair, Lucinda, the president, a few dozen agents—they were all in the kill zone if what this woman said was true about a bomb on one of the cars, and she could do nothing for them except listen and search for a chink in the UNSUB's plan. She had to stay clearheaded and think. She took a breath and listened.

"This is simple," the Jane Doe said. "Have Jennifer Pattee transported to the train station in Washington DC. There she will buy a ticket for a departing train and be allowed to travel freely. She will be provided a phone to call me at the number you've traced by now, once she is on the train. When she has left the train and entered a cab, she will call me again. As soon as I have confirmation she is en route to a safe location, I'll deactivate the drone detonators and the train may continue. You have thirty minutes to transport her to the train station."

"I'd like to know who I am negotiating with," Andrew Powell said.

"You don't need to know anything about me. All you need to know is this. I'm prepared to shoot anyone attempting to dismantle the drones. If you attempt to drop an incendiary on me or send a kill team to neutralize me, I'll trigger the explosives. If I die, a signal from a heart-rate monitor will initiate a relay to automatically detonate the drones. There's enough C4 on the train right now to take out half of it." She paused. Her breathing was quiet and steady. "As long as everyone stays exactly where they are and you follow my instructions, we will all be done with this and everyone can go on their way."

"If you—"

The line went dead.

"Cam, Tom?" the president said. "Did you get all that? Is it credible?"

"Yes, sir," Cam said tightly. "We can't be sure of the capability of the drones, but what she says is theoretically possible. You, Mr. President, must be evacuated. As soon as we get a satellite feed of the probable location of the UNSUB, we can move a team forward to get you out."

"How safe is that?" the president said. "If you can see her, how can you be sure she can't see you?"

"There's a small chance of that," Tom Turner said, "but we can't leave you in the present situation."

"You'll have to for now," the president said.

Lucinda broke in. "Andrew, that's an unacceptable risk, and you know—"

"What I know is my daughter and dozens of our people are also at risk. Right now, if I continue to converse with this woman, I'm the best chance everyone has to stay alive."

Lucinda said, "Tom, what about evacuating the other cars?"

Tom glanced at Cam. "We can try to move everyone to the rear of the train, but we have no proof they'll actually be any safer. We need to keep everyone calm and on the train. Evacuating anyone but you is our second choice."

"What's the first?" Andrew said.

"In our opinion," Cam said, "our best option is to deactivate the drones."

"How?"

"First we have to locate them." Cam nodded to Phil Virtucci, who leaned toward the mic.

"Sir," Phil said, "this is Virtucci, the K9 chief. I'm sending out an agent with our best dog. We all agree a solo team has the best chance of getting close to the drone on the train without being detected. We'll have a visual feed and can assess the best way to neutralize it."

"How soon?" the president said. "We're on the clock."

"Now, sir."

Dusty eased down between the two K9 kennel cars and dropped to the ground. Atlas jumped down beside her and pressed close to her leg. She dropped onto her back and pushed under the car in front of her. She was eight cars back from the private presidential cars. She turned her head, met Atlas's calm brown eyes gazing at her from where he crouched by the side of the car.

"Find it, boy," she murmured to Atlas.

He seemed to understand that they had to work close to the train, and he moved slowly ahead of her with his big body almost brushing the wheels of the cars as she shimmied forward, pressed flat to avoid the undercarriages of the cars. Ice seeped into the neck of her jacket and cold water soaked her hair. She sweated inside her thermal camos. Seventh car. Sixth. Fifth.

Atlas worked quickly, but thoroughly, checking the wheels, poking his nose beneath the undercarriage ahead of Dusty, and sniffing the platforms between the cars. He had the best nose of the lot. If the drone carried a payload, Atlas would scent it. Snow drifted under the train on swirling eddies of wind and coated Dusty's lashes and face. The world beyond the narrow window of light at the edge of the track was gray and bleak. She and Atlas were alone in a cold, barren world. She blinked the salt and snow from her eyes. Fourth car. Third.

Atlas stopped abruptly and jumped up with his paws against the side of the car. He woofed once, deep in his chest.

"Where, boy, where?" Dusty rolled to the edge of the track and peered up.

He whined and scrabbled, trying to get onto the platform between the two cars. She couldn't see anything above her and chanced rising. Atlas circled, his ears quivering, his eyes bright with excitement. Dusty's skin prickled in anticipation of a shot. When none came, she spoke into her wrist mic.

"Chief, we've got something. Roof of the third car, right at the junction with the second."

"Have you got a visual?"

"Not yet. I'm going up for a better look."

"Nash, don't touch it."

"Roger that."

Dusty cautiously climbed the ladder attached to the side of the car, trying to avoid any vibration that might trigger a sensor on the drone. She didn't know the exact capabilities of the device, and she didn't want to accidentally set off the charge. She peered over the top of the car. The bird was bigger than she expected.

"I see it. Explosives taped to the body. Blinking lights—sensors probably. Multiple charges, but I can't see a detonator. Chief, I can get it."

"Can't take that chance. We need to see the detonators."

"Video's rolling. I just need to get a little clos—"

The blow slammed into her shoulder and she flew backward off the car. She landed on her back and the cold claimed her.

❖

Stark jumped up from where she'd been sitting and swore, something Blair almost never heard her do.

"What is it, what's happening?"

"Agent down," Stark said, a thread of fury in her voice. "God damn it. We're hostages in here, and someone's taking shots at us out there."

"Who?" Blair said, a hand squeezing her heart. "Who?"

"One of the K9s."

Viv gasped. "Dusty."

Blair turned, stared. Vivian's face was stricken, white and pinched. "We don't know who."

"This is insane," Vivian railed. "This is the United States of America. People with bombs don't threaten the president! They don't shoot—" She broke off, visibly pulled herself up straight. "I'm sorry." Her voice was flat, devoid of everything but rage. "Of course they do.

They shoot presidents, they blow up buildings filled with innocents, they send planes to crash into the Pentagon. These things *do* happen here."

"How bad is it?" Blair said.

Stark shook her head. "I'm not sure. Reports are scattered. I'm linked to command, but they don't know yet."

"We have to do something," Blair said.

"Believe me, I'd love to get you out of this car. We don't know where the shooter is or the range of the bombs. Right now, we're paralyzed."

"My father will never negotiate," Blair said. "Whatever they want, they're not going to get it."

"No," Stark said, a gleam of satisfaction in her eyes. "They're not."

Blair glanced at Vivian. She was holding up better than most civilians might under the circumstances. And she was smart enough to know what was happening.

"We're not going to die in here," Blair said with absolute certainty. "No one on this train is going to let that happen."

"I know that." Viv took a deep breath. "Can you find out about the agent? I...It's personal."

"As soon as we hear, I'll let you know." Blair gripped her hand. "But if it helps at all, I've been where you are now. And let me tell you this...our agents are the best there is. They'll take care of whoever is down."

"Thank you." Viv lifted her chin, steel in her gaze. "And you're right. Whoever is out there, they've already got one agent by their side. They've got their dog."

CHAPTER TWENTY-SIX

Dusty stared at the jumble of blurred shapes four inches above her face. She blinked and objects slowly swam into focus. Grease-covered rods, enormous bolts. Mud- and rust-coated sheets of metal. The undercarriage of the train car. Rails pressed into her back. The base of her skull throbbed as if someone had hit her with a sledgehammer. She shivered, glad for the cold. The discomfort convinced her she was alive. When she tried to sit up, her stomach rolled and she abruptly turned her head. Bile erupted. Her insides settled, but a blazing pain in her left shoulder took its place. She couldn't remember what had happened, and that couldn't be good. Slowly she became aware of welcome warmth spreading along her side and a distinctive scent—wet fur and all the other tangy odors that said dog. A sense of safety spread through her and the ball of fear in her belly eased. Atlas lay pressed against her left side.

"Hey, guy," she croaked.

He whined softly and licked her face.

She closed her eyes, trying to reassemble the bits and pieces of the last moments. The pictures coalesced as her mind sluggishly cleared. She'd climbed up the ladder on the side of the train car. An image jumped into sharp focus, and her pulse kicked into overdrive. The drone, she'd needed to see the drone. And when she'd leaned forward just a little, something had slammed into her and knocked her off the car. She tried to make a fist with her left hand. Nothing happened. Her left shoulder was a ball of fire. Fuck, she'd been hit. And then...

Falling. Her last sensation had been of falling. But she was under the train car now. Protected, warm from Atlas's body heat. She swallowed. "You dragged me under here, didn't you, boy." She reached over with the arm that was working and gripped a handful of his coat. Wet, thick, reassuring. "Smart boy."

He nosed her neck, his big body tight, guarding.

"It's okay, boy. I'm okay."

He seemed to relax a fraction, but he didn't move away from her side. She found her com link and activated it. "This is Nash. I'm down."

"Nash." Virtucci's voice blasted into her ear, loud and hard. "Are you hit?"

"In the shoulder. I'm functional, though, Chief."

"What's your location?"

"I'm under one of the cars." Millimeter by millimeter, she lifted her head and peered down the length of her body. "The three car. The same car as the drone."

"Can you move?"

"Affirmative." She dropped her head to the ground. The little bit of motion had spurred a wave of dizziness that made her stomach curl. After a few deep breaths, the nausea settled and she tried digging her feet into the snow-packed surface of the track underneath her. She pushed with her legs and slid forward an inch. Her heart pounded as if she'd run twenty miles. "I'm not sure how far or how fast."

Her vision dimmed, and she floated. Damn cold. Not so bad now.

"Nash! Nash, you read me?"

Dusty jerked. She'd almost been asleep. She wet her chapped lips. "Yeah. I'm here. Sorry."

"We need to get you inside," he said. "Can you make it to the junction between the cars? There ought to be enough cover to pull you in there."

"I can try."

"Go. But stay under the cover. We think the shooter is stationary, but we can't be sure."

"Roger that."

Dusty dug in her heels again and pushed. She made it a foot or two and had to stop. The jostling and bouncing sent shafts of pain into her neck and down her injured arm. Sweat broke out on her face and ran into her eyes. The more she struggled to move, the weaker she felt. If she just rested a minute…

Atlas growled and tugged her sleeve.

"Right." Dusty forced her eyes open. "Okay. One more time."

This time when she pushed, Atlas scrambled on his belly behind her, gripped the back of her flak jacket, and pulled. With a hundred and fifty pounds of pure muscle assisting her, she managed to make progress. A torturous five minutes later, she was staring up at the couplers between two train cars.

"I'm at the rear of the three car," Dusty said into her com.

"Can you stand up?"

"Yes, sir," Dusty said, hoping she was right.

"Stand by. We'll have people to you in a minute."

Dusty rolled out from under the cover of the car. Ice crystals blew into her face and her eyes watered. Atlas bellied out beside her, his dark head swinging from side to side, scanning. He hunkered down protectively, hackles up, a low growl rumbling in his chest. The sound of a door sliding open above her was possibly the most beautiful music she'd ever heard—after Atlas.

She gripped a handrail on the side of the car with her good hand and pulled herself to her knees. Pain rolled through in waves and spots danced before her eyes. Hands gripped her and tugged. Atlas barked a warning.

Dusty groaned, "Left shoulder," right before she was swallowed up in a tunnel of blackness.

❖

Jane checked her watch. Eighteen minutes since she'd given the ultimatum. She'd expected them to try to stall, knew it wouldn't be easy. She needed more leverage. She couldn't beat them with firepower, not as long as they stayed under cover, but sooner or later they'd send ERT and CAT teams against her and she'd be overpowered by sheer numbers. But she had the second drone she'd used to stop the train. Now the train was stationary, and she could deploy it again. If she had to take out one of the train cars to convince the president she was serious, she would. She didn't want to kill innocents, but innocents died as a consequence of war every day. Casualties couldn't be helped. And everyone on that train was in some way an enemy. Everyone except Robbie. She'd told him to get to the rear of the train where he'd be safe. Had he done it? Was he safe? And she couldn't deploy the second drone until she knew he was out of range. Improvisation was a part of any plan. She started the timer on her watch and picked up the phone. Twenty-two seconds later, she slid her phone into her pocket.

Now she would prove she wasn't afraid to engage the enemy. Jane powered the remote, and the drone lifted off from the track and swept upward toward the train.

❖

"I've got another communication," said Cheryl Wilde, the com tech, an edge of excitement in her voice. The trim, thirty-year-old African American wore a navy USSS polo shirt and pressed khaki pants and looked like an all-American advertisement for a job in government service. She'd been the best hacker at MIT when they'd recruited her.

"A call?" Cam asked quickly.

Cheryl had already traced the number on the phone the UNSUB used to contact the president, but the UNSUB had been wise enough not to have used it before. They hadn't been able to pull up any previous contact info, but Cheryl could monitor the number now and tell when it was in use. If the president was able to keep the UNSUB talking just a little longer the next time she called, they might be able to triangulate a location with enough accuracy to neutralize her with a missile strike. F-15 fighter planes were scrambled and waiting for the order. For now they were working blind, and if they couldn't find a way to alleviate the threat to POTUS, they'd have to send a counterassault team out and hope their firepower would overwhelm the UNSUB before the team sustained significant casualties. They could not risk her triggering the drones out of retaliation or in an attempt to force the president to negotiate.

"Not a call," Cheryl said with a note of frustration. "A data burst."

"Can you read it?" Cam asked.

"Working on it."

"What about the recipient," Turner said. "Can you track that?"

"The burst is too short and gets lost in traffic. I was lucky to grab it at all."

"That's okay," Cam said. "You're doing great—we just need the text."

"I know," Cheryl said, fingers flying over the keyboard, sorting and downloading data packets. "It's in here somewhere."

Lines of scrolling text filled the screen. Cam, Tom, and Phil leaned forward together, shoulders touching. They were running out of time. The president, Lucinda, Blair—they were all in range of the drone if the UNSUB detonated it. Initially they'd waited to evacuate POTUS, judging the likelihood of the UNSUB triggering the drone while he negotiated with her to be less than the threat to him if they tried to pull him out of the car before she was neutralized. But they couldn't wait any longer. They needed a weapon of their own. Cam needed the inside man.

Cheryl slammed back in her chair and pointed at the screen. "There!"

Where r u
15
Stay

"What?" Virtucci exploded. "What the fuck is that?"
"That," Cam said grimly, "is from someone else on the train."
"Son of a bitch," Tom murmured.
Cam smiled. "Gotcha."

❖

Stark and a big dark-haired agent Viv didn't know carried Dusty into the lounge. Atlas bounded in beside them, his eyes riveted on Dusty.

"Put her on the sofa," Stark said.
"Who is it?" Blair asked.
"Dusty," Viv said, "Dusty Nash." She pressed forward, sickening fear twining through her. Dusty wasn't moving. Her eyes were closed, her skin a waxy white. Her wet hair was plastered to her forehead. Viv didn't see any blood. Was that good? She didn't even know.

Dusty moaned and twitched. Atlas growled, his lips pulled back and two inches of gleaming canines directed at the agents.

"We need a dog handler up here," Brock said, his eyes riveted on Atlas.

"No one is coming up here," Stark said. "Just don't make any sudden moves."

"How about no moves at all," Brock muttered from a spot near Dusty's feet.

"He thinks you're hurting her." Viv inched over and slowly knelt at the side of the sofa by Dusty's head. "Hey, Atlas. She's going to be okay. You can stay right there and look after her."

He glanced at her once quickly, and then back at Dusty. His hackles rose but the warning growls quieted.

"Go ahead," Viv said. "He's just protecting. Just try not to get between him and her."

"Good dog," Stark said. She unzipped Dusty's camo jacket, pulled the Velcro flaps on the vest underneath, and eased off her body armor. "We're going to fix her right up, fella."

"Shot?" Viv's voice sounded foreign to her ears, feathery and tight. She clenched her fists, willing herself to stay grounded, clearheaded. She had to help. Screaming was not an option.

"Can't tell," Stark ground out, swiftly opening the buttons on Dusty's shirt. She parted it to reveal a tight green tank underneath.

Viv's stomach tightened. A purple bruise extended from Dusty's left shoulder down onto her chest, and a fiery lump as big as a softball rose from her collarbone. Viv caught her lower lip between her teeth, wanting to look away but needing to see. "Blood? Is there—"

"Don't see any yet." Stark cut the tank straps with a pocketknife and pulled the stretchy cotton down to the tops of Dusty's breasts. "Looks like the vest caught the force of the round. I don't see any penetration. Might have broken her collarbone, though, and there could be some internal bleeding."

"Here…" Blair slipped up behind Viv and passed a towel-wrapped bundle to Stark. "Ice."

Stark pressed it to Dusty's shoulder. "Thanks."

"Why isn't she waking up?" Viv asked.

"Don't know." Stark slipped her hand behind Dusty's head. A few seconds later she pulled her hand away, her fingers streaked with blood. "Got a scalp laceration. Must have hit her head."

"I can hold the ice," Viv said.

Stark narrowed her eyes, then must have decided Viv wasn't going to fall apart, and nodded. "Good, thanks."

Viv said, "Atlas, let me closer, boy."

Atlas shifted a fraction of an inch, and Viv sat on the side of the sofa, holding the ice to Dusty's chest with one hand and stroking the damp hair from her forehead with the other. Atlas rested his head on Dusty's arm and watched her face with total concentration.

❖

Cam gritted her teeth and listened as the president answered the ringing phone.

"I didn't want to have to do that," the woman said. "I asked you not to interfere with the drones. I'm trying to be reasonable here. I'm not interested in shooting anyone else, so don't make me. Now you've got nine minutes to put Jennifer on the phone to me."

"That's not enough time," the president said. "Holding this train hostage is not—"

"I'm not going to negotiate with you," the woman said calmly. "I either hear from Jennifer or you're going to have more than one dead Secret Service agent. Car eight is your command center, isn't it? Don't bother lying. There's a drone on the roof."

Chapter Twenty-seven

Son of a bitch," Virtucci echoed. "Do you think she's bluffing?" He stared up at the ceiling of the command car as if he could see through it to the roof.

"I doubt it. We can't take the chance. Game's up." Cam linked to Evyn Daniels, lead on the PPD in the president's car. "Do you have eyes on the track ahead? Is the drone still there?"

"It just lifted up a couple of seconds ago," Evyn said, her voice calm. "What's the situation? Do we wait?"

"The bird is in the air, two minutes out, but the UNSUB's got live ordnance on the roof. If she sees the bird coming in, she could detonate it."

"Roger that. I've got Eagle armored up. We can get a hundred feet from the car in under a minute if you can lay down cover fire."

"We're trying to get a fix on the UNSUB's position now, but until we can concentrate our firepower, it's too risky trying to blanket the area. She claims she's got a suicide switch."

"What's the range of the explosives?"

"Unknown. We're waiting for intel from the agent on scene. The video didn't pick up the drone, but she had eyes on."

"We'll be ready to evac anytime."

"Stand by." Cam switched to Stark's channel. "How's the agent?"

"Still unconscious," Stark said, "but as far as I can tell, nothing's life-threatening unless the head injury's worse than I think."

"The UNSUB's moved the second drone to the top of the command car. She's threatening to blow the first half of the train. Prepare to evac."

"Right," Stark said. "I've got a civilian here."

Cam didn't need to tell Stark what she already knew. Egret was the priority. "We'll get a second team up there as soon as we can."

"Understood, Commander."

Cam knew what Stark wouldn't say. They'd been more than colleagues for a long time, had saved each other's lives more than once. She trusted Stark to take care of Blair when she couldn't. "Let me talk to her."

"Cam?" Blair said a moment later. "Are you all right?"

"Yes. You?"

"What's happening? Can you get my father off the train?"

"Soon. Listen to me. You need to go too." Cam pushed away the thoughts of the payload of C4 a few feet above Blair's head, the explosion, the death. Fear would cripple her, and too many people depended on her right now. Blair wouldn't want to leave—would resist efforts to safeguard herself while others were at risk. Blair needed to do what neither of them wanted to do—leave those they cared about behind. "We're bringing in a helicopter for you and your father. Evyn will be with POTUS. You will stay close to Stark and keep your head down."

"I've got a reporter here with me, an injured agent, and *two* of my detail." Blair whispered, but she might as well have been shouting. Her anger came through loud and clear. "Just who do you want to leave behind?"

"Stark will get you on the helicopter."

"What about you?"

"I'll be here until—"

"Until what, Cam? Until she detonates the damn bombs?"

"That's not going to happen."

"How can you be so sure?"

"Because I think her brother is on the train," Cam said. "And I plan to find him."

"How do you know?"

"If I tell you, will you promise to evacuate when we give the word?"

"That's blackmail."

"I'll use anything I have to keep you safe."

Blair sighed. "I'll do what has to be done. If you promise me you won't be a hero."

"You're tough to bargain with." Cam blew out a breath. "We intercepted a transmission. We think he's in one of the press cars."

"One of the corps?"

"Probably, but we can't be sure. Anyone could have gotten into that car. We're running checks on every male in the press corps from here, right now."

"That's it? That's all you've got? Hell, Cam. How long will that take?"

Cam gritted her teeth. Blair had been around too long—she knew how these things worked. "I've also got Jennifer's photo, and one of the techs here is running an algorithm to adapt it for a related male. I might recognize him from that."

"There's a reporter here with me," Blair said. "Could she help ID him?"

"Possibly. I'll send the photo as soon as I get it. One minute."

"You're going after him no matter what, aren't you?"

Cam sorted through her options. She'd run out of bargaining power. She wouldn't lie to her, but she needed Blair safe. She couldn't do anything until she was sure of that. "Blair, I—"

"Damn it," Blair said. "I already know the answer. I love you."

"I love you too. Wait a second…we've got the image." Cam downloaded the computer-adapted image of a man with Jennifer Pattee's hair and eye color, similar eye shape, and general facial structure. She didn't recognize him. "Sending through to your phone now."

Blair said, "You don't have much time, do you?"

"No. Get ready. Stark will know when it's time."

"Cam," Blair said, "don't get hurt."

"I'll see you soon."

❖

"You need to put this on, Ms. Powell," Stark said, holding out chest armor.

"I'm not leaving unless my father leaves," Blair said, "*and* we get everyone off this car."

Stark straightened, her face taking on that calm, intense expression Blair had seen a thousand times before. At first glance, Stark always impressed people as being too young for the job. Too green, too pliable. They didn't know her well at all. Blair braced for the upcoming argument.

"Ms. Powell," Stark said without raising her voice, "if and when the word comes to evacuate, you will be evacuated." She glanced at Brock. "Pick her up and carry her if you have to."

"Roger that, Chief."

"Paula," Blair said threateningly.

"This is not a drill," Stark said. "And it's not negotiable."

Blair bit back a retort. She was beaten and she knew it. She glanced at Vivian. "They're not going to abandon you. It's just—"

"It doesn't matter." Viv met Blair's gaze, looking as calm and steady as Stark. "I'm not leaving here without Dusty."

"We're not leaving anyone behind," Stark said to Viv. "As soon as Ms. Powell is evacuated, we'll have other agents in here to cover you and Nash."

"Maybe it won't come to that," Blair said when her phone signaled and incoming message. She held out her phone to Vivian. "Do you know this man?"

Viv took the phone, her brow furrowed. "Should I?"

"Cam thinks this man is part of the attack, and she needs to find him."

"She thinks he's on the train?" Viv asked. "But why would I know him?"

"He might be in the press car."

"You're not saying he's one of us?" Viv stared at the image. She didn't know him. "He could be one of half a dozen guys. Is there anything else she knows about him?"

Blair shook her head. "They think whoever is behind the attack on the train is a woman, and this man is probably her brother."

Viv shook her head, unable to make sense of the information. "How can it be? Every one of us is vetted and background checked."

"Backgrounds can be fabricated. Some members of sleeper cells are undercover for decades."

Viv worked to absorb the news. She understood the idea of a sleeper cell in theory, but trying to imagine that someone she knew, someone she talked to on a daily basis…her mind shied away from the reality. She thought back over the faces of the people she greeted in the morning, said good night to long after the sun had set, traveled with, ate with. She couldn't put a face to an enemy. "I don't know him."

"Don't look at it for a minute," Blair said.

Viv turned the phone away, happy to oblige. She wanted to know him, if it meant possibly saving them all. But she couldn't point a finger at an innocent man.

"Think about the last few days," Blair said. "Has anyone seemed off to you—excessively nervous, maybe disappearing unaccountably, off their game in some way?"

"I don't know," Viv said, frustration a bitter taste in her throat. "We're cooped up on a train and the only time we leave is to cover an event. I haven't noticed anything."

"Something you heard, then?"

"No! I—"

You know what security is like. We might as well be trying to breach the White House.

That couldn't mean anything, could it?

"What is it?" Blair said.

"I'm not sure. Just something—probably nothing."

"Look at the picture, Viv," Blair said sharply. "Who is he?"

❖

Cam's com clicked and she switched to Stark's frequency. "Tell me she's refusing to go."

"No, Commander," Stark said. "Egret is perfectly cooperative."

Cam marveled at Stark's ability to lie with such absolute confidence. "What—"

"We might have an ID from the photo."

"Do you have a name?"

"Gary Williams."

"Stand by for evac." Cam closed the link and signaled for body armor.

❖

Jane dialed the president's number for the last time.

"In three minutes, I'll detonate the second drone. It will take out your command center and half a dozen other cars."

"You never told me your name," the president said.

"My name doesn't matter."

"Yes, it does. Right now, though, I'd like you to fly the drones to the following coordinates." The president calmly read out a series of numbers. "You're to leave them there so we can defuse them."

Jane laughed. "I'm afraid you aren't giving the orders, Mr. Powell."

"If you would look at the command car," the president said quietly, "I think you'll change your mind."

Jane sighted through her rifle scope at the center of the train. Her drone sat atop it, and she could clearly see its payload. "What—?"

A tall, dark-haired woman and a man stepped down from the car into the snow. Robbie's hands were cuffed in front of him. Ice stole through her blood. She knew the woman. Cameron Roberts. She'd held Roberts captive for twelve hours, and then Roberts had killed her father. She focused on the center of Roberts's forehead.

"We have your brother," the president said. "You can't detonate that drone unless you want him to die with a lot of other innocent people."

"We are prepared to die for the cause," Jane said, but the words were acid in her mouth.

"No one has to die. Remove the drones and surrender. You and your family will be safe."

Jane cut the connection. Lies. She didn't need to hear his lies. If she killed Roberts right now, they'd still have Robbie. If she detonated the second drone, Robbie would die, but so would Roberts. Then the president would know she was not bluffing and she wouldn't bargain. He would have to set Jennifer free. Robbie would die but Jennifer would live.

Her father's words sounded loudly in her head.

We all must be prepared to sacrifice. Even those we love.

Robbie stared up toward the hillside, his eyes searching for her. He couldn't possibly see her from that distance, but she felt as if he did. Could she trade Jennifer for him?

A brother for a sister? She had only seconds to make the choice.

Chapter Twenty-eight

G o, go, go!" Stark shouted.

The door at the rear of the car slid open and a blast of icy wind struck Blair in the face. Tears welled in her eyes, blinding her for an instant. A hand gripped her jacket in the center of her back, half guiding, half propelling her forward. She focused on the ground a few feet below and jumped down from the platform into knee-deep snow. Her body was instantly numb. Brock charged ahead, forging a path, and she followed him on autopilot, thinking of nothing except placing one foot in front of the other. The body armor encasing her chest was a lead fist constricting her heart. Was Cam somewhere close by, safe? Or on her way to face another madman?

The helicopter emerged from the thick soup of fog, a prehistoric beast rising out of the underworld. The rotors kicked up sheets of swirling ice, and she stumbled forward with one arm shielding her face. The side doors slid open and figures in armor, bristling with weapons, appeared in the doorway. Then they were reaching down and she up to them. Her feet left the ground, and her body flew the few yards into the helicopter. When she got her balance on the ice-slick floor, she wiped moisture from her eyes and peered around frantically. The ball of terror in her midsection loosened a fraction. Her father was beside her. "Where is everyone else? Dad, where is Luce?"

"There," he shouted, and she looked where he pointed.

Two agents lifted Luce into the helicopter as the floor tilted and the helicopter rose. Blair gripped Stark's arm for balance and leaned forward into the open doorway. The train rapidly grew smaller as they picked up speed. The drones perched atop the train cars, the one she'd been in and another one a few cars down, looking like primeval predators from a science fiction movie. Her heart seized. She braced for the explosion, the fireball erupting, the train engulfed in flames. The end of her world.

"It's going to be all right," her father shouted, his arm coming around her shoulders. His words were nearly lost in the whir of the rotors and the clatter of the engines.

The door rolled shut and she pulled away, needing to see out the small portholes, unable to breathe, unable to think of anything except Cam. And so many others. The train looked like an abandoned toy in a sea of white.

And then they were over the top of a mountain and the train disappeared. She kept watching, waiting for the flare of red to rise above the purple crests. Sensation returned to her fingers and toes, and her mind started working again.

"What about the others?" she shouted to Stark. "What's happening on the train?"

"No word yet," Stark said.

Frustration choked her. She was more a captive here than when she'd been trapped in the train car with a bomb over her head. She knew she was supposed to be safe now, but all she wanted was to escape. She recognized the feeling, she'd had it all her life. But she knew better now. She took a deep breath, searched for what she could do until she had word from Cam.

Lucinda sat on a jump seat, her arms wrapped around her torso, her face pale but composed. Her father was huddled with Evyn Daniels, who had a headset pressed to one ear. Evyn was relaying something to the president that Blair, isolated in a roaring tunnel of silence, couldn't hear. She crouched next to Lucinda and took her hand.

"All right?" she shouted.

Lucinda nodded and leaned close. "Pissed off."

"Me too."

Lucinda squeezed her fingers. "We *will* get them."

"I know."

"And Cam will be fine. She's the best there is."

Blair swallowed hard. Cam was everything. "I know."

Ten minutes later the helicopter circled in a wide arc and set down behind a sprawling log cabin in the foothills, surrounded by evergreens and ringed with familiar black SUVs. The door opened and agents poured toward the helicopter like a black tide, weapons in hand. Stark helped her out of the helicopter and jumped down beside her.

"Where are we?" Blair called as she raced toward the house in the middle of a scrum of agents.

"Safe house," Stark yelled back.

"What about the train?"

"Command center is inside. Come on." Stark pushed open a set of french doors and sprinted toward a wide hallway on the far side of a rough-stone-floored foyer.

Blair scarcely noticed her surroundings. All that mattered now was the train.

❖

Cam heard the helicopter lift away. Blair and the president were safe. The play was in motion. All that remained was to see it through. No second guesses, no second chances. If she'd misjudged Jane Doe, a lot of people would die.

"Come on," she said to Gary Williams. "Back up. We're getting back into the train. She's seen you now."

"It won't matter," he said dully. "She won't give up."

"No," Cam said. "I don't think she will. But the game is over for today. She won't sacrifice you."

"How do you know?"

"Because you're family." Cam gripped his collar and pushed him ahead of her into the command car. "And that's her Achilles heel."

He snorted. "You really think you understand what makes her tick?"

Cam thought of Blair and Andrew Powell and Lucinda Washburn and Paula Stark. Of what she would do, what she would give, to keep them safe. "I know I do."

❖

Jane watched through the high-powered scope as Robbie climbed back into the train. He looked frightened and younger than she remembered. He looked resigned too, as if he knew she would not back down. She had never relented when they were growing up and he'd lagged behind in training, always pushing him to try harder, practice more, be stronger. She'd never had to push Jenn—she'd had to struggle to keep up with her sister. Robbie had always believed she and her father had loved Jenn more than him. Maybe he'd been right. None of that mattered now.

Robbie disappeared, and Jane knew she'd seen him for the last time. She set the rifle aside and picked up the remote.

CHAPTER TWENTY-NINE

Jane kept the rocky outcroppings rising from the pristine white slopes like bad teeth between her and the train in the valley below. The rifle slung across her back was a comforting weight. She'd set the delays on the drones for forty-five minutes and left her backpack and the rest of her supplies behind. She could cover a lot of distance in forty-five minutes, and if she didn't make it out of the canyon before the feds descended in force, she wouldn't need food. All she'd need was ammo, and she had plenty of that.

She'd been training all her life for action like this, and within minutes she was over the ridge and out of sight of the train. They'd follow her, once they realized she'd left before the drones were activated. But they wouldn't send a team out immediately. They'd think she was debating what to do, probably expecting her to take time to choose between her brother and her sister. They didn't know her. They didn't know the way the three of them had been raised. But then, she hadn't really known herself until Roberts had forced her to declare who she really was. She angled upward to the road, barely discernable now under the accumulated snow, and took a calculated risk. The chance of a vehicle traveling along this road was slight, but there was always a chance. If she could commandeer a vehicle she might still get away.

She hadn't heard another helicopter since one had dropped from the sky a hundred yards from the train. They must have evacuated the president when they'd made the play with Robbie, but they weren't chancing an all-out assault with the drones still in play. Her window was shrinking fast, though. Before long, the only vehicles traveling this stretch would be in pursuit of her, but for now, she had a clear path. She kept close to the cover of the trees along the shoulder and ran on through the gathering storm.

She'd traveled three miles when the sound of an oncoming vehicle forced her to jump behind a cluster of trees. She shouldered her rifle and sighted on the curve in the road ahead. A familiar red Jeep careened into view, spewing snow as it cut a path toward her. She stepped out and Hooker skidded to a stop.

Jane threw open the passenger door and jumped in. "What are you doing here?"

"It's getting late. I figured you might need a ride." He did a 180 in the middle of the road and slewed around the curve the way he'd come. "Besides, there's nothing to do in that one-horse town." He glanced at her as she pulled a water bottle from her inside pocket and drank deeply. "Mission abort?"

"Yes," Jane said, staring out the windshield but seeing nothing. Nothing except Robbie's frightened face. He was her little brother. He trusted her.

"They on your tail?"

She glanced at her chronometer. "They will be in about seven minutes."

Hooker whistled. "Guess we better find us a busier road pretty quick so we can blend in."

"Take a left a mile up the road. You'll hit the interstate five miles farther on."

"Huh. You think of everything," Hooker said.

"Not everything," Jane said softly and closed her eyes. She'd never expected to be faced with choosing between the last two people she loved.

❖

Before Dusty opened her eyes, before she knew where she was or why she felt as if she'd been flattened by a tank, she knew she was going to be okay. Atlas's breath blew across her throat. He was keeping her safe. And something else, something new and deeply comforting. Warm fingers gripped her hand. She recognized the softness and strength of that hand. Eyes still closed, she said, "Did I miss all the action?"

"Most of it," Viv said quietly. "How are you feeling?"

Dusty looked up and just as she'd hoped—dreamed—Viv was there, smiling down at her. Viv's eyes looked worried but her smile was brilliant. All Dusty wanted was for Viv to keep smiling at her like that, pretty much forever. "I'm okay. Headache. Shoulder hurts like a son of a gun, but I'm mostly good." She turned her head carefully. So far so good. "Atlas—you okay, boy?"

"He's perfect." Viv scratched behind his ears. "He's just the best, aren't you, big handsome boy."

"Hey, hey," Dusty said, laughing. "Stop spoiling him."

"I can spoil him. He's been looking after you."

Images of the drone jumped into sharp focus. Dusty glanced around the empty car. She didn't recognize it. "What's happening? What about the bombs?"

"I'm not sure. They just evacuated Blair Powell. So I think—"

"Why are you still here?" Dusty tried to sit up and her head swam. "You should get off this—"

"Don't do that," Viv warned, pressing down on Dusty's good shoulder. "You need to lie still."

"You have to get off this train. It's not safe. Let me u—"

The connecting door slid open and Dusty reached for her weapon.

"Stand down, Agent Nash," a man in a flak jacket said. "We've got this."

Dusty recognized Mac Phillips from Egret's detail. She relaxed and let out a breath. "Hey, Mac. What the hell is happening?"

"The UNSUB is playing chicken with the director." Mac grinned. "Want to place a bet on who's winning?"

"Hell, no," Dusty said. "POTUS?"

"Safe house. We've been slowly relocating civilians to the rear of the train, out of range of the second drone."

Two more agents and the first doctor crowded in behind Mac Phillips.

"Agent Nash—Captain Wes Masters," Mac said. "The captain needs to look you over, Nash."

"I'm good," Dusty said.

Viv exclaimed, "No, you're not."

"How about I decide?" Wes leaned over and shined a light in Dusty's eyes. "How are you doing, Agent?"

"Fine, Captain."

"Vision okay?"

"A little blurry earlier. Clear now."

The doctor asked her a few more questions and straightened. "As soon as we're cleared to evac, we'll be giving you a lift to the ER."

Viv asked, "Is there something wrong?"

Wes smiled. "Precautionary. I want a CT scan to be sure that head bump didn't shake things up too much on the inside. And we need to x-ray that shoulder."

Atlas growled softly when one of the agents moved closer. Mac raised a brow at Dusty. "What about the dog?"

"Radio Dave Ochiba to come and get him," Dusty said. "Atlas will go with him if I tell him to."

Mac nodded, contacted Ochiba, and told him he was needed when he was free to move around. "As soon as Ochiba gets your partner here settled, you're out of here."

"I'm going too," Viv said.

Mac gave her an appraising look. "You're press corps, aren't you?"

Viv smiled down at Dusty and grasped her hand again. "Yes, but this is personal."

"Yeah," Dusty said, not caring who was watching. "Very personal."

❖

Cam regarded Gary Williams. With his well-cut hair and bland good looks, he could have been any of a dozen reporters on the White House beat. Except that he sat on a bench in the lounge next to the command car in his dark suit pants, wet shoes, and wrinkled pale blue dress shirt with his hands cuffed in front of him. Two ERT agents stood guard at either end of the car. "What's your real name?"

He stared straight ahead.

"Gary is actually your last name. Youngest child of Augustus Gary. How about your first name?"

His jaw clenched.

"We've got three assault teams readying to go after your sister. You might want to take this chance to reason with her." Cam held up a phone. "Tell me about your plans to attack the president, who's behind it, and you'll earn a call."

His dark eyes flicked to Cam. "She won't change her mind."

"I know the three of you didn't plan this on your own—I doubt it was even your father's idea. Where is the money coming from? Who's pulling the strings behind the scenes?"

"I have nothing to say."

"Now is the time to help your sister," Cam said quietly. "She's not going to win this fight, but she doesn't have to die. Help me so you can help her."

He shook his head. "She wouldn't thank me."

"Not today, maybe, but—"

Tom Turner burst in from the adjoining car. "The drones are active."

Cam turned her back on Gary Williams. The time for testing the field with pawns had passed. The battle was on. "Deploy the assault teams."

CHAPTER THIRTY

Blair paced in front of the window fronting the cabin's wide front porch. Someone had started a fire in the stone hearth on the far wall, and the room smelled of sweet pinewood smoke. The place would have been rustic-homey under any other circumstance. Two agents holding assault weapons stood on either side of the walkway leading up to the cabin. Paula was still in the command center in the adjoining room, monitoring what little communication was coming from the train. Her father and Lucinda were in a makeshift office at the far end of the hall.

Communication techs from the local Secret Service office had arrived and set up a secure room to keep her father in contact with DC. No one knew what was going on out here, and no one ever would. As far as anyone knew, her father had simply chosen to leave the train for a little private R&R. Now he was probably carrying on business as usual.

Business as usual. That's what Cam was doing now too. Putting her life on the line again. Risking herself for others. Blair gave herself a mental shake. She'd never really believed that a change in Cam's job description would change Cam or what she felt compelled to do in the line of duty. Added to that, Lucinda would never let Cam get very far away from the president's security needs, and Cam would never *want* to be very far away. All that meant their life would never be without risk. She could never wake up in the morning and not feel a few seconds of fear that something would happen to threaten everything that mattered to her.

She turned away from the window, annoyed with herself. None of this was news. Cam, her father, Paula, Lucinda, every agent back on the train or here at the cabin did what they needed to do day in and day out because that's what they had signed on for. She might not have had a choice about her life when she was only her father's child, drawn into the tangle of politics and pressure that came with being the first daughter. But she'd married Cam with her eyes wide open and her heart as well. Lucinda was right. Cam was the best there was. And she trusted Cam to take care of herself and the love they shared.

The sound of vehicles approaching drew her back to the window. Her heart lifted as the convoy of SUVs came up the snowy drive and parked in a ring in front of the cabin. Doors opened, a flood of armed agents emerged, and she raced to the cabin door.

Cam reached her when she was halfway across the porch. Blair didn't care who was watching. She threw her arms around Cam's neck and kissed her hard. Cam's arms circled her waist, holding her tight.

"It's over?" Blair asked.

Cam brushed her cheek with a bare hand. "Yes. Are you all right?"

"Couldn't be better," Blair said softly. "You?"

Cam nodded. "Never better."

"The train?"

"Everyone is fine." Cam let her go. "I'll have to see your father now."

"I know. Can I come?"

"Of course."

"I love you, you know."

Cam grinned. "I'm counting on it. Every minute of every day."

❖

"She withdrew the drones?" Andrew Powell said.

"Yes," Cam said, "forty-five minutes after our last communication they lifted off and flew to the coordinates you'd provided. The bomb containment unit is on it now."

"She couldn't sacrifice her brother," Blair said.

"No," Cam said. "She couldn't."

"What about her?" the president asked.

"We've got teams out on foot, in the air, and on the roads."

Andrew gave Cam a penetrating stare. "What are the chances of finding her?"

"Fifty-fifty." Cam sighed. "She has a head start, she's undoubtedly a trained survivalist, and she likely had an exit plan already in place. It's rough territory out there and the storm's not helping."

Blair said, "What's the chance she'll try again?"

"Tom and I agree," Cam said, "the chance of another up-close attack on the president is small. At this point, she represents the same threat level as any other UNSUB, and we're well prepared for that."

"So you're not going to cancel the rest of the tour?" Blair asked.

"We can't," Lucinda said. "There's far too much advance press and investment in the scheduled appearances. We'd never be able to give a plausible explanation for cutting things short."

"The train is already en route to the next stop," Cam said. "The press secretary gave a statement to the press corps about the president's unscheduled departure from the train. We're using the old national security excuse for not briefing them any further. We'll all meet up again in Trinidad and carry on."

"Vivian knows about Gary Williams," Blair pointed out. "And she knows what happened out there."

"This time the national security card is a legitimate one," Lucinda said. "I've already talked to her by phone. She understands the situation."

Blair nodded. Vivian was someone she could trust.

The president asked, "Did Gary Williams give you anything?"

Cam shook her head. "He didn't put up a struggle when we went to pick him up, but that was the extent of his cooperation. I don't think he'll talk."

"Like his sister Jennifer." Blair sighed. "I wish this trip was over."

"I might as well add to the misery," Lucinda said. "Franklin Russo has decided to capitalize on all the press around the president's trip. He's staging an appearance opposite the president's in Flagstaff. So, of course, you and Cam will have to be there onstage to power up our finale."

"Political maneuvering," Blair said. "It never ends."

Lucinda smiled. "That's the name of the game, after all."

"When do we head out for the train?" Cam asked.

"Later this afternoon." Lucinda glanced at the president. "I think everyone has earned a few hours' rest."

Blair stood. "I'd rather a few days, but I'll take it."

Out in the hall, Cam grasped Blair's hand. "Hey. Care to join me for a shower and a nap?"

Blair leaned against her. "I can't think of anything else I'd rather do."

In the room they'd been assigned, Blair closed the blinds and pulled back the covers on the bed. They showered quickly and crawled naked under the sheets. She curled up next to Cam and put her head on her shoulder. "How are you doing?"

Cam sighed. "I'm tired. But I'm okay."

"Do you really think she's going to quit?"

"She's tried twice now and failed. She's a good strategist—she has to know she's beaten."

"How did you know she wouldn't destroy the train with him on it?"

"Because everything she's done has been motivated by love for her family," Cam said. "She's been raised from the time she was a child to place loyalty to cause and family before herself. Her father's dead, her sister's incarcerated. Her brother is all she has left, and I couldn't see her trading him for her sister."

"Now you have her brother and she has nothing," Blair said. "Won't that make her even more dangerous?"

"I don't know. Maybe seeing her whole family fail will be enough to make her reconsider what she's really doing." Cam kissed Blair's temple. "I hope so."

"You sound a little sorry for her," Blair said.

"I'm not, not really." Cam stroked Blair's hair, staring at the tiny shafts of sunlight dancing across the ceiling. "She made her choices. She might have been molded, maybe even warped, as a child, but she knows the difference between right and wrong. She knows what they were doing was treason and an act of terrorism. But part of me wonders what choices she would've made if she hadn't been raised the way she was."

"What will you do if you have a chance to capture her?"

"Bring her in and leave her to the justice system." Cam kissed Blair. "Because that's how this country is supposed to work."

"I love you."

"I love you too. More than anything."

"I wouldn't change a single thing about you or our life," Blair murmured, feeling sleep dragging her down. She could sleep safely, because Cam was here and Cam was hers.

"Neither would I," Cam said softly. "Go to sleep now, baby. I'm here."

EPILOGUE

Flagstaff, Arizona: the end of the line

"Pull over here," Jane said.

Hooker turned into a roadside lookout that would be crowded with tourists in a few hours. At an hour before dawn, no one was around. Flagstaff lay three miles away in a basin in the Ponderosa pine forest, the sprawling city marked by the lights of the Northern Arizona University campus, the downtown area, and the sporadic headlights of cars speeding along Route 66.

"Plenty of spots up here for me to lay low for a while," Hooker said. "You might need a ride out of this place a little later."

"No, I won't." Jane handed him a slip of paper. "You'll need this to pick up the package at FedEx in Sedona. It should be there already."

He looked at it, his jaw working. "The money's been there all along?"

She smiled. "Most of the time."

"I don't suppose you're going to let me in on this op either?"

"No need for you to know."

He drummed his fingers on the wheel. "You know, you can't really change things by taking out one man. Just because he's got the title doesn't mean he's really in command of anything. The kinds of things you want to change—there's usually a lot of people wielding power behind the scenes, people who won't necessarily stop even if you take out the figurehead."

"Sometimes a big statement is the only thing that makes an impression," Jane said, having heard the refrain repeated thousands of times by her father and his friends. She still believed it, mostly, but it didn't much matter anymore. Jennifer and Robbie were looking at life in prison. The chance that she would ever see them again was zero. Her father was gone, and along with him, the organization he had built. She'd told Robbie they could find another militia to join, but when she tried to imagine putting her faith in someone the way she had her father, she couldn't picture it.

"I've gotta get going," she said.

"Yeah," Hooker said. "Me too."

"Russo," she said. "You're a liability to him, you know that, right?"

Hooker laughed, the sound like gravel crunching under tires. "Oh yeah, I've always known that. Always knew I'd have to get out before he decided I wasn't any use anymore. Since I haven't been returning any of his boy Derek's calls, I think that time is now."

Jane pushed open the door and stepped out. Hooker must know he'd be running for the rest of his life, if he was lucky. "You might want to get rid of this Jeep when you hit Sedona. They'll figure out who it belongs to sooner or later."

"I could leave it somewhere for you."

"I won't be needing it."

Jane closed the door, shouldered her pack and rifle, and strode to the edge of the drop-off leading down the mountainside. She turned and watched Hooker pull out and drive away. When his taillights disappeared around a curve, she quickly dropped down the slope and disappeared into the trees.

❖

"I hadn't realized how much I missed the big bed," Blair said, stepping out of the hotel-room bathroom and toweling off her hair.

Cam grinned. "The berth was cozy, but there's a lot more you can do with a little extra room."

Blair laughed. "I noticed that last night."

"Ready for today?"

"Considering we'll be headed home after this one is over, more than ready."

"Me too."

Blair pulled the white terry hotel robe from the closet and slipped into it. "I got an email from Vivian Elliott. She, Dusty, and their dog made it back to DC just fine and apparently they're going to spend the rest of Dusty's medical leave at a shore house somewhere down

South. Viv says it's a great place for a picnic. Do you think picnic is a euphemism for sex?"

"You know, baby," Cam said, sliding her arms inside Blair's robe, "sometimes a cigar is just a—"

Blair nipped at Cam's jaw and smoothed her palms over Cam's spectacular ass. "Yeah, but I'm thinking in this case it's more."

"Maybe we can get away for a while and have a few picnics of our own." Cam kissed Blair's neck and eased free. "And that *is* a euphemism."

Blair grinned and sprawled in the big chair by the window to watch Cam dress, something she never tired of. She loved Cam naked, she loved her in a suit. She just loved her. By the time Cam donned a pale charcoal shirt the same shade as her eyes, Blair couldn't wait any longer to touch her. She smoothed the shirt collar down, pressed her palms to Cam's chest, and kissed her. "I couldn't be prouder to stand up there onstage with you and show the world you're mine."

"Adam said he wanted us to be low-key, remember?" Cam ran her hands through Blair's still-damp hair.

"Oh, and I so care what Adam Eisley wants. He's Dad's campaign manager, not mine."

Cam laughed. "You still going to wear that little red dress?"

Blair laughed. "Damn right I am."

"Then let's go make a statement."

❖

Jane stretched out on top of the water tower. By eleven, the metal surface would have been too hot to tolerate if she hadn't spread out a thermal barrier blanket underneath her. By the time her perch became too uncomfortable, she wouldn't need it anymore. She sighted on the stage through her scope and watched as the faithful arrived. The distance was at the farthest range of her weapon and her skill, but she wasn't worried. She wasn't going to miss, not this time. This time, she'd have justice—if not for Jennifer and Robbie, at least for her father.

Chances were they'd reach the water tower or cut off her exit routes before she'd have a chance to get away. That was fine too. She didn't really have anyplace to go.

The minutes ticked by and the motorcade arrived, a line of black limos and SUVs gleaming under the winter sun. She watched through her scope as people filed into the stands facing the stage and the man of the hour stepped out from the line of vehicles, surrounded by a handful of security. She tracked him across the stage, patiently, like stalking a deer from a blind. She had nothing but time now. When he finally stepped up to the podium, a thrill of satisfaction coiled in her belly. She settled her cheek against the stock, her heart rate slow, her breathing even slower. As she focused on Franklin Russo's face, she saw her father's.

Honor thy father, she thought, and squeezed the trigger.

About the Author

Radclyffe has written over forty-five romance and romantic intrigue novels, dozens of short stories, and, writing as L.L. Raand, has authored a paranormal romance series, The Midnight Hunters.

She is an eight-time Lambda Literary Award finalist in romance, mystery, and erotica—winning in both romance (*Distant Shores, Silent Thunder*) and erotica (*Erotic Interludes 2: Stolen Moments* edited with Stacia Seaman and *In Deep Waters 2: Cruising the Strip* written with Karin Kallmaker). A member of the Saints and Sinners Literary Hall of Fame, she is also an RWA/FF&P Prism Award winner for *Secrets in the Stone*, an RWA FTHRW Lories and RWA HODRW winner for *Firestorm*, an RWA Bean Pot winner for *Crossroads*, and an RWA Laurel Wreath winner for *Blood Hunt*. In 2014 she was awarded the Dr. James Duggins Outstanding Mid-Career Novelist Award by the Lambda Literary Foundation.

She is also the president of Bold Strokes Books, one of the world's largest independent LGBTQ publishing companies.

Find her at facebook.com/Radclyffe.BSB, follow her on Twitter @RadclyffeBSB, and visit her website at Radfic.com.

Books Available From Bold Strokes Books

Making a Comeback by Julie Blair. Music and love take center stage when jazz pianist Liz Randall tries to make a comeback with the help of her reclusive, blind neighbor, Jac Winters. (978-1-62639-357-8)

Soul Unique by Gun Brooke. Self-proclaimed cynic Greer Landon falls for Hayden Rowe's paintings and the young woman shortly after, but will Hayden, who lives with Asperger syndrome, trust her and reciprocate her feelings? (978-1-62639-358-5)

Price of Honor by Radclyffe. Honor and duty are not always black and white—and when self-styled patriots take up arms against the government, the price of honor may be a life. (978-1-62639-359-2)

Mounting Evidence by Karis Walsh. Lieutenant Abigail Hargrove and her mounted police unit need to solve a murder and protect wetland biologist Kira Lovell during the Washington State Fair. (978-1-62639-343-1)

Threads of the Heart by Jeannie Levig. Maggie and Addison Rae-McInnis share a love and a life, but are the threads that bind them together strong enough to withstand Addison's restlessness and the seductive Victoria Fontaine? (978-1-62639-410-0)

Sheltered Love by MJ Williamz. Boone Fairway and Grey Dawson—two women touched by abuse—overcome their pasts to find happiness in each other. (978-1-62639-362-2)

Searching for Celia by Elizabeth Ridley. As American spy novelist Dayle Salvesen investigates the mysterious disappearance of her ex-lover, Celia, in London, she begins questioning how well she knew Celia—and how well she knows herself. (978-1-62639-356-1).

Hardwired by C.P. Rowlands. Award-winning teacher Clary Stone and Leefe Ellis, manager of the homeless shelter for small children, stand together in a part of Clary's hometown that she never knew existed. (978-1-62639-351-6)

The Muse by Meghan O'Brien. Erotica author Kate McMannis struggles with writer's block until a gorgeous muse entices her into a world of fantasy sex and inadvertent romance. (978-1-62639-223-6)

No Good Reason by Cari Hunter. A violent kidnapping in a Peak District village pushes Detective Sanne Jensen and lifelong friend Dr. Meg Fielding closer, just as it threatens to tear everything apart. (978-1-62639-352-3)

Romance by the Book by Jo Victor. If Cam didn't keep disrupting her life, maybe Alex could uncover the secret of a century-old love story, and solve the greatest mystery of all—her own heart. (978-1-62639-353-0)

Death's Doorway by Crin Claxton. Helping the dead can be deadly: Tony may be listening to the dead, but she needs to learn to listen to the living. (978-1-62639-354-7)

The 45th Parallel by Lisa Girolami. Burying her mother isn't the worst thing that can happen to Val Montague when she returns to the woodsy but peculiar town of Hemlock, Oregon. (978-1-62639-342-4)

A Royal Romance by Jenny Frame. In a country where class still divides, can love topple the last social taboo and allow Queen Georgina and Beatrice Elliot, a working-class girl, their happy ever after? (978-1-62639-360-8)

Bouncing by Jaime Maddox. Basketball coach Alex Dalton has been bouncing from woman to woman because no one ever held her interest, until she meets her new assistant, Britain Dodge. (978-1-62639-344-8)

Same Time Next Week by Emily Smith. A chance encounter between Alex Harris and the beautiful Michelle Masters leads to a whirlwind friendship and causes Alex to question everything she's ever known—including her own marriage. (978-1-62639-345-5)

All Things Rise by Missouri Vaun. Cole rescues a striking pilot who crash-lands near her family's farm, setting in motion a chain of events that will forever alter the course of her life. (978-1-62639-346-2)

Riding Passion by D. Jackson Leigh. Mount up for the ride through a sizzling anthology of chance encounters, buried desires, romantic surprises, and blazing passion. (978-1-62639-349-3)

Love's Bounty by Yolanda Wallace. Lobster boat captain Jake Myers stopped living the day she cheated death, but meeting greenhorn Shy Silva stirs her back to life. (978-1-62639334-9)

Just Three Words by Melissa Brayden. Sometimes the one you want is the one you least suspect…Accountant Samantha Ennis has her ordered life disrupted when heartbreaker Hunter Blair moves into her trendy Soho loft. (978-1-62639-335-6)

Lay Down the Law by Carsen Taite. Attorney Peyton Davis returns to her Texas roots to take on big oil and the Mexican Mafia, but will her investigation thwart her chance at true love? (978-1-62639-336-3)

Playing in Shadow by Lesley Davis. Survivor's guilt threatens to keep Bryce trapped in her nightmare world unless Scarlet's love can pull her out of the darkness back into the light. (978-1-62639-337-0)

Shadow Hunt by L.L. Raand. With young to raise and her Pack under attack, Sylvan, Alpha of the wolf Weres, takes on her greatest challenge when she determines to uncover the faceless enemies known as the Shadow Lords. A Midnight Hunters novel. (978-1-62639-326-4)

Heart of the Game by Rachel Spangler. A baseball writer falls for a single mom, but can she ever love anything as much as she loves the game? (978-1-62639-327-1)

Prayer of the Handmaiden by Merry Shannon. Celibate priestess Kadrian must defend the kingdom of Ithyria from a dangerous enemy and ultimately choose between her duty to the Goddess and the love of her childhood sweetheart, Erinda. (978-1-62639-329-5)

The Witch of Stalingrad by Justine Saracen. A Soviet "night witch" pilot and American journalist meet on the Eastern Front in WWII and struggle through carnage, conflicting politics, and the deadly Russian winter. (978-1-62639-330-1)

Soul Selecta by Gill McKnight. Soul mates are hell to work with. (978-1-62639-338-7)

Night Mare by Franci McMahon. On an innocent horse-buying trip, Jane Scott uncovers a horrifying element of the horse show world, thrusting her into a whirlwind of poisoned money. (978-1-62639-333-2E).

Pedal to the Metal by Jesse J. Thoma. When unreformed thief Dubs Williams is released from prison to help Max Winters bust a car theft ring, Max learns that if you want to catch a thief, you have to get in bed with one. (978-1-62639-239-7)

Dragon Horse War by D. Jackson Leigh. A priestess of peace and a fiery warrior must defeat a vicious uprising that entwines their destinies and ultimately their hearts. (978-1-62639-240-3)

For the Love of Cake by Erin Dutton. When everything is on the line and one taste can break a heart, will pastry chefs Maya and Shannon take a chance on reality? (978-1-62639-241-0)

Betting on Love by Alyssa Linn Palmer. A quiet country girl at heart and a live-life-to-the-fullest biker take a risk at offering each other their hearts. (978-1-62639-242-7)

The Deadening by Yvonne Heidt. The lines between good and evil, right and wrong, have always been blurry for Shade. When Raven's actions force her to choose, which side will she come out on? (978-1-62639-243-4)

One Last Thing by Kim Baldwin & Xenia Alexiou. Blood is thicker than pride. The final book in the Elite Operative Series brings together foes, family, and friends to start a new order. (978-1-62639-230-4)

Songs Unfinished by Holly Stratimore. Two aspiring rock stars learn that falling in love while pursuing their dreams can be harmonious—if they can only keep their pasts from throwing them out of tune. (978-1-62639-231-1)

Beyond the Ridge by L.T. Marie. Will a contractor and a horse rancher overcome their family differences and find common ground to build a life together? (978-1-62639-232-8)

Swordfish by Andrea Bramhall. Four women battle the demons from their pasts. Will they learn to let go, or will happiness be forever beyond their grasp? (978-1-62639-233-5)

The Fiend Queen by Barbara Ann Wright. Princess Katya and her consort Starbride must turn evil against evil in order to banish Fiendish power from their kingdom, and only love will pull them back from the brink. (978-1-62639-234-2)

Up the Ante by PJ Trebelhorn. When Jordan Stryker and Ashley Noble meet again fifteen years after a short-lived affair, is either of them prepared to gamble on a chance at love? (978-1-62639-237-3)

Speakeasy by MJ Williamz. When mob leader Helen Byrne sets her sights on the girlfriend of Al Capone's right-hand man, passion and tempers flare on the streets of Chicago. (978-1-62639-238-0)

Myth and Magic: Queer Fairy Tales, edited by Radclyffe and Stacia Seaman. Myth, magic, and monsters—the stuff of childhood dreams (or nightmares) and adult fantasies. (978-1-62639-225-0)

A Spark of Heavenly Fire by Kathleen Knowles. Kerry and Beth are building their life together, but unexpected circumstances could destroy their happiness. (978-1-62639-212-0)

Venus in Love by Tina Michele. Morgan Blake can't afford any distractions and Ainsley Dencourt can't afford to lose control—but the beauty of life and art usually lies in the unpredictable strokes of the artist's brush. (978-1-62639-220-5)

Rules of Revenge by AJ Quinn. When a lethal operative on a collision course with her past agrees to help a CIA analyst on a critical assignment, the encounter proves explosive in ways neither woman anticipated. (978-1-62639-221-2)